BL: 5.0- Pts: 10.0

# BELLE'S SONG

# BELLE'S SONG

## K. M. GRANT

WALKER & COMPANY
NEW YORK

*To MS, with love*

Originally published in Great Britain by Quercus Books in 2010
First published in the United States of America in November 2011
by Walker Publishing Company, Inc., a division of Bloomsbury Publishing, Inc.
www.bloomsburyteens.com

For information about permission to reproduce selections from this book, write to
Permissions, Walker BFYR, 175 Fifth Avenue, New York, New York 10010

Library of Congress Cataloging-in-Publication Data
Grant, K. M. (Katie M.)
Belle's song / by K.M. Grant. — 1st ed.
p.    cm.
Summary: In 1387, fifteen-year-old Belle joins Geoffrey Chaucer, his scribe Luke, squire
Walter, and others on a pilgrimage from London to Canterbury to atone and pray for a cure
for her father's crippling injury, but political intrigue threatens them all.
ISBN 978-0-8027-2275-1
[1. Pilgrims and pilgrimages—Fiction. 2. Voyages and travels—Fiction. 3. Knights and
knighthood—Fiction. 4. Chaucer, Geoffrey, d. 1400—Fiction. 5. Middle Ages—Fiction.
6. Great Britain—History—Richard II, 1377–1399—Fiction.] I. Title.
PZ7.G7667755Bel 2011      [Fic]—dc22      2010038026

Printed in the U.S.A. by Quad/Graphics, Fairfield, Pennsylvania
2  4  6  8  10  9  7  5  3  1

All papers used by Bloomsbury Publishing, Inc., are natural, recyclable products
made from wood grown in well-managed forests. The manufacturing processes
conform to the environmental regulations of the country of origin.

# 1

# London, August 1387

*It happened in that season that one day*
*In Southwark, at the Tabard . . .*

Tragedy and opportunity, conspiracies and compulsions. And love. Unexpected love. Once-in-a-lifetime love. Love as real and true as I am. I'll find it hardest to tell of the tragedy, since it was partly—no, entirely—my fault. And it was a real tragedy, at least for my father. It altered his life and not in a good way, although, like most tragedies, the actual tragic event was not the end of the matter. The opportunity, indeed, emerged from the tragedy, and love sprang from the opportunity. How can anybody wish opportunity and love away? Yet the opportunity and how I live now doesn't make the tragedy less tragic. Life's a bit of a muddle like that, I find.

Why tell my story? you may ask. That's easy. Somebody should know the whole truth. People know parts, you see, but only one person knows everything and I'm frightened that he's dead. So if I die too, and of course one day I will, then nobody will know everything except God, and he won't be telling because he's only interested in his own story. If you've got a story, better tell it yourself.

So, here goes. My father was a bell founder: that is, he made bells, which is a difficult profession involving large weights, hot metal, and hairbreadth calculations. Until the tragedy, he was always busy. London, where we lived, was greedy for bells, and the bells my father made pealed proof of his talent and diligence several times an hour. If my father was downcast or worried, my mother would stand outside our door, hands on flirtatious hips, and identify each individual tone. "St. Martin Vintry, St. Jude's, St. Mary's on the Wharf, St. James Garlickhythe, St. Michael at Paternoster, White Friars, St. Paul's, St. Mary Overie." My father would pretend he wasn't listening, but as her litany drew to an end he'd throw out long arms to catch her waist and then whirl her about until she had to remind him that whirligigs cannot make dinners. Their love reminded me of a bell. It resounded, if you know what I mean.

I was an only child, which, for a bell founder, is an unhappy circumstance. It's really a family trade. I was also the wrong sex, being a girl, although this did at least allow my father to call me Belle, which was the kind of joke he liked. "Sound the bell, Belle!" "Peel your apple, Belle!" "Belle, get your clapper swinging!" when I lingered in my bed. He denied himself no pun, no wordplay, no easy joke. As my figure grew more bell-like, others took up the chant. My name, I have to say, has been a trial.

Nor, to my father's great disappointment, did it generate an interest in bell founding. Not then and not now. I've never been a practical girl. I've no feel for the workman's lathe or even the domestic broom, which is why, after my mother died, our house was a mess.

I can see now that the loss of his love nearly killed my father, half through grief and half through anger. For months, tears streaming down his face, he raged against a God who decreed that a good woman, his woman, and a woman who, incidentally, had already survived the plague, should be unexpectedly and hideously carried off by a stupid pox. No priest could supply the answer. Nor could I fill the ache in his arms for the feel of her waist or even cheer him with the bell litany. I had no gift for that. My gifts were all to do with the made-up, not the real. So we fell into bad habits, he and I. After my father's tears had dried into a salty riverbed of wrinkles, his rants were directed not at God but at me, as though the dirty pots and disheveled laundry were somehow a betrayal of my mother's memory. I'm afraid I simply took no notice. I mean, what did the house matter? It was just an extension of my father's workshop, and without my mother to fill it with light and baking, just a place for eating and sleeping. More and more, I lived in my head and, by and by, through my compulsions.

If you're also a life-in-the-head person, you'll know

that it's half joy, half trouble. I found it made me few friends, and I could hardly complain. If, most of the time, you're pretending to be somebody else, people soon lose interest in who you really are. Indeed, I didn't really know who I was myself and concocted a variety of persona, sometimes human, sometimes animal. Goddesses, ermine, and unicorns were my favorites. Sometimes I even imagined myself a knight, although I didn't want to be a man.

Worse than my imaginings, so far as my father was concerned, was the undoubted fact that when you're a goddess battling with the devil or a unicorn caught in a thicket, you just don't smell scorching bread. Nor, when you're an ice-white queen straddling the back of a blood-red horse or a dear little ermine snug against a knight's breast, do you bother about soiled linen or remember to feed the chickens. Chickens! I only ever fantasized about them in a pot.

My most pressing compulsion began as a game and became serious only after my mother died, probably because she wasn't there to laugh it away. Not that the compulsion was sinister, unless you find the number three sinister. I'd say it was more of a nuisance. It began by my having to do a kind of three-skip bounce before mounting our pony and progressed to cutting all my food into three or multiples of three and going up the stairs only in threes. With eight stairs, this meant that at the top or the bottom I had to put in an extra step so that there were nine footfalls. If I forgot—well, I never forgot. I couldn't really, because the counting was soon accompanied by bargaining. Once, for example, it came to me that if I didn't see three gray ponies by the time I reached the end of our street, something bad would happen on my way home. I did see three, only one of them was really a horse. On my way home, a woman emptied a bowl of slop onto my head. Another time, I saw two one-horned oxen and had to scour the city to find a third, because if I didn't, the next visitor to the house would bring bad news. Luckily I did find another and the next visitor to the house was the apothecary, who told my father the plague was not expected to return. Had I not seen that third one-horner, I know the news would have been different. Then there was the morning I had to catch three leaves between the first toll of the compline bell and the last. If I failed, God would take three days off my life. I did catch a third leaf, but only just, and it had another leaf attached to it. I'm still uncertain whether this was a good or bad sign. I think I may live three extra days, but I'm pretty sure that the last one will contain a surprise. In my experience, bargains have to be very precisely kept.

Why three? I don't know, except that three is the number of the Trinity, the number of tasks a knight usually has to perform on a quest, and the number of curses an old beggar woman once showered on me to make me give her three pennies.

I might as well tell you now that life-in-the-head and my obsession with three weren't my only peculiarities. For my twelfth birthday—my second motherless one—I wanted a company of musicians to follow me about. Not the tiddly-taddly horn and drum offered by every tinker in every marketplace, much as I loved dancing to jolly rhythms at the midsummer fair or during the Christmas feast. No. The music I craved was as yet unwritten for instruments as yet uncrafted—music, so I rather pompously told my father, to wrench tears from the driest of eyes and swell the soul even of the godless. In other words, music to go with the stories I inhabited. My father, who, despite his grief and my domestic failures, had tried hard to make my birthday as my mother would have made it, listened with some patience and was not unsympathetic. However, since a perfect bell peal was the only music he really liked (I'm fond of triple peals, any others make me nervous), I know he didn't fully understand.

He did understand, though, that the house was a pigsty and, birthday or not, told me that if he came across yet another rotten egg, never mind swelling the souls of the godless, he'd make music like the devil. We ended that birthday with a row that contained no music of any kind, and though I found I couldn't leave him without an embrace, it was three cold kisses that I planted on his cheek before we parted for the night.

Later, when the poxy strummers who played at the Tabard Inn next door struck up their chorus, I crept out and hurled six rotten eggs through their window. The rest I dispatched into the brothel farther down the road. How dare those ladies be happy?

Now to the tragic event itself. I say only one thing in my defense. I was so sorry afterward I thought I might die and I must have relived the moment a million times, pinpointing the very second, less than a second, before which everything was normal and after which nothing was normal again. I would lie awake, rubbing the doll my mother knitted for me against that special place between the bottom of your ear and your chin, and as I rubbed, would rewrite the moment, rewrite the whole day, then go on to rewrite my whole life so that I was a different person, a nice person, a daughter of whom my father could be proud. But rewriting would not change the facts. Indeed, the only thing to change was Poppet, who I rubbed so hard that all the features of her face were scoured away. Soon, just like me, she didn't know who she was anymore. In the end, to stop her vanishing altogether, I covered what was left of her face with a washcloth.

I think it was the day I covered her face that I took to

rubbing my shins with a pumice stone. It was a surprise, the first time they bled. I'd started with the pumice stone before, taking one from my father's toolbox to help get rid of the smoky stubble that was beginning to speckle my legs. Hair should only be on your head, although the priests want even that covered. They say it leads a man to sin. That's ridiculous. No man would be led to sin by my red tangles. Nevertheless, the priests are right about one thing: only a man-God would allow hair to grow where no girl wants it. Anyway, after the tragedy, as well as the hair on my legs, I rubbed away my skin. It was an accident at first, and I was frightened by the blood. It was also a curious, biting pleasure. After that I couldn't stop myself. Every time my flesh tore, part of me was horrified, but a greater part rejoiced in the ugliness and the pain because it obliterated everything else. I suppose a gallon of wine would have done the same, but I didn't like the taste. For several years now I have tried to keep the pumice out of reach. I'm not always successful. Even as I write this, I'm tempted, and when I'm tempted, I sometimes rub my ankle for a second or so. Ankles bleed a lot.

Back to the tragedy.

For all our arguments, my father indulged me. He didn't rely on me to dig the bell pit, shape a core, or mold a cope. He mixed the copper and alloy himself. He sharpened his own lathe. He didn't even press me to keep his account book or clean his overalls. Far from it. He employed a boy as well as an apprentice so that I could spend time learning to read and write. The only thing I was occasionally required to do, and only if the work was local and the boys were busy or unwell, was watch the ropes when the bell was swung into the tower, to see that they uncoiled properly as the pulley wheel strained. For big bells, the ropes were thick and the pulley turners were huge men, often from the local tug-of-war team. To get the biggest heave, they set their heads low between great shoulders and kept their eyes on the back of the man in front. Hence the need for someone to watch.

I wasn't required to touch the rope. I just had to watch and shout if something seemed amiss. Just watch and shout.

It was a big bell, perhaps the biggest my father had founded, and he was so proud of it. The Black Friars had had a competition for the privilege of crowning their huge new church, and my father had won. At the announcement, he smiled properly for the first time since my mother's death and set to work with a will. It was quite an undertaking. The boards from the mock-up mold were as tall as me, and the wax filled one of his biggest vats.

I'm putting the real moment off, I know. It's just that writing this down is like picking an old wound. Even now the rawness catches me, although not unawares. I'm always aware. Not, of course, that my wound is anything like my father's.

The bell tower was of solid stone, so my father was confident it could take the weight. Indeed, as the work progressed, he was confident about everything. Perhaps we should have learned from the pox that tragedy takes advantage of confidence.

I wasn't really watching the rope. When had it ever tangled? I stood, half slouching, reading a little book that my father had purchased at Paternoster Row and given me on my fifteenth birthday just past. It was tales of King Arthur's knights. I had nearly finished it and was sighing for the flawed chivalry of Lancelot, Arthur's broken heart, and Guinevere's faithlessness. I was at Camelot, rising mistily through the lake. I pressed my arms flat against my sides and was the sword in the stone, being slowly drawn by Arthur. A living sword! Why not? In a second I was no longer aware of my father shouting, the wheel beginning to turn, the bell rising inch by inch, the clapper swinging like the tongue in a dead hog's head. All I knew was Arthur running his hand over me. I was glittering at his touch.

Four men cranked the wheel, treading their circle, muscles bulging under rolled-up shirtsleeves and pearl-sized beads of sweat bouncing into the dust. Perhaps

if there had been six, or even just three, what happened wouldn't have happened. Anyway. Up, up went the bell, a smooth hoist, a perfect hoist, the ropes uncoiling in copybook style. Now Arthur had raised me above his head, every fiber of my being thrilling. I was flashing in the sun, twisting and turning as he swiped me through the air. Up and down, round and round. He would never let me go. He whirled me so hard that I was suddenly giddy. To stop myself falling, I stepped sideways and put out my hand. Such a little step. Such a tiny mistake. That's the second I relive and relive as though through reliving it I could change it. Why did I move *sideways*? Why didn't I step forward or backward, or just fall over? Sometimes it seems impossible that I didn't.

I'm gritting my teeth. I'm forcing myself to continue.

I'm slight and not very tall but I broke the stride of one of the hoisting giants and he faltered. That's all it took. Just a momentary falter and the momentum was lost. There was no hovering of the bell, no hesitation. It plummeted, its huge weight blowing two birds clean out of the tower window. My father didn't think first about himself: he thought about me. His head whipped around to make sure I was safe before he leaped. It was too late. The rim of the bell caught his legs and, with the clapper gently booming, broke them into pieces.

Everybody was kind. Not your fault, they said. One

of the hazards of bell founding, they said. But it was my fault, and they knew it and I knew it, and God knew it and would punish me. My father had asked me to watch out for him. I had agreed and then been quite elsewhere. After he had been carried off, I threw King Arthur into the corner. Though the book was expensive, I never retrieved it.

Over the next few days, the neighbors crowded about. Look on the bright side, they urged. It's a miracle that your father isn't dead! But his legs were dead, quite dead. Even the best physician, summoned and paid for by Master Miller, could do nothing about that. I suppose it was a miracle that both limbs were saved from amputation, although it's not much of a miracle to avoid the doctor when you can no longer even piss on your own.

I won't dwell on the pain my father must have suffered. Not that he didn't shout and swear and even scream, particularly when the bone setter tried to straighten things out. I think that the noise was for my benefit. My father knew that a martyrish silence would have been worse for me, so once he was conscious again he hollered when he felt the need, and sometimes even when he didn't so as to give me a decent excuse to hold his hand and pretend I was doing something useful. When I was not home he was completely silent. I know that because the plump and garrulous widow, who appointed herself his nurse, told me. I suppose she thought it would make me feel better. At mealtimes, she took to answering for him when I asked him a question. Pretty soon I longed to take her by the scruff of the neck and hurl her into the cook pot.

Sometimes, at night, when the widow was snoring by the fire, my father and I would both cry for my mother. When he comforted me—him comforting *me!*—a stone formed in my stomach. The pumice was my best friend then, and I think it must have taken the place of the unicorn and the ermine because I don't remember ever being either of those creatures again.

Enough of that. Now for the opportunity—well, perhaps more an adventure, except that traditional adventures are organized affairs where people make plans and stick to them with courage and determination. My adventure wasn't at all like that. For a start, it occurred quite by chance and most of it, just like my life, was haphazard. My death will be like that too, I expect. I'll be dreaming of glory as I'm squashed by the butcher's cart.

Anyhow, in the late summer following the accident, my father was in the Tabard. He had recently taken to going there in a wheeled chair constructed by Peter Joiner and decked out in fine style by the ladies from the brothel. Even that tiny journey was exhausting, for August storms bring August mud, but the lure of the

Tabard's host, a man of vast and irrepressible cheer, was as strong as the lure of ale.

Master Host was always full of gossip and kept a good deal of company. He was also a man of opinions. Where others were more circumspect, he spoke freely about our current king's troubles, making his own views perfectly clear, though what they were I couldn't tell you because his views were as changeable as the tide. One day he loved King Richard, the next he despised him. One day we absolutely must make peace with the French, the next we most certainly must not. I wasn't much interested. I did know that England's king was wayward and that France was a trouble, but only because kings are always wayward and France had been a trouble my whole life. I'd never met King Richard, of course, and I wasn't frightened of the French. There is a rough sea between us and them, and any French merchants I encountered at the Tabard, or even the occasional captive French knight I saw paraded through the streets, winked rather than threatened, particularly as my childish body bloomed into something a man could get his hands around. And anyway, men are always fighting. It gives them something to talk about.

In keeping with his forthright manner, Master Host didn't skirt around my father's helplessness as others did. He called Father "the Emperor" and, when he heard the grinding of the chair's wheels, would shout,

"Make way for the imperial chariot!" When he could see my father struggling against the deep gloom into which he had sunk, he devised entertainments, one of which was using a row of tankards as skittles and seeing how many my father could down with a stuffed goat's bladder. It pained my father to throw, I know, but the host whispered that the exercise would make his back stronger. Nor was any money accepted, for as you may imagine, money was now short. "You can pay for your liquor when you're back on your feet," Master Host declared, sweeping the proffered coins into Father's lap. Though the phrasing made me wince, he didn't apologize. "There's more ways of standing than on a couple of flat soles," he said, looking my father directly in the eye. It was a robust approach, certainly.

This day, the host was busier than usual. Having heard of its fine food and clean wines, a whole party of persons had arranged to meet at the Tabard. When I went to fetch Father home for his dinner, the place was so busy I could scarcely push my way through, and when I did I found him being berated by a man whose face was so red and warty he could, without disguise, have played Lucifer in the mystery play. "*Questio quid juris?*" the wart man kept repeating amid a glaze of spit and breakfast remains. "What's the point in law?"

When I appeared, Father seized me. "This is my daughter, Belle," he said. "She's come to take me home."

The man took no notice. "I ask you again, my crippled friend. *Questio quid juris?*" he bellowed. Only when he looked at me properly did his voice descend into a tomcat purr. "Your daughter, you say? Legs still working when you conceived her, I would imagine." He winked outrageously. My father's face set like stone. The man belched. "Well, as I say, a very creditable daughter, to be sure, though I prefer more flesh in those places a man looks for it." He belched again. "Tell me, little lady, do you call the color of your hair 'warning sunset' or 'moldy pumpkin'? Never mind. You've eyes pretty enough to make up for it. Let me kiss your hand. The name is Aristotle Seekum." He wiped his mouth and leered over my fingers. "I'm Archdeacon Dunmow's summoner."

His title was meant to impress, but since he was clearly a toad, I pulled my hand away. "Dinner's ready," I said to my father and tried to push the chair out.

But Master Toad stood his ground, smacking thick lips. "Not so fast, my fine mistress, for your father's sake. You see, I've been trying to root out who was to blame for his accident. He tells me it's a personal matter and I say nonsense to that! There may be a point in law! And if there is, he may be entitled to some redress. What man doesn't want money for his pain? Just because your father lacks the will to pursue the point himself doesn't mean somebody more knowledgeable can't pursue it for him. Indeed, there is amongst our company a sergeant from the Inns of Court personally known to me. For a small fee, I'm certain he'd gladly take up this worthy cause." He flicked my locks with a pointed fingernail. "Compensation is always useful. You'd like more ribbons and silks, would you not, poppet?" He peered about, trying to find the sergeant in the crowd.

Every hair on my father's head bristled, and mine too. I should have been more circumspect, but how was I to know all that was to follow? "The accident was my fault," I said loudly, "and I prefer parchment and pen to ribbons and silks. By the way, I'm sorry for your boils. Who's to blame for them? Do you get more compensation if even your mother won't kiss you?" The summoner's mouth still agape, I shoved past.

Sitting near the door, slightly apart from the crowd, sat a quick-eyed older man and a youth with skin white as whey. They'd not heard the exchange with the summoner, but when they saw me struggling and my father being uncomfortably jostled, the youth—really just a boy—got up. He was tall, for all that he stooped like a strand of windswept barley, and he wore hinged eyeglasses cracked in lens and frame. His arms must have been strong, though, for my father's no feather and the boy lifted him clean out of his chair, hoisted him above the melee, and carried him into the street. It was much easier to manage the chair without my father in it and though I clobbered a few shins, I maneuvered out of the inn without further difficulty. The boy carefully lowered my father back onto his cushion, awkwardly accepted some equally awkward thanks—being rescued was hard for Father—and quickly turned away, leaving a smell of something pungent but not unpleasant that I couldn't quite place.

Dinner, which Widow Chegwin had cooked and sat with us to eat, was taken in silence. She'd made the house neat as a new pin, my father's bed all fluffed up and inviting. She'd even untangled the knots in the wool for the three-sided cushion I was clumsily trying to embroider. I'd been furious with her in the morning because, can you believe it, she'd washed Poppet. Washed her! Of course Poppet was dirty and of course I only imagined she still carried Mother's scent, but the widow, thrilled that Poppet now smelled of violets, simply couldn't grasp that inside the doll's worn and battered body had nestled dust from happier times. As long as the dust was there, some of that happiness remained. Now it was all gone. As a consequence, I'd spent much of the day pumicing my legs. Yet even as I'd bitten down on a piece of leather, for the pain was very great, and cursed the widow in the language of the gutter, I'd been ashamed. For all her inconsequential cooing and dementing interference, what would my father's life be like without her? I gave him nothing: not a clean house, not a decent meal, not even an embroidered cushion. Even now, as we were sitting at supper, a meal which, naturally, I'd had no hand in preparing, I wasn't concentrating on being considerate. Instead, I was telling myself a salty tale in which the milky fish on my plate was going to eat me rather than me eat it.

"They're pilgrims, all," the widow warbled, watching me cut my fish carefully into three, "and on their way to Canterbury so I hear, each wanting a miracle at the tomb of St. Thomas." At mention of St. Thomas she crossed herself. She was a firm believer in keeping the saints sweet. "Such a diverse company! There's a knight amongst them and a cook! Fancy that! A knight and a cook traveling together. Times are changing, are they not, Master Bellfounder? Even the king's going to have to accept that. The knight's brought his son as squire"—her little eyes blinked at me. She couldn't help herself. Matchmaking was in her blood. "A handsome boy by all accounts, full of accomplishments. He's interested in books too, I'm certain."

I cut my three pieces of fish into another three and threw half to the cat. "I think we may have met the squire already," I said politely. I wanted to show my father, who had witnessed the morning's row, that my fury had abated. "Would you like more bread, Father?"

"He only eats one piece," said the widow.

I clenched my teeth and gave Father a slice anyway. "The squire helped us out of the Tabard. He's not particularly handsome. Thank you for unknotting the threads in my cushion. I'll try to get it finished."

"Don't you worry about that," the widow twittered more kindly than I deserved, "but you do get the colors mixed up. I wonder whether all your reading hasn't weakened your vision? A wife needs sharp eyes, you know, not just for sewing but to make sure she's not cheated by her servants."

"We don't have any servants," I pointed out, all my good intentions dissolving.

"No, dear, not now, but who knows . . ." She chattered on. I pushed my plate away. "I think you're right about my eyes," I said, "and there's no time like the present. I'll find the oculist."

"Don't go out," said my father at once. "It's not safe. Even you must know that with the king and Parliament still at loggerheads, mobs form out of nothing."

"The king's squabbles don't bother me," I said, "and it's months since there was any trouble around here. Why, we've even given up setting the window bars at night."

"We'll start setting them again right away," said my father shortly. "Please see to it, widow." He rapped his fork on the table, making her jump. "Anyway, it's a silly time to go. The oculist will be at his dinner."

My father was not really worried about a mob or the oculist's dinner. He was really railing against his own inability to escape the domestic hearth. I just had to get out, though, so I got up, crossed myself three times while the widow intoned the grace, then collected Poppet, lest I should come home and find her lips and eyes reworked. When I stepped into the street, I saw a girl balancing three jugs of milk. She dropped one. I didn't help her pick up the pieces because I needed to pretend it hadn't happened.

# 2

Then people long to go on pilgrimages
And palmers long to seek the stranger strands
Of far-off saints . . .

I never went to the oculist's house, but so as not to be entirely deceitful, I wandered to his shop and stood outside the window gazing at the frames and stoppered vials. "No better spectacles in all Southwark! Curative drops for all conditions!" declared curly writing set above a wooden puppet sporting two rondels joined with a rivet. I leaned my head against the open shutters. This evening I wasn't Belle Anything Nice, I was Belle the Rude.

My father was right. The shop was closed, but somebody was knocking tentatively on the door around the other side. I moved. It was the stooping boy from the inn and he peered at me, lank hair flopping over his face. In the thinning light, he looked not so much interestingly pale as unhealthily pasty. If I had not seen him carry my father with my own eyes, I would have said such an effort was beyond him. Immediately, my compulsion kicked in. If he didn't speak before I'd counted to three, I'd walk away. *One, two, thr—*

"Do . . . do . . . do you know when the shop will be open?"

His voice was deeper than I'd expected. "In the morning," I said. "That's when shops usually open."

His face fell. "Of course. Stupid of me. And we're off at dawn."

"You'll not be off at dawn," I said. "Tabard breakfasts are famously long. You'll be up early but the shop'll be open by the time you pass."

He looked relieved. "Th–thanks." It struck me that he was very tongue-tied for a squire—not that I had met many squires, but in stories they were always full of easy words.

I thought he would shuffle off, but when I went back to the window his reflection was beside me. "My spectacles are broken and I'd better choose new frames now. I don't want to be messing about tomorrow," he said.

I looked at him and then at the eyeglasses on display. "Black rims," I said, "so that people can see you. You look as though you might vanish."

He smiled nervously. "Perhaps I shall."

"Are you ill?"

"No."

I faced him properly. "Why then?"

He twisted long fingers. "I may be a bit fermented."

I laughed and this encouraged him. "My father's an alchemist," he explained, "and I've spent my whole life breathing in vapors from his experiments." Now he stood a little straighter and pushed his hair back.

"Oh," I said. "Of course."

"Of course?"

"The widow who helps with my father said there was a squire staying at the Tabard. I thought it might be you, but then no squire I've ever read about wears eyeglasses, and even without your glasses you don't really look like a squire." It was clear at once that I'd hurt his feelings and I felt bad so I rushed on. "Was that your father, the man sitting beside you at the inn?"

He shook his head. "No, no. That man is my master and my mentor." He blushed. "My savior, really, I suppose."

I was surprised. "You need a savior?"

"Don't we all sometimes?"

I thought of my father and myself and the years stretching ahead. I hugged Poppet hard. "You never introduced yourself."

"Oh! I'm so sorry! I-I—"

"I'm Belle," I said, cutting through his stuttering and stretching out my hand.

"Luke," he said, avoiding my hand. "Belle. It suits you."

I dropped my hand. "You think I'm shaped like a bell?"

"Not at all! I meant it as a compliment."

"It's all right," I said, "I was joking. It doesn't matter."

"It does matter. A man of letters should be able to pay an ordinary compliment."

"You're a writer?" Only now did I began to pay him properly serious attention.

"It's what I've always wanted to be."

"And that man—your master—is teaching you how?"

"Yes. I'm his scribe."

"What's he writing?"

"He's got an idea but his wife's ill, so he's going on pilgrimage to Canterbury to ask St. Thomas to cure her. I heard that he was looking for somebody to help him write a report of the journey, and so I applied for the job."

I was disappointed. "I thought you might be learning to write stories."

He leaned his back against the wall. "My master writes tremendous stories," he said with more confidence. "That's why there was a line of people wanting my job."

Jealousy stirred. "Why did he choose you?"

Luke bit his lip.

"I suppose you're very, very clever," I said, disliking myself for goading him but doing it all the same.

"No," he answered at once. "I'm not very clever. I've got a very good memory."

"Oh? For what kinds of things?"

"Pretty much anything."

"All right," I said, "what's in the window behind you—and no cheating."

He took off his spectacles and stared hard into the distance although his eyes seemed somehow turned inward. "Three shelves on the left, two on the right. The poppet in the middle with a sign above her."

"I know the sign," I said. "That's easy." I glanced across the road to make sure he was not staring at a reflection. He was not.

He went on. "On the top-left shelf there are six eye-glass frames, all round and of black leather, with ties. On the second shelf are four vials, two brown and two red, one with a pointed stopper, the rest pear-shaped. On the third shelf are fifteen—no, fourteen—sheets of horn. On the right-hand top shelf is a book entitled *Of the Eye and All Its Ailments*, and on the lower shelf are two boxes, with twenty pairs of spectacles in one and six crystal reading stones in the other."

I pressed my nose to the window and began counting. "How many sheets of horn did you say?"

"Fourteen. The fifteenth is on the table farther back in the shop, with one pair of frames cut out of it. Next to it is a box of rivets but I can't tell how many rivets there are because the box has a lid on."

It was impossible not to be impressed. "It's magic," I said. Now I was nervous. Widow Chegwin was always

warning about magic. I tapped my fingers together three times.

"Not at all. My father pretends it's some kind of supernatural power but it's really just a trick. Anybody can learn to do it. I can remember words as well, and numbers, and it's very useful because it means that my master can dictate as he rides and I write everything down when we stop. He tells me puzzles too, though he says not to write those down. I think it amuses him to test me. So far I've not forgotten anything." He was nervously proud.

"What a useful person you are," I said, not very nicely.

He was immediately bashful. "There are lots of people like me, I expect."

"I shouldn't think so," I said.

"You're just saying that."

"Well, you got the job, didn't you?" I said more gently. I was always losing friends by saying the wrong thing and though this boy would hardly qualify as a friend, I didn't want him to dislike me. "You must have had something that the others didn't have."

"I did. I had God's blessing. You see, I made a bargain that if the Master chose me as his scribe, I'd place my alchemist's tools on the altar of St. Thomas at Canterbury and become a monk at St. Denys in Paris. God kept his part of the bargain, so now I'm really a monk. When I've delivered my tools, I'll deliver myself."

"Jesus Mary!" I was genuinely horrified. "A poor, chaste, and obedient monk, and in a foreign place! You must have wanted the job really badly."

He gave an uncertain smile. "I did," he said. "I wanted this job more than anything else. When you're a monk you can write to your heart's content. I'm looking forward to it, and if I'm out at sea, I'll never have to go home again."

"Is home that bad?"

"Have you ever met an alchemist?"

"I don't think so."

"Can you smell anything?"

I sniffed, recognizing the smell I'd noticed earlier. He removed his spectacles again and edged close enough for me to see that his eyes were goose gray and slanted at the corners. His skin was smooth as white lead. I sniffed again. "Sulfur," I said, wrinkling my nose, "and brimstone."

"That's the alchemist's smell. That and the smell of deceit. My father turns base metal into gold."

"Really?"

A red fork flashed in the goose gray. "Of course not really. It can't be done. My father's a peddler of lies and false dreams. He's tried to teach me how to do it, but that was one lesson I refused to learn. Nobody should

pretend they can make gold. It's the worst deceit of all because it drives men to murder. He beat me, but I wouldn't give in." He didn't look cowed by the memory of that beating; he looked livid.

"But isn't anything possible through alchemy?" I asked. "Master Host says that alchemists cured lots of people of the plague."

The red fork flashed again. "That's what men like my father would have you believe, but it's only through God that anything's possible and, believe me, God's as far from being an alchemist as I am from being St. Peter."

I tossed my head. "You really believe in God's power?"

"I believe in his power for good. He got me my job."

"Your memory got you your job."

"And who gave me my memory?"

"Your father."

"And who gave me my father?"

"This is silly," I said.

The red spark flickered and went out. Soon, dusk thickened into dark and the poppet and the eyeglasses smudged and disappeared. Somewhere across the river, a bell tolled for evening prayers. I held my breath. Six strikes. I let my breath out again. "If God really could do anything, he'd mend my father's legs," I whispered when I was sure my face was shadowed.

Luke caught the whisper. "What happened to him?"

"Has nobody at the Tabard told you?"

"I didn't speak to anybody except my master."

So I told him, adding nothing and taking nothing away, which is unusual for me, but he seemed to draw the truth out by listening with his whole self. When I finished, he was staring at me intently. "Do you believe in miracles?" he asked eventually.

"I believe God could have caused the bell to fall away from my father," I said, "but the bones . . ." I could still see them, stained and sharp through the broken skin, and my father's feet flopping like a couple of dead herrings. "I do believe in bargains, though," I added, surprising myself, since I'd never admitted this to anyone before. "They seem more powerful than miracles."

Luke touched my arm. "Come with us to Canterbury," he said, and the moon came out, lighting his face like the church on Easter Sunday. "You never know what God can do."

I wagged my finger. "Aha! You'll not trick me like that, Master Monk-in-the-Making. I'm not promising to be a nun."

"Even to give your father back his legs?"

A horrible coldness trickled down my throat. That was one bargain I'd never thought of. I began to edge away. "You're a peddler in dreams just like your father. God's never going to cure my father, whatever I promise. That's my punishment." I turned on my heel; then, I don't quite know why, I turned back. "Remember, black rims for your new glasses." After that I ran.

My father didn't have a good night, nor did I. The widow muttered prayers and incantations and stoked up the fire. When necessary, she helped my father turn over and resettled him with surprising deftness. Only when she had to do the most intimate things was she silent, knowing her muttering would add to his humiliations. I couldn't like her, but I couldn't say she wasn't thoughtful. And it was my fault we couldn't do without her. I stared at the ceiling. *Why had I moved sideways?*

At dawn I rose, dressed, and went to the bedside. The widow was snoring noisily in her chair, her mouth wide. I lit three candles and sat down. My father's face was ashy and mottled. Pain had made him old. "Well, Belle," he rhymed, trying to banter. But his mustache drooped into his beard.

"Do you believe in miracles?" I asked him, straightening blankets that didn't need straightening.

He closed his eyes. "What happened happened," he said, "and what's done is done. Time can't be reversed."

"What about miracles?" I persisted.

He made a tiny movement. "Life's a miracle. A perfect peal of bells is a miracle. Your red hair's a miracle."

"You know what I mean."

He suddenly opened his eyes. "Hope of miracles

makes people mad," he said, "and I won't be mad as well as crippled."

I took a deep breath. "I want to go to Canterbury with the pilgrims at the Tabard," I said, gripping his hand. "I want to take a lock of your hair to St. Thomas's tomb, and if God will cure you, I'll . . . I'll . . . I'll stop living in my stories and become more like the son you should have had. I can be a bell founder—a good one. I know I can. If St. Thomas can persuade God to mend your legs, that's what I'll do. I swear—"

"You'll swear nothing, do you hear me!"

I wasn't to be stopped. "I swear it, I swear it, I swear it," I said. "There. As you say, what's done's done."

My father's head fell back. "You shouldn't have sworn. You know you'll break your word and then what'll God do with you?"

"I won't break my word." I was on my feet. My skirt against my pumiced legs. I didn't wince. "I won't. If the boy can become a monk, I can become a bell founder."

"What boy? What are you saying?"

"Never mind," I told him. "I just need a lock of your hair."

"For God's sake, Belle."

I snipped a lock before he could stop me and put it in a hinged pendant. I fastened the pendant around my neck with a leather thong. "Isn't it worth a try, Father? Isn't it?"

He raised his hands, then dropped them. "If you

want to get away from this sickroom, at least be honest enough to say so. Don't hide behind the pretense of miracle seeking."

"For once I'm not pretending," I said, and hoped this was true. "I've made a promise."

"How many times did you promise your mother to keep the house tidy? How many times did you promise to learn to bake? How many times did you . . . ?" His voice petered into nothing. "I don't want another argument. I haven't the strength."

"Listen," I said as the bell that had been the cause of our misfortune tolled. "What do you hear?"

"I hear the end of my life drawing near," he whispered.

I was suddenly terribly afraid. "Father!"

He turned his face to the wall. "Go to Canterbury, Belle. I can't stop you. But don't pray for me, pray for yourself."

"There's no rule to say I can't do both," I said. He didn't smile, but at least he looked around so that I could kiss both his cheeks and his forehead. Then I patted the blankets and picked up my belongings. I held the pumice stone tightly before, with an effort, putting it down. I should have left Poppet behind too. I know I should. Pilgrims don't take toys. But I didn't feel strong enough for that, so with my pendant swinging and clutching my doll under my arm, I said three Our Fathers and left my father to the widow's mercies.

# 3

Some nine and twenty in a company
Of sundry folk happening then to fall
In fellowship . . .

The Tabard yard was heaving with horses, mongrels, chickens, tradesmen, servants, squabbling pages, itinerant hawkers, and pilgrims fussing over their baggage. It was still early but already I could smell the sewage. The day would be hot. Three pigs had joined the melee, snuffling about between the pack mules' hooves and upsetting the better-bred palfreys. I stood with my pack on my back and felt a fool. My father's horse had been sold. Was I going to be the only pilgrim walking? And how was I going to pay for food and lodging on the way? I had brought no money. I couldn't see Luke. Summoner Seekum pounced. He'd not forgotten my jibe about his boils. "Ah," he said, oozing greasy malice, "you've come to atone for your wicked carelessness? Last evening, I learned how you crippled your father. There'll be a very particular place in hell for you."

This morning he was less toad and more snow-spattered volcano, for he had pasted his eruptions with cream of tartar using the back of one of Master Host's horn spoons. I could see the top of the spoon sticking out of the large leather pouch attached to his belt. The spoon wasn't of value, but I knew Master Host would miss it because it was one of a set with unusual pigtail stalks. For a man of means like a summoner, it was a strangely petty thing to take. "Stay out of my business," I said. "It's nothing to do with you."

His eyes bored into mine, crafty and inquisitive. "When times are troubled, no man's business is just his own, nor woman's neither."

"Well, troubled times don't trouble me," I said, standing my ground. He moved closer in, his many rings flashing in the sun, and before I could move, pressed a sweaty palm against the swell of my shift. I leaped back into two strong arms. A voice lively as a flute exclaimed, "Whoa there, my lady! You don't want to be kicked."

Though I had never seen him before, I recognized my rescuer at once. *This* must be the squire, the knight's son, and I could see why the widow had been so taken. On the cusp of what was obviously going to be a magnificent manhood, his handsomely bearded face was fresh and open and his eyes full of romance. My pack slid from my back and Poppet to the floor. "Whoops!" he said, dusting her down and replacing her under my arm. "The poor poppet." It was impossible not to twinkle at him, for his eyes were the twinkliest I ever saw.

The Toad quickly lowered his hand and coughed. "I'm attending to this girl, which is only fitting, since she's coming to Canterbury to atone for sin."

"As are we all, are we not?" The squire's response was so quick and his manner so pleasant that the Toad was left floundering. "Now, sir," said the squire, "as summoner, your office naturally means you're an important person on our journey. I believe you'll be required to ride up front. One who summons sinners before the archdeacon carries enough responsibilities without cluttering himself up with the rest of us."

The squire's tone was firm and the Toad allowed himself to be flattered. "I suppose so," he said, spraying spittle. "I shall take my place as you suggest." His fingers twitched to chuck me under the chin, but in the end he left us, closing his pouch over the stolen spoon and waggling his thumb in a gesture both childish and obscene.

The squire released me. "Now," he said, rather absent-mindedly straightening the crush of my clothes and picking up my pack. "Where's your packhorse?"

"Right here," I said. Tucking Poppet into my belt, I held out my arms.

He laughed, showing very white teeth. "No, really."

"Really. I've no horse, neither to ride nor to carry my pack. But I've two sturdy legs and I'll manage perfectly well."

When he saw that I was serious, he cocked his head

to one side, sizing me up. I must have passed muster. "Wait right here," he said, and disappeared, taking my pack with him.

The yard became a little more orderly as somebody shooed the pigs out and the pilgrims began climbing into their saddles, though some, having taken full advantage of the host's liquid hospitality, found this quite difficult. The widow was right. They really were a disparate lot, as was clear from mounts ranging from two high-stepping warhorses, clearly belonging to the knight and the squire, to a stumpy pony more used to pulling a plow than having the plowman as jockey. There were, all told, eighteen men if we count Sir Knight's page and the wagoner and his boy, and nine women, including myself and a lady who traveled in a wagon with her daughters, one a baby and the other just walking. There were also two lapdogs wearing pilgrims' cockleshells on their collars, but I'm not counting them. Twenty-seven, being nine times three, is the number I prefer.

I strained my eyes for Luke and eventually spotted him, already mounted and waiting by the gate. When he saw me, his face lit up and he bent to speak to his master. His master glanced over, frowned, asked a question, then nodded. Luke vaulted neatly off his horse and made his way toward me. He had his new glasses. They were black rimmed. It was, I suppose, a little unfortunate that he reached me at the same time as the squire. There was a tinderbox moment as Luke clenched his fists, and I was conscious of an explosive energy that was decidedly unmonklike. But he held back as the squire shook his curls and bowed.

"I've brought the lady a horse," the squire said.

"So I see," said Luke without enthusiasm.

A horse! That was like calling a silk dress a rag. The horse was nothing like the workaday, thick-legged animal my father had kept. Round-flanked, dish-faced, and soft-muzzled, this palomino sweetheart was a creature from myth. Unlike the other horses, even the warhorses, her coat was not thickening in early anticipation of winter, but retained its summer sheen of waxed cherry wood. She carried her tail high, as a princess carries her head.

"She's beautiful!" I exclaimed.

The squire was delighted. "Yes, isn't she? She belonged to my sister. She has no more need of her." His lips puckered slightly as he checked the girth and made sure the bridle was properly fitting.

"Is your sister sick?" I ventured.

"No," he said. He patted the mare. "I'm sorry. That was rude. The truth is that my sister has run away with a French knight, damn his black hair and dirty fingernails. We're making a pilgrimage to pray for her return. My father wanted to bring the pony because she is—was—so fond of it and for some reason he thought—well, he just thought."

My spirits rose. Of course, at the same time, I asked myself the question you may be asking. Was it sinful to feel cheerful on pilgrimage? I didn't know. All I can say is that when the squire handed over reins of soft red leather, I pinched my wrist to make sure I wasn't dreaming. "That is not a sidesaddle," he said. "Can you ride astride?"

"I've never ridden any other way," I told him, "though I've only ever ridden over harness, never with a saddle. Does your sister always ride astride?" The squire linked his hands to make a step for me to mount, his silence polite but eloquent. I bit my lip and performed my three-skip mounting bounce. If this flower of chivalry didn't wish to tell me about his sister, I shouldn't pry. To make up, I tried to make myself as light as possible, but in the end I scrambled because the mare wouldn't stand still. It was mortifying when my skirts rode up, revealing the scabs on my legs. I knew what to expect: the squire would flinch first and then comment. He did neither, only laughed as the pony danced about, and his laugh was like music.

"Could you hold her still while I tighten the girth?" he asked Luke. To tell the truth, I'd forgotten Luke was even there. As soon as the girth was fixed, Luke retreated.

The squire called his father's page. "Fling a leg over so

that you're sitting sideways," he ordered when the page had gone. He produced a pair of the softest woolen hose. "Shuffle into these," he said, meeting my eyes with unexpectedly sympathetic candor. "They're fashionably tight, so they should protect your legs from saddle sores. Here. Use my shoulders as footrests." He stood with his back to me. When I was ready, he placed my feet carefully into the stirrups. "There," he said, smoothing my skirts. "You and that poppet look very fine."

"I don't really know how to thank you," I said, rubbing Poppet's threadbare head hard against my crimson cheeks. I knew he understood what I meant. "I'll pray that it's not long before your sister sits in this saddle again."

He bowed. "The pony's name is Dulcimer," he said. "My sister called her Dulcie. And I'm Walter de Pleasance."

"Belle," I said.

"Ah! *Une belle jument pour une belle dame.* A beautiful mare for a beautiful girl."

I blushed. Nobody had ever paid me such a compliment before, or in such a voice, and I never thought somebody would, particularly after they'd seen my legs.

"I've taken the liberty of stowing your pack in our armor cart," Walter said. "It's the one painted blue—I do like blue—and it's drawn by a spotted riding horse.

I thought of painting him blue too, but I don't think he'd have appreciated it much. Now I must go and tend to my father. Will you manage? Dulcie's high-spirited but I think she'll carry you well."

I nodded, happily bemused by the blue and the spotted horse and the kindness of this new friend. "Please thank your father," I called out.

"The pleasure's entirely ours," he answered, and doffed a ribboned cap. Altogether it was a most unexpected start to my journey.

When the whole company was ready, the priest blessed our venture: "May our prayers be answered according to our just deserts. May St. Thomas of Canterbury bless us, and may God keep us together in a pilgrim's pact of friendship." Three invocations. We all began to say Amen. The summoner called out, "And may God's blessing fall only on loyal Englishmen." My fellow pilgrims shifted uneasily. "We're just pilgrims," somebody murmured angrily. "There should be no politicking here." I wasn't angry about politicking. I was angry because the summoner's invocation knocked out the symmetry of three and cast a shadow over a shadowless morning.

We were off very quickly after that, and many envious looks came my way because of Dulcie, particularly from the lowly nun acting as the prioress's secretary. It was the prioress who owned the traveling lapdogs:

two yappy, woolly bundles who really had no place on a pilgrimage at all. Poor Sister Secretary, who was riding an ugly mule with one of the yappers perched in front, could hardly go two paces without the prioress exhorting her to take care. I'd have been tempted to strangle both prioress and dog, but with pretty Dulcie beneath me and Walter swinging himself onto a dashing bay, I couldn't but think there had been a small miracle already.

The reeve, charged with bringing order to the group, chivvied us into a column. "Now," he called, pecking like a crow with indigestion, "I don't want to see a gaggle. We're pilgrims, not geese. Come along! Come along! Sir Knight, you should be first, for you can protect us, and Walter—goodness, Arondel's decked out like a maypole but never mind, never mind—will you go behind your father? At least Granada still looks like a warhorse. Good. Then—"

"Then me," said Toad Seekum.

The reeve stopped short. "You?"

"I believe so." The Toad rocked, and his mangy horse rocked too, with the weight.

"I entirely disagree." The reeve swung his rusty blade.

"You may be in charge of hauling sinful wretches before the church court, but you're nothing but a paid official."

The Toad pushed his roan behind Arondel's rump. "I, as the archdeacon's summoner with jurisdiction over immortal souls, clearly take precedence over somebody who simply oversees worldly accounts. Ask the squire."

Walter and the reeve exchanged glances. "Very well," said Master Reeve, "but watch out for Arondel's heels. The horse isn't as polite as its master."

The summoner scowled. "I'll have my friend next to me," he announced. "Pardoner Bernard, ride alongside." Pardoner Bernard, long-nosed and with hair like yellow dribbles, was thrilled to be the summoner's friend. He kicked his shaggy pony smartly in the ribs.

"Excuse me," said the reeve, "but since when did a pardoner, even a pardoner of Bernard's standing"— the irony in his voice was palpable—"take precedence over an apothecary or, indeed, a franklin, who we also have amongst us? Master Franklin does, after all, own enough land to represent a shire in Parliament and is a justice at the court sessions. A pardoner just sells pardons, and in my experience, not always for the right price."

"The apothecary's a woman and Master Franklin's not at the Parliament or in the courts now," said the summoner, stubborn jawed. "And are you suggesting that Pardoner Bernard's a crook?"

"I've never met a pardoner who wasn't," the reeve muttered.

The pardoner caught that. "Take care, Master Reeve."

He wagged a crooked finger. "I've a piece of Our Lady's veil about my person that's been known to slice like an ax."

"Gentlemen, gentlemen!" The knight suddenly exerted himself. "Squabbling before we've even set out? And over rank? Shame! Let each man choose his place, and each woman too, according to his fancy. If Master Summoner wants to ride with his friend, and if both are willing to risk Arondel's heels, let them do just that. God doesn't stand on precedence and, during a pilgrimage, nor should we."

"Why are you still at the front then?" somebody shouted. I think it was the cook. "Let's see you give up your place."

"Gladly," said Sir Knight, drawing Granada to the side with a gesture simultaneously grand and humble, and signaling for Walter to do the same. "Whosoever wishes to lead the procession, let him make himself known right away. I shall gladly hand over the responsibility of finding the way and of being the first to cross swords with any enemies we may meet." There followed a long minute during which nobody moved. Without further comment, Sir Knight remained in the place he thought rightly his. It was, indeed, the reeve who gave up. Muttering into his chin, he mounted his plump stallion and used his spurs unnecessarily. "We'll stay at the back, Scot," he said to the horse, and the animal's dappled ears flattened as its master's irritation flowed down the reins.

Storing all this away to amuse my father on my return, I managed to avoid being corralled with the other ladies by a thick-necked, honey-tongued friar but then risked being swept up by a mountainous dame of some age whose deafness caused her forever to clack, "What? What?" like a garden crow. What with her, the wailing of the mother over her baby's lost rattle, the trilling of Sir Knight's page, the cries of an escaped hawk, and the yapping of those silly dogs, we were really more traveling circus than journeying penitents.

"May I ride with you?" I asked, slipping Dulcie between Luke and his master. Luke glared at Dulcie through his glasses. I knew he was thinking of Walter, and not fondly. My heart gave a small flutter. Nobody had ever been jealous on my behalf before. "The black rims suit you," I said before he could open his mouth, "and here I am, all because of you, seeing if dreams can come true." I didn't want him to glare the whole way to Canterbury.

He pushed back his hair though he refused to smile. "This is Belle," he said by way of introduction to the man at his side, "and Belle, this is Master Chaucer."

"Master Chaucer?" I grasped Dulcie's reins so hard that she squealed. "Geoffrey Chaucer?" Master Chaucer gave a nod, those quick eyes missing nothing. "Jesus Mary! You never told me your master was famous."

"Would it have been important?"

"It would have been *something*," I said nippily. "I'm so glad to meet you, sir."

"Are you indeed," said Master Chaucer, and I was conscious of a sharp appraisal. I was sure he could see straight into my head, which made me nervous. I was also very aware that Dulcie was hardly the right mount for a girl who had crippled her father.

"Walter de Pleasance, the knight's squire, lent Dulcie to me," I explained. "She really belongs to his sister but the sister's run off with a Frenchman and they're going to Canterbury to pray for her. I didn't like to refuse because I didn't have anything else to ride." There followed a silence too awkward to leave unbroken. "Luke told me that your wife's ill," I blustered on. "I'm sorry." I wanted to say something brilliant. After all, Master Chaucer was the most famous person I'd ever met. I could think of nothing beyond the horribly ordinary.

"Thank you," he said.

"You're quite welcome," I replied.

Master Chaucer rode his gray horse carefully, mindful both of its feelings and the safety of the writing box strapped firmly behind him, to which his hands—clean and not ink stained, I was surprised and a little

disappointed to see—kept straying. The horse, one ear permanently forward and one back, seemed as mindful of its burden as Master Chaucer himself, and also rather conscious of its saddlery, which was blue, like Arondel's, though not as exuberantly so. I think it had been chosen to match the bonnet that grew from the Master's head like a large mushroom, a short tail flapping behind to protect his neck from the sun. All in all, he did not look as I expected a writer to look, which was yellow as a dusty parchment and with no care for clothes at all. This, I decided, was because he wasn't only a writer but also a man of business and politics, and I scolded myself for not having listened more carefully when my father and the host had spoken of the famous trial at which Master Chaucer had given evidence. Had he also been a Member of Parliament? Was he still? I struggled to remember so that I could impress him with my knowledge. I failed.

"I'm on pilgrimage for my father," I said. "I expect Luke has told you."

"Luke's the soul of discretion," said Master Chaucer, letting go of the writing box for a second and patting Luke's hand. "He learned early that I like people to tell their own stories in their own time."

"Stories that Luke writes down?" I couldn't help sounding envious.

The Master scrutinized me again, and then, touching

his box, said, "I'm not doing too well with my stories at the moment. I must be getting old."

"Nonsense. It's because your wife's sick," I said. I know it was impertinent, since we had only just met, but I didn't want the conversation to end. "It's hard to write when you're worried."

He shot me another look. His horse stumbled. I wasn't surprised. Its mane was so thick it must have weighed almost as much as a fleece. I tried to make a little joke. "You could hide a library of stories in there and nobody would ever find them," I said.

"What? Oh. Yes. Very amusing," the Master said. "Are you on a special pilgrimage?"

I began to explain and the Master seemed to be listening. "The truth of it is that wives are curious creatures," he suddenly interrupted. "I don't know that I even liked mine much until she became ill. Only now, when I may lose her, do I find that the prospect of life without her makes me gloomy." He glanced apologetically, not at me but at Luke. "Even for a man who's made monkish promises, I'm afraid I'll be dreary company."

Luke's return glance was full of affection. "You don't know how to be dreary."

"Dear, dear." Master Chaucer shook his head. "That sounds very exhausting."

"I didn't mean—I mean—I don't—I just—" Luke

tied his tongue in such knots it was a wonder his spectacles didn't steam up.

"Easy, boy, easy." Master Chaucer patted his hand again. "It's just my way of taking a compliment."

Luke met my eye by mistake and shifted in his saddle, hitting his head on a low-hanging branch. It must have hurt, but his expression was so funny and I was so nervous that I laughed. Master Chaucer jumped as though he'd forgotten I was there, and his hand sprang back to his writing box. I noted the gesture and thought I'd copy it myself when I was a writer.

"So, flame-haired Belle on the horse of a girl who has run off with a Frenchman, what do you like to do with yourself when you're not looking out for bell ropes?" he asked, giving me his full attention.

I flushed. "I like to make up stories, just as you do," I said. It was arrogant, I suppose, but the truth.

"Do you indeed. And do stories come readily to you?"

"Quite readily," I said. "Sometimes I make up my own and sometimes I hear one and make it more . . . more—"

"More colorful?"

"Yes," I said. "More colorful, because it's God's honest truth that God's honest truth can be a bit dull."

Master Chaucer's mouth curled in a delightfully foxy smile. "Not a bad reply, child. I myself often exaggerate, or even change things a little. Why not, so long as the purpose is entertainment and not malice. Do you agree, Luke?"

"I agree when you do it," Luke replied, still pulling twigs from his hair, and then added pointedly, "but beginners must be careful."

I bridled at being thought a beginner. "Stories have their own kind of truth," I pointed out. "And there's not much story if you don't make things up. I mean, you can't be a writer and just write about real life."

"Why not?" Luke snapped a twig.

I was amazed he even had to ask. "Because real life's only bearable if you don't have to live in it all the time," I said.

"Amen to that," Master Chaucer echoed. Two red spots dimpled the pallor of Luke's cheeks and he fiddled with the handle of the small meat knife he kept at his waist. Perhaps it was fortunate that at that moment a caterwauling arose, a duet between what sounded like a billy goat and a trumpet. "*Come hither, love, come home!*" I recognized the billy goat and so did Master Chaucer. "Ah!" he said, "so our summoner's a songbird!"

"He's a toad," I said with some feeling. "I'll bet he prizes out everybody's secrets and then stores them as little jars of poison."

Master Chaucer's foxy smile vanished. He leaned hard on his box and aged twenty years before my very eyes. "You think so?" he said. "What do you make of Summoner Seekum, Luke?"

"He asks too many questions," said Luke.

The Master blinked. "He does? What about?"

"He wants to know everybody's business," Luke said. "I mean, he asked why you were going to Canterbury and what you were writing. The effrontery!"

"And what did you tell him?"

"Why, the truth, of course." Luke gave me a look of small triumph. Then his face became grave. "But you should be careful, Master."

"I should?"

"Yes," Luke went on. "I'll bet he'd not hesitate to steal your ideas." He gestured to the box. "Make sure you keep them locked up."

"Ah, my ideas," said the Master, and some of his foxy look returned. "He's already tried that. He writes poetry, or what he imagines is poetry, and, most gratifyingly, he copies my style. We both sang our own works to the king a little while ago." He paused as the humility of the pilgrim battled the pride of the poet. "It would be dishonest of me to say that laughter didn't greet both our efforts." Another struggle. "I think it would also be dishonest not to say that the king laughed *with* me but *at* our friend, whose performance, if I remember correctly—and I do— he compared to the brayings of an ass." Though the recollection clearly pleased Master Chaucer, it can hardly have pleased the summoner.

Luke relaxed. "His hat's pretty asslike too."

"Asslike as mine?" the Master teased.

Luke's tongue again twisted into knots. "No, I didn't mean—I really meant—I mean yours isn't—"

"Calmly, boy, calmly!" Chaucer admonished, laughing. "If we're to get on, you must learn that I'm seldom looking to take offense. Untie your tongue. I was just about to remark that hats tell a great deal about a person."

"You're right," I said, pointing ahead. "Just look at Pardoner Bernard. He's warbling away, so dignified and holy. Yet by sewing that enormous bulgy thing on the top of that quite fetching little cap, he's turned himself into a clown."

"It's supposed to be St. Edmund's knucklebone," Luke said, at which the Master hooted like a naughty schoolboy, making Luke and me smile at each other. In moments, though, the hoots had gone and the Master closed his eyes, the years pressing down on him again.

The road grew too narrow for the four of us and there was a bit of barging. I wanted to continue to ride by Master Chaucer. Luke didn't want to give up his place and a skinny cleric persisted in pushing between us. In the end, I admitted defeat, gave Dulcie her head and caught up with Walter. He was countering the boredom of the walking pace on which his father insisted by braiding small bows into Arondel's mane and was very pleased to see me. When Summoner Seekum and his friend stopped to draw breath, he and I settled on singing a roundel my mother had taught me.

*Summer is a-coming in, merry sing cuckoo,*
*Bloweth mead and groweth seed and merry sing*
  *cuckoo.*
*Sing cuckoo!*
*Ewe bleateth after lamb, loweth after calve coo.*
*Bullock sterteth, buck averteth, merry sing cuckoo.*
*Cuckoo! Cuckoo! Now sing we all cuckoo,*
*Never swick thee never noo.*

"What a pretty voice you have," Walter said.

*Such* a gallant lie. I sing like a strangled cat. Even Walter didn't suggest an encore and instead told me of a tournament in which he and his father had taken part. After he had described the maneuvers of his third encounter, lance by lance, and exactly which tunic he'd chosen for each new joust, I began to wonder what kind of silken favor I would give a man who wanted to fight for me. Would I make a virtue of my red hair by reflecting it or would I simply dye it raven black, perhaps, or sun gold? What color was Guinevere's hair, or Sir Galahad's? I'd tried not to think of King Arthur's court since my father's accident and now I couldn't remember. Walter tapped my arm gently. He'd stopped talking. "I'm afraid I was boring you," he said, and grinned, "though your poppet's still listening."

"Not at all," I said, quickly tucking Poppet into my sleeve. "I was just wondering what kind of a favor would suit me, with my red hair and all."

"Oh," he said, happily nodding. "Yes, yes. Red can be a problem. Let's see, though. We can either be brave and go for orange—make a virtue of the clash—or perhaps green would be safer?"

"Can you remember what color Guinevere's hair was?" I asked.

"I can't remember Guinevere's, but I do remember that Arthur's hair was yellow." He twisted in his stirrups. "Let's see. I have it very exactly in my mind. Yes. Arthur's was the same color as Master Chaucer's scribe's if his were clean and properly cut."

It was true. Luke's hair, which had seemed so dull, suddenly seemed full of possibilities. "You're quite right," I said, and before I knew it, we were talking about hair fashions, the new vogue for belted tunics, and trying to decide whether tapering points on shoes made men's feet look elegant or ridiculous. I thought what a kind person he was, particularly since I was sure he preferred talking about swords and battles. It was nice, too, that for now at least I could live in a fairy tale in which famous writers, rich squires, alchemists' sons, and bell founders' daughters could get along as easily as cows at cud.

At dusk we headed for the glow of a town and walked in procession through the gate amongst a trickle of laborers who had been clearing out an overgrown moat. Set amongst the stone houses of the town's merchants and officials we found an inn that could put up all of us for the night. It was quite a grand place, considering. How I would manage to pay my bill I had no idea. I told myself that if Dulcie sneezed three times before I dismounted, something would turn up. Though I dismounted as tardily as possible, she only sneezed twice.

I thought of pretending I was fasting and refusing dinner, but I was starving, so let myself be seated between Walter and Sir Knight and opposite Luke and Master Chaucer. Though Luke said little, the conversation flowed, and, from those who opened their souls, it turned out that there were not two people amongst us who had the same reason for making the pilgrimage. St. Thomas was going to be very busy.

Walter carved for his father, and then, slightly to my embarrassment, for me. He set meat on my plate with a little jeweled dagger and cut it neatly into three. "We don't want to see any of your silver, Belle. For this journey, you're Dulcie's guest," he whispered. Walter wasn't a fool. He must have realized that I had no money. I thanked him and then I sneezed, which was a relief.

We ate too well for pilgrims, Sir Knight and Walter with the carelessness of those who have only known plenty, and the poorer pilgrims with the enthusiasm of those who've never been sure of enough. The friar simply speared something from every platter that passed him, often cramming his prize straight into his mouth, while Master Reeve cut all his food into tiny pieces and darted at them with long fingers. Everybody's patience was tried by the prioress, whose dogs, at her insistence, sat at the table like drooling empresses. The prioress herself refused all food, but though her plate was always empty, I noticed her mouth always full. The Toad, of course, ate hugely and messily, and scarcely concealed his fascination with the lady apothecary's hideously scarred face. She had only three teeth and when people spoke to her, drew her gaze back from some place beyond the walls and answered so sharply that nobody addressed her twice.

After the plates were cleared, we settled ourselves around the room and Sir Knight read a long account of a battle from a little book whose cover, so he told us, was splotched with blood from one of his own wounds. The blood was much more impressive than the story, which was dull enough to send a sheep to sleep. It was then that the trouble started, because Walter asked the Master if he'd ever witnessed a battle and when the Master said that he hadn't, remarked that it must be much nicer to write about war than fight in one. I'm sure Walter didn't mean to imply any cowardice on the Master's part, but Luke chose to take offense on the Master's behalf and sprang up, red fork flashing again in those goose-gray eyes, skin like molten silver. Our Christian monk had a very pagan temper. Some of the pilgrims sniggered. But I didn't. Walter sprang up too, hands up, palms out. "I'm so sorry. I meant no harm, I really didn't." He offered a conciliatory smile but it was only at the Master's insistence that Luke slowly unclenched his fists. By the time he sat down he was just an angry, lank-haired boy again.

Order restored, the landlord banked up the fire and brought out cakes to dip in our wine. In the sweetness of it all I must have dozed off because the next thing I knew, everybody was getting up to prepare for bed and I needed to relieve myself. There were internal latrines hanging over the stream that bypassed the inn, but since there was a line, I decided to go outside. As I straightened my skirt I was seized from behind, and I knew who it was from the stench of must and garlic. "Jesus Mary, Master Summoner!" I cried loudly. "What on earth are you doing?"

"Make a noise and it'll be something you'll not forget," he hissed, and the pungency of his breath scattered the sweetness and peace. I could feel my skirt riding up and regretted bitterly having taken off

Walter's hose before supper to give my legs an airing. The Toad pressed my back against a tree trunk, then squashed his chest hard over mine, squeezing my calves against the bark until my scabs tore. His lips were a greasy slash far too near my own.

"What do you want?" I tried not to breathe any of him in. I knew, of course, what he wanted. It was what all men want. But I was quite wrong. "I want to know what you were discussing with our famous Master Chaucer," he said.

"Master Chaucer?" I was stupid in my surprise. "Nothing."

His shins scraped my bare knees. "A whole day's a long time to discuss nothing."

I couldn't imagine where this was leading. "We were talking about the pardoner's hat," I said rather desperately. A bead of his sweat dripped onto my neck.

"The pardoner's hat?" He jolted, forcing my skirt up farther. His knee followed my skirt. "Very clever."

"Please," I said. I wanted to wriggle my skirt down, but instinct told me not to move. "Let me go. I've nothing of interest to you."

His answer was to squeeze my waist until tears started in my eyes. His mouth was so close now that his spittle peppered my chin. I thought that if he kissed me I should be sick. I wished I hadn't been rude to him when we first met. Perhaps this was my punishment for that. But he never mentioned it. Instead, he echoed what he'd said in the Tabard yard. "Are you loyal to England, Belle the bell founder's daughter?"

I thought maybe he'd gone mad, so I wrenched my head around, away from his mouth, although now his whiskers were like fleas in my ears. "What are you talking about? What on earth do you mean?" Why didn't somebody come to rescue me?

"Come, lady. You know exactly what I mean. Do you take the side of the king or the commission?"

"Commission?" I really had no idea what he was talking about. "What commission?"

He squeezed harder. "I suppose you know who the king is?"

"Of course I do. King Richard II." I had to get him off me. If I'd had a meat knife I'd have stabbed him.

"And you know that his taxes and fancy friends have brought England to near ruin?"

"I know as little of the king's affairs as he knows of mine," I replied with as much spirit as I dared. "I know that he finds your poetry laughable, though." Such a stupid thing to say and had the summoner bellowed his fury, I would have been less alarmed. But he simply said, "Ah, Master Chaucer has been gossiping. Quite the writer. Quite the wit. *Quite the operator.*" He narrowed his eyes to slits. The memory of that unfortunate poetry performance clearly still made him seethe.

However, even this wasn't what he was referring to. "We'll come to the Master later. I want to talk first about the company your father keeps."

My heart stuck in my throat. "My father keeps no company. His injury sees to that."

"He keeps company with the host of the Tabard." The summoner rolled the words around his mouth. "And Master Host's not very loyal to England; not very loyal at all."

His grip loosened a little. He knew he had me. I tried to recover some bravado. "My father's just a bell founder," I snapped, "and Master Host's just a neighbor."

"In times such as ours nobody's 'just a neighbor.' Even a silly girl like you must know that the king's mustering an army to use against those who object to the way he lives. Why do you think even this paltry little town's busy restoring defenses that probably haven't been used since the godforsaken days of King Stephen?" He shook me, and visibly enjoyed it. "A monarch should have the good of the realm at heart, and our king, God curse him, has only the good of the king." He leered into my face. "Master Geoffrey Chaucer favors the king."

"And why shouldn't he? Whatever his faults, the king's set above us by God," I retorted.

"A *good* king is set above us by God," the summoner contradicted, "and a bad one by the devil."

"You're calling the king the devil?" My terror increased rapidly because only a true madman would dare to make such an accusation.

The summoner pressed so close I could feel the end of his nose. "King Richard certainly takes the devil's advice." He squeezed my waist again. "He also forgets the law, and where once he met with his people, now he flees from them. The commission, on the other hand, meets with everybody. It speaks for the people. It speaks for England. It speaks for me and it should speak for you. The king cares only about being king. That makes him a very bad king—an unworthy king, a king we cannot trust." His knee lodged in a place no knee should lodge. I grew faint. "But you knew all that, my pealing Belle. Of course you did. You're not a fool and you've got two pretty ears which, I'll warrant, hear more than they should." I felt something sticky. His tongue! It slimed over my earlobe. Now I tried shoving violently. He enjoyed that too, for he easily contained me. "You may also have heard, since you're such a fan of his, that Master Chaucer has occasionally been a royal messenger boy." His tongue was right in my ear. "*And I believe he still is.*" I tried to think of myself as a statue. "He's on a royal mission to ask the king of France to make sure the commissioners don't tip King Richard from his throne."

That was so ridiculous that I couldn't help myself.

"Nonsense," I burst out. "King Richard won't have anything to do with the king of France. How could he? The French king's our enemy."

The summoner withdrew his tongue. "Good for you! You've at least grasped that! The king of France *is* our enemy—at least he's the enemy of the commission and all real Englishmen. But to keep his throne, Richard may choose to make him a friend." He wiped the spittle from my chin with his thumb. What kind of man wears a ring on his thumb? Oh, where was somebody to rescue me?

"You're saying the king's not loyal to his kingdom?" I said, terrified that if I remained silent I would feel that tongue again.

"I'm saying that King Richard would prefer to see England overrun by French knights than have to submit himself to the will of an English parliament." He shifted his knee down a little.

I breathed. "Well, the French king's not in Canterbury," I said, "so it would be a funny place for King Richard to send Master Chaucer to find him."

He raised his knee again. I sprang onto my tiptoes. "Of course the French king's not in Canterbury," he said, snarling, "but Canterbury is stuffed full of French pilgrims, or at least people pretending to be pilgrims. It's the perfect place for conspirators to meet. Once we've arrived, Master Chaucer'll pass on a message inviting

King Charles to send French knights to help King Richard keep his throne, even though they both know that King Charles wants the English throne for himself."

I made a last bid. "French pilgrims, English pilgrims! French kings, English kings! French knights, English knights! What does any of this matter to me?"

"Your father matters to you," the summoner said.

My blood drained to my toes. The summoner could feel it. At last he stood back. He knew I wouldn't run. "Now you're listening, eh, Miss Belle Who Thinks She's So Clever." He placed his hands either side of my shoulders. His pouch swung away from his belt and, inside it, something shifted and rattled. One hand shot down to silence whatever it was and then was back, stroking my left cheek. "Are you listening properly?" I didn't nod, which made him click that horrible tongue and stroke harder. "I've a little job that needs doing and I think you're just the person to do it." Stroke, stroke, stroke, those dirty fingernails scraping my skin. "I've been watching you. You're a clever minx. Set your mind to it and you could get any man to trust you. The job's hardly difficult. All you have to do is pluck out the Master's secrets as we travel and deliver them to me."

I flattened my palms against the tree. My legs were jelly. "Why pick on me? Why not get Luke to do your dirty work?"

"Because he'd refuse."

"How do you know?"

"He's that sort." He spat over his shoulder, then grinned. "And his father doesn't frequent that hotbed of treachery, the Tabard."

"Please," I begged, though to beg stuck in my craw, "my father's not a plotter and as for Master Host, his opinions about everything from the king to boiled eggs change all the time."

"Ah! So you do admit that the Tabard's a center of gossip?"

"I admit nothing of the sort."

"But Master Host talks about the king. You just said so."

"I said Master Host talks about everything—"

"Everything includes the king. And your father listens."

"He *hears*, but that doesn't mean to say—"

"You've said enough. *Questio quid juris?*"

"What?"

"Never mind. Have you ever seen a cripple hanged?"

We stood in awful silence. Then suddenly the summoner was gasping. Pale fingers had wound themselves around his thick neck, and through the garlic I smelled brimstone. "Master Summoner?" Luke's voice was ice-cold. "What on earth are you doing?"

The summoner choked.

"Oh, thank God!" I was so relieved I almost cried.

"Has he hurt you?"

Seekum's eyes were bulging, but even in the dark, the threat they contained was strong and clear. He retracted not a word. "No. He hasn't hurt me."

Luke held on a second longer before letting go. The summoner gurgled and spluttered. "We were simply passing the time of day," he said, a picture of aggrieved innocence.

"At this time of night?" Luke was completely disbelieving.

"Is there a law against it?" Seekum wiped his face on his sleeve. "And is it not the truth, Belle?"

"Yes." I stared at my feet.

"And was it not so pleasant that we'll speak again?"

I didn't reply.

"Sweet dreams to you both." The summoner made a crude pout with his lips. "Very sweet dreams."

We waited until he'd gone. "He followed me out here," I said. "You know the type. He's just an old lecher taking advantage. Believe me, I've dealt with worse." I sounded too bright.

"So I needn't have come looking for you?" The leather thongs that were supposed to keep his glasses firm had loosened. Luke had to keep pushing the glasses up.

"I didn't mean that," I whispered.

We began to walk back to the inn. I wanted to feel

him against my shoulder. I just felt the need. But he didn't invite me to get that close, and anyway, I felt defiled and deceitful. I was glad of the dark.

"Walter would doubtless have challenged that animal to a contest." He kicked an abandoned wooden stool in the yard. "I wish—"

"Walter didn't notice I was missing."

We reached the ladies' chamber. "I always know where you are," Luke said.

The water in the pitcher was cold, but I turned the posy of night herbs the prioress had placed on my pillow into a scraper and scrubbed myself from head to toe. Even after I'd scraped and scrubbed until I was sore I felt dirty. I couldn't get the feel of saliva out of my ear. Only when the water ran out did I kneel in front of my bed, saying three Our Fathers on one knee, three on the other, and three on both. Then I pulled on Walter's woolen hose, buried myself under the blankets, and curled myself into the tightest ball possible.

The other ladies were already snoring but I remained awake a long time, scrunching Poppet into my neck. I'd once seen a man hanged—not even a man, just a boy, about the same age as the king. It had been the year of the great revolts, the year of my mother's pox. I was nine, the king thirteen. There had been riots over a poll tax and the king had been brave. I never knew the details. All I knew was that for days and days the air was full of howling and ash as people were dragged from their beds and London burned. Because the victims were mainly people of position, I don't think my father feared for us particularly, so we didn't flee as others did. Anyway, my mother was dying, so the outside world seemed unimportant.

The day my mother was taken from us, I went to buy corpse candles to burn beside her body. Outside the shop a crowd had gathered around a boy, a gentleman's son by the look of his clothes. I don't know what he was doing in Southwark or what he had done to annoy them, but the crowd attacked him violently. Without any warning, so it seemed to me, they rose like wild animals, plucked him from his horse, and strung him up with his own belt. He kicked and kicked, his arms jerking up and down, and he wet himself. That seemed worse than everything else. As the stain darkened his silk leggings, I hurried away.

Tonight I could see him again, only he wasn't a boy, he was my father, unable to kick of course, but with that spreading stain. "God help me," I whispered as the ladies snored on and the dogs snuffled, only there seemed no reason why he should. I got out of my bed and said another nine Our Fathers, then nine more. I made three circles of the room. I looked out of the window until I'd seen three rats. I missed my pumice stone. When I shut my eyes, I could see the summoner, and he was pushing me and my father into an abyss. Only when I remembered Walter's kindness and Luke's jealous concern did I find something to cling to. It was only then that I slept.

# 4

Take counsel ere you speak, let nothing slip.
My son, too often by some babbling speech
Many are blasted . . .

The cock crowed early, and though the room was muggy
from the sleepy heat of so many bodies, I shivered as
I pulled on my dress. The joy of yesterday morning
had vanished. I ate no breakfast. Walter again helped
me to mount and made no comment when I increased
my usual three compulsive skips to six. I tried to smile
at Luke but he was not looking. As I passed the summoner, he wagged his thumb, which made Pardoner
Bernard smirk, though I'm sure he knew nothing of
last night's encounter. I shrugged. I did not go near the
Master. In the light, it was easier to convince myself
that if God didn't protect my father, he wasn't worthy
to be God. I tried to be nonchalant.

Dulcie welded herself close to Arondel. As we jogged
back onto the road, Walter began to describe the pen-
nants of each Knight of the Round Table and, with his
father's obvious approval, followed this with a highly
intricate but not altogether fascinating assessment of
the defensive benefits of a great helm over a basinet,

the essential nature of an aventail, the development of the fauld, the discomfort of a besegew, and the possible blistering potential of ill-fitting sabayons. I had no idea what any of these things were, but I didn't care. The boredom was comforting, and Walter's bobbing curls and lark's voice shone a light on last evening's dark nightmare until, after an hour or two, I gave myself a stern lecture. The summoner was just a summoner, not the Lord Chief Justice. He had no power over life and death. His threats were horrible but they were just threats. Master Chaucer was a pilgrim on a pilgrimage. I was a pilgrim on a pilgrimage. The king, the commission, and France were nothing to do with either him or me. As for my father, he had friends, some in high places. If anybody came to take him, he would have his protectors.

After passing three vagrants locked in the stocks, I was calm enough to note the neatness of Walter's eyebrows and the suppleness of his waist. With those pearly teeth, he was really quite perfect.

"How do you keep them so white?" I broke in during an exposition of the benefits of chainmail against plated armor.

"And so plate is really—keep what white?"

"Your teeth?"

"Oh," he said, abandoning armor in an instant, "I mix up mint and chalk in a mortar, and of course I'm

never without a twig to pick out bits of food. Nothing nastier than a mouth full of leftovers. The smell! *Brrrrr.*" He flashed a smile. "Luke's got white teeth too. Have you noticed? I wonder what his secret is."

"We could ask him," I suggested.

This made Walter uncomfortable. "No, I don't think we should ask something like that."

"Why ever not?"

"Well, you could ask. But it's not the kind of thing men ask each other." He changed the subject. "What's the worst story you know?"

"That's easy," I answered, and without further ado began to tell not a tale of my own, but one I'd heard Master Miller tell to make my father laugh. To this day I don't know why I chose it. Perhaps because I was upset. Perhaps I knew Summoner Seekum was listening and thought, in some way, to show that his threats had not cowed me. Perhaps I wanted Walter to realize how worldly-wise and sophisticated I was. Honestly, who knows why we do things that, in the cold after light, are clearly silly. Anyhow, the story I began was a thoroughly bawdy one involving an idiotic carpenter; his neat, sweet, lecherous wife; a lovesick parish clerk; and a sly student. The miller had told it when he thought I was asleep and only realized I was awake when, at the very rudest point, I had giggled. My father had been furious. Now, even as I began, I knew I'd made a bad choice, and as the story got bawdier and bawdier, I became more and more flustered.

Then, God be thanked, there was a roar. "Foulness! Utter foulness! This tale's unfit for pilgrims' ears, or anybody else's for that matter! And you, a girl, *a girl*, think it right and proper to repeat it? Cover your ears, Madam Prioress!" The skinny cleric, hovering behind us, almost burst out of his jerkin. He brandished his whip. Believing the whip was meant for her, Dulcie bolted.

The cleric could never have guessed how grateful I was. Thank the Lord not to have to finish the tale! My cap flew off. My hair erupted like an autumn storm, and in the thunder of Dulcie's hooves, the last of the summoner was blown away. We flew, Dulcie and I. Out of habit, I turned myself into Queen Eleanor of Aquitaine speeding toward the tower at Châlus-Chabrol to see her favorite son, King Richard the Lionheart, as he lay dying. It was wonderful, being somebody else. "Will we be in time?" I cried. "Faster, Dulcie, faster, faster." She flattened into a streaming arrow.

Only when I had left everybody at least a quarter of a mile behind did Queen Eleanor fade and panic set in. What would happen if Dulcie swerved? If I was thrown and hurt, my father would suffer further. "Enough, now, Dulcie, please steady!" I shouted, but she, still dreaming her own dreams, sped on. I clung to the saddle. Not being a magic horse, she would tire eventually. But when? My gut and my leg muscles were already beginning to dissolve. Soon I would be as easy to shake off as a leaf in a breeze. I couldn't turn around. I couldn't look ahead. I couldn't do anything.

But others could, and I was suddenly aware, as was Dulcie, that we had company: on our right Picardy, Luke's workmanlike bay, and on our left Walter's blue-clad Arondel. Arondel, long-legged and oat-fueled, was barely trying. Picardy, however, was struggling, and Luke had to force him on. Dulcie, sensing a race, galloped faster. Walter was shouting instructions. "Take her rein and pull her around until she's galloping in a large circle."

"No," cried Luke, "she'll fall if you do that. She's going too fast and the ground's too slippery."

"Aim toward the river, then." Walter's face was shining. He was finding the speed as exhilarating as I had.

"No," cried Luke again. "Dulcie'll jump in."

"She can't gallop in the river!" Walter was almost singing.

"I can't swim," I yelled.

Now Walter took things much more seriously. He grasped the rein and dragged it over Dulcie's head, then, by unlucky accident, dropped it. Flapping dangerously, it threatened to loop her forelegs and bring her down. I screamed, Walter cried out, and Dulcie galloped joyfully on.

Luke wasted no more breath. He forced Picardy to gallop faster and when he was a little way in front, threw something into the air. At once a mist arose and Dulcie, surprised and disconcerted, faltered. With some dexterity, Walter leaned over and flicked the reins back over her head. When I took hold of them, Dulcie no longer set her elegant neck against me. The mist, now thickening and swirling, disoriented her, and she was grateful for a guiding hand. Within minutes we were all cantering, then trotting, then walking, the horses' flanks billowing. As quickly as it had arisen, the mist dissipated until you could believe it had never appeared. I wiped my eyes and nose and felt for my pendant. Thank God it was still there.

"Idiot clerk." Walter was furious. "Poor Dulcie, and poor you, Belle. How could a man brandish a whip when there are ladies in the company! It was monstrous." He glared behind him. We could hear Master Cleric still expostulating. "Did you hear her story? I did what any decent man would have done. Where are this creature's parents? They should be ashamed." He waved a small wooden crucifix in which, so he boasted, was embedded a relic of the true cross, brought back by a warrior uncle from the Holy Land.

The company was noisily divided, those who hadn't overheard the story supporting me, those who had supporting Master Cleric. Walter, who would certainly have been appalled had I finished the tale, politely avoided mentioning it at all.

"It was a miracle that God sent the cloud so low," he said. "He must love you very much, Belle, if he directs the weather to help you."

Luke raised his eyebrows, opened his mouth, and then shut it again. I would have smiled at him had my lips not still been clamped together.

"Mind you," Walter went on blithely, "even without God, a low cloud can sometimes be very useful." He patted Arondel's sweating shoulders. "Once, during a foggy tournament in Ghent, two knights chalked up their horses to make them invisible. Then it rained and how we laughed. As bits of the chalk were washed away, their horses looked just like ghosts in need of darning."

I coughed and loosened my lips. "Holy ghosts," I said.

"Indeed! Indeed! Holy ghosts!" Walter crowed. "Belle's quite brilliant, Luke, isn't she?"

"Brilliant," Luke said abruptly, and dropped back to find the Master. I turned, wanting him to stay, and instead found Summoner Seekum closing in. I was lucky. Sir Knight pushed past him, fussing, and, though he could see I was unhurt, insisted that I ride close beside him until he could be certain Dulcie would not bolt again.

Like his son, Sir Knight was also much too well bred to mention my story, and the general chatter now was the miracle of the cloud. When Luke, resuming his place next to the Master, tried to explain that it was a trick and no more miraculous than the dew, he was shouted down. This was a pilgrimage. They would have their miracle.

Only Master Chaucer remained quizzical. "Clouds are clouds," he said, "and miracles are miracles."

Summoner Seekum pushed his horse's nose against the Master's leg. "Indeed, Master Chaucer, indeed. Yet not everything is always as it seems, I find. Is that not right?" Master Chaucer said nothing. As he passed me, Summoner Seekum made a noose with his reins. I saw the hanging boy again.

We spent that night in a barn with the farmer's cattle and pigs, which Sir Knight's horse didn't like at all. Shortly after we left the next morning, there was a rumpus over the priest's crucifix. He'd been boasting of it to the half-witted swineherd and now it was gone. It seemed that even pilgrims weren't safe from villainy. This diverted attention from yesterday's goings-on, but the delay meant we'd only been going about an hour before a messenger shouted for us to stop. The summoner had made me so nervous that my heart leaped into my mouth. But the message was not for me. It was for the Master, and it was a very gloomy message indeed. The worst, in fact. His wife had died. I know I should have been sorry, but since I'd never met her, all

I felt was relief. With Mistress Chaucer dead, the summoner's plans were quite foiled. Even if the Master was up to something, which I didn't believe for a minute, I couldn't find out because he would have to return home.

The messenger didn't tarry and when he had gone, the Master dismounted. He handed Dobs's reins to Luke. Respectful of death, we all dismounted too. The Master unstrapped his writing box, tucked it under his arm, and wandered off the road toward the river. For all his bright clothes, he was a shrunken, melancholy figure as he settled himself on a stone and set out his writing tools. "Looks like we'll be here for a bit," said the wagoner, loosening the carthorses' traces. Sir Knight, with Walter and the page in attendance, took the opportunity to fly his hawk. I hooked Dulcie's reins over a tree and went to Luke. "I don't think he expected her to die," Luke said, never taking his eyes off the Master, "at least not while he was away."

"You'll be setting off back to London very soon."

Luke's lips tightened. "No need to sound so pleased."

How could I explain? "Has he got children?" I asked.

"Two that I know of, but the oldest, Thomas, is with the Duke of Lancaster in Spain, and I don't know where the younger one is."

The Master was hunched over a parchment, his quill trimmed and poised but no words coming. It was a miserable sight and it suddenly struck me hard that if God had let good Master Chaucer's wife die, he was never going to do anything for my father's legs. The seed of miraculous hope that Luke had sown in my soul outside the oculist's shop began to wither. I bit my pendant. "God doesn't seem to have listened to the Master's prayers."

At first Luke thought I was being pert and he stiffened against me. Then, just as quickly, he melted, and I saw myself reflected in two milky irises, not so much gray today as violet and deep enough to drown in. This wasn't without its discomforts. Drowning eyes are all-seeing eyes, and there was plenty about me that I didn't want Luke to see. Without Poppet to steady me I had difficulty keeping my chin from wobbling. "Luke?" It came out as a gurgle.

"Yes?"

"Will you pray for my father? God will listen to you, I'm sure. After all, you're practically a monk."

He put his glasses back on. The purple dulled. "Of course I'll pray for your father," he said. "I'd be honored." His touch on my shoulder was light as a butterfly. "Now, take Dobs. I must see to the Master's baggage."

I held the reins, wiping my tears on the cob's sturdy shoulder. Why hadn't I been born a horse? They were afflicted by neither conscience nor nightmares. Then I felt disloyal. If I were a horse, I'd want to be pretty Dulcie, not loyal Dobs, though Dobs was easily the more useful and dependable. I was rather disgusted at myself. How could I be daydreaming *now*? Dobs sighed. I patted him. "You're a better horse than I am a girl," I told him. One ear twitched, but not for me. He had eyes only for his master.

"We're all ready," Luke said when Master Chaucer returned to us. "I've got your baggage and the lady apothecary has lent us her pack pony." He took the writing box and reattached it to the saddle. Master Chaucer leaned heavily against Dobs's flank. "You'll feel better when we're on the move," Luke said, trying to comfort him. "Here, use my hands as a stirrup."

The Master grunted, keeping both feet on the ground.

"Are you unwell?" Luke asked anxiously, as minutes passed and the Master still made no move to mount.

Master Chaucer slowly shook his head. "I'm going on to Canterbury," he said.

"Yes," Luke said. "We'll set off again after the funeral."

"No, I'm not going back for the funeral."

"Not going back?"

I noticed how Master Chaucer avoided Luke's eyes as he spoke. I couldn't believe anything bad of the Master, but I felt a chill. "My wife's friends can bury her just as well as I can," he said too quickly. "And that would be more fitting. I've not been a good husband but I'll be a better widower and start by praying to St. Thomas for her immortal soul." His tongue clicked. His mouth was dry. Mine was too.

"But won't people expect—I mean, wouldn't she want—?"

"She's dead, Luke. She wants nothing now except heaven. Anyway, the messenger said her body was not in a good state, so even if I gallop back as fast as Dobs can carry me, she'll most likely be in the ground before I get home."

"If we hurry, we could be there in a day—less." Luke couldn't abandon what he thought was right.

Master Chaucer slapped his hand hard against the writing box. "You're my scribe, not my inquisitor."

Stung, Luke walked the pack pony back to the wagons.

Master Chaucer caught me staring. "What's the matter with you?" He fussed with his sleeves. I was acutely aware of the summoner lounging against a tree, observing. I hung on to my pendant and took a deep breath. My legs were jelly again.

"Why must you go on, Master Chaucer? What's the rush?" My voice sounded strained and false. The Master's features settled into stone.

"I don't inquire into your business."

I swallowed. "That's because I have no business."

"And you think I do?" His top lip twitched. Such a tiny movement, but my legs jellied further. Our eyes met. I don't know what mine were full of but whatever it was it made him blurt out, "Oh dear! I'm good at stories but so bad at—" He stopped and was very discomfited.

Sickness rose in my throat. Master Chaucer was just a pilgrim. He must be. The summoner's suppositions must be nonsense. They must. I fixed my eyes on Luke and bargained frantically. *If Luke turns around before he takes another three steps, I'll . . . I'll do what? I'll get on Dulcie and gallop home? I'll do as the summoner wants? I'll . . . I'll . . .* Luke took two steps and hesitated. *What will I do? What will I do?* Then somebody called and he turned. I spoke very fast, not knowing before I spoke what words were going to emerge. "Please say nothing more, Master Chaucer. Summoner Seekum suspects you've other business apart from the pilgrimage and he wants me to be his spy. But I can't tell him anything you don't tell me so don't tell me anything. Please."

The Master raised his head wearily. "Ah yes. The summoner. I suppose I'd really guessed."

"Don't look at him!"

The Master drooped. "I'm so sorry, Belle. The summoner had no business to involve you." There was an awkward silence.

"Look, Master Chaucer," I said, "I don't care what you're doing. I just want to pray for my father and that's what I'm going to do."

"Quite right." There was another long pause, then, just as I was about to go back to Dulcie—"Walk with me," the Master said.

I should have refused, but his fame and his grief

made me naturally deferential. "We'll be watched," I said rather hopelessly.

"I know. Walk with me anyway."

"I'll get Luke." I felt hysterically anxious.

"Do you have to? Luke believes nothing but good of me."

That stopped me in my tracks. "And I don't?" Then I was walking. "Whatever you do, it must be for a reason," I said, more to reassure myself.

"That's kind." The Master knotted his fingers behind his back. We got to the river. "Do you know what a trimmer is?" he asked, turning his full gaze on me.

"No."

"Can I tell you?"

It was so odd that the Master should ask permission. "I suppose so," I said in the end.

"Thank you. A trimmer, Belle, is the worst kind of person. A trimmer's somebody who doesn't want to end up on the wrong side." He gave me a very frank look. "In my public life, that's what I've always been, and very successfully so."

"Nobody wants to end up on the wrong side," I mumbled.

He unknotted his fingers and reknotted them again. "In some ways, you know, Summoner Seekum's a braver man than I am." He shook his head when I tried to disagree. "No. It's true. Seekum may be lecherous and scab

ridden, but he's run his colors up the mast and doesn't care who knows it. Did he tell you that he's joined those who have declared themselves the king's enemies?" I looked at my feet. "Yes," said the Master, "I can see he did. And it's brave, Belle, because he knows that if the king wins, his own life may be forfeit. I, on the other hand, who have been in Parliament and should disapprove of the king, at the same time take the king's wages, thus neatly keeping a foot in both camps." He paused. "It's also a matter of public record, as Seekum must well know, that I've occasionally undertaken private missions in royal service."

My mouth opened.

The Master waited until I shut it again. "If that disappoints you, I'm sorry. Perhaps I should add, though, that the summoner's wrong if he imagines I believe our present king to be a good king. I don't. That's the truth and you can tell him I said so."

"I'll tell that toad nothing at all," I declared with more conviction than I felt.

"Oh, you will if you have to, I daresay."

I glanced back. Luke was standing beside Dobs, hands on hips. I had usurped his place and his hurt was palpable, even from a distance. I wanted to run to him, to explain, but the Master hadn't finished. He bent down, plucked a reed, and held it in the breeze. "Look how it bends," he said. "That's how it withstands the wind that snaps an oak's fat branches." He let go and the reed curved a graceful descent. "I bend, just like that reed." He grimaced. "You see, Richard shouldn't be king yet, and wouldn't be if his father had lived. It's one of God's poorer jokes that we're ruled by a mercurial boy. Have you uncles, Belle?"

"None," I said, wondering if grief had made the Master lose his reason. What had uncles to do with anything? "I've no relations except for my father."

"King Richard has uncles, some good men amongst them. Unfortunately, he also has friends, and friends and relations are an unhappy mix. The king listens to his friends when it might be wiser to listen to his family, particularly his uncle John, Duke of Lancaster, who has been very kind to me." The Master plucked another reed. "He's quarreled with Duke John and behaves very high-handedly with all the great lords whose support he needs. Now he's made his other uncle, Thomas, Duke of Gloucester, so angry that a rebellion is threatened."

"The king's uncle is going to rebel against the king? How dare he!"

"Oh, Belle, men do all manner of things for power. Thomas of Gloucester thinks he'd make a good king himself. Moreover, he's a cantankerous fellow who loves war, just as Richard's father did. It's public knowledge that he thinks Richard disgraces both God and the kingly office by not being nearly keen enough on fighting."

"But I thought God didn't like fighting."

"Only certain sorts of fighting. Apparently, if men fight in his name, he doesn't mind that at all." The Master's mouth kinked into an unwilling grin that almost immediately vanished. "The truth is that a rebellion would have support. Richard did so well during his early years, but that's all forgotten now. Many whisper that far from upholding his father's memory, he's turning into his great-grandfather."

"What happened to him?"

"Deposed and murdered," Master Chaucer said, and stared over the river as though trying to see into the future. "I don't want Richard to suffer the same fate."

I spoke slowly, filling in the gaps. "So you're going to ask King Charles of France to send men-at-arms to England to help King Richard keep his throne." As soon as the words were out I regretted them. "Don't—" I began.

The Master spoke quickly and firmly. "Listen. Nobody with any sense wants to see Richard deposed, but not everybody has much sense. If Richard is to stop his uncle Thomas of Gloucester, the Earl of Arundel, and the Duke of Warwick seizing power—" I looked quite blank. "These names mean nothing to you, I know," the Master said, "but believe me, Belle, they are powerful men and they seem quite determined to destroy the king and rule England themselves. They've even made up a—"

"Commission," I said.

"A Commission of Government," the Master corrected, frowned, then softened. "Yes, a commission, which they say is acting on the people's behalf and to which men should rally." He shook his head. "They've humiliated the king, demanding to see his household finances as though he were a troublesome child, and they're unlikely to stop there. With enemies like this, is it really surprising that Richard has resorted to enlisting help from abroad?"

"Why are you telling me this?"

"I want you to understand that whatever Seekum insinuates, I carry no letters or documents and I'm meeting nobody. I'm going to Canterbury for my wife just as you go for your father." The Master's voice was suddenly very tired. "Come. I've delayed everybody long enough."

There were raised eyebrows when the other pilgrims learned that Master Chaucer was not going home to bury his wife, and, inevitably, we'd not gone half a mile before I found the summoner beside me. I didn't bother to avoid him. Indeed, I told him, in as deadpan a manner as I could, exactly what the Master had told me, except for the stuff about the Master being a trimmer and the compliments he had paid to the summoner himself. Nothing would drag those out of me. "That's all," I said. "The Master's made it very clear that he's carrying nothing and meeting nobody because he's going to Canterbury to pray for his wife's immortal soul. So, I've done what you asked and from here on, you've no reason to speak to me ever again." I trotted smartly off. I wanted to ride with Luke, but it was clear he didn't want to ride with me. He had sacrificed the rest of his life to be the Master's confidante and scribe on this journey. He was not inclined to welcome a rival.

That night I dreamed of Luke and Walter, and we were all saving the hanging boy together. Only the hanging boy turned into the summoner, and after we'd cut him down he made three nooses with his fingers and hanged the three of us. It was a horrible, feverish dream and I was glad to wake early, even though what woke me brought complications all its own.

# 5

Quick-eyed, as horsely as a horse can be . . .

Despite Walter's hose, the saddle had chafed the inside of my thighs and calves, and when that chafing was added to the damage left by my final, vicious pumicing, my legs were completely on fire. The moment they woke me, I could think of nothing but plunging them into cold water, so I ran down the stairs without even dressing properly and rushed to the brook behind the stables. It was full of stable boys filling buckets. Stifling a moan, I fought my way through undergrowth until the brook narrowed and cut deep banks between overhanging trees. It wasn't far enough away, really, but I couldn't wait any longer. Panting, I pulled off the hose, biting my lip as the scabs tore, and plunged into the water. Icy cold and running hard, it foamed above my knees and nothing had ever felt so good. It took several moments for the burning to ease. When it did the relief was so great I laughed out loud. I leaned against the bank and let my skirts billow about in the current.

As my skin cooled, so did the fever of my dream. I'd done what the summoner asked. He had no hold on me anymore. Now I had to get on with praying for my father—that, and repairing the rift with Luke I had never meant to cause. I spread my palms to the water's bubbles. Luke. What was it about him that intrigued me? Certainly, Walter was much easier to talk to. And anyway, it was silly to be bothered by Luke. In less than a month he would be a monk, and he was already committed to those awful promises: poverty, chastity, obedience. I shuddered and rolled the soles of my feet over the pebbles. What must it be like for a man to swear never to know a woman as a man should know a woman? I couldn't imagine, and for a moment held a picture of Luke in my head that was decidedly unmonkish. On impulse, I bent my knees and dunked my entire self.

I heard nothing in the water's gurgle, but suddenly I was fighting something. Dreading the summoner, I kicked and kicked. My attacker and I broke the surface together and I came face-to-face with Walter. "Jesus Mary!" I choked. "You nearly frightened me to death!" I tried to stop my skirts swirling. Walter mustn't see my legs now. They were far worse than the glimpse he had caught in the Tabard yard. "What on earth are you doing? How dare you sneak up on me!"

Water streamed from Walter's hair and beard. There was a moment when his eyes were unfathomable. "You vanished, Belle. I thought—I thought—"

"How dare you! How dare you! I suppose you thought

you'd see something to give you a thrill." My skirts seemed determined to show off my terrible legs. The more they swirled, the more incandescent I became.

"It must seem like that. It's not like that." Walter wiped his eyes. He looked so stricken that my nightmares returned and for the most awful of moments I thought he might have the same kind of news for me as Master Chaucer had received. "What's wrong? Tell me quickly."

Walter shook himself and spray flew like teardrops. His eyes were quite light again. "Wrong? Only that I was up with the lark and now I'm wet as a duck." He splashed me. "And so, dear Belle, are you. That's what's wrong." He seized a low branch and hung from it. "Now I'm a fish on a line. Come and join me. We'll be a pair of kippers."

"For God's sake, Walter." Relief made me snappish. "I came here to wash. Leave me be."

"You've no soap."

"The water's enough."

He dropped beside me again and the water swirled merrily around us both. "I've brought you something." He nodded toward the bank. There was a bag and his face was suddenly very tender and very serious. "I know about wounds," he said. There was a pause. I pretended I still had water up my nose. Walter found my hand. "You say nothing. I say nothing. Just let me help with your legs. Dulcie will be so disappointed if you have to ride in the wagon."

Many objections bubbled up. None got further than the back of my throat. I could not—ever—tell him about my pumicing. Slowly and firmly, I was lifted onto the bank. What happened next should have been mortifying, but Walter settled my skirts to preserve my modesty and worked so swiftly and deftly that I could almost pretend he wasn't there. True to his word, he asked no questions, just dabbed and patted before producing a small jar of salve, the contents of which he worked in with three fingers, never prying where he shouldn't, never pressing harder than he needed, never interfering where he was not welcome. When he'd finished, instead of another pair of woolen hose, he produced silk bandages, which he dextrously wound and fastened firmly, then handed me a pair of silk trousers with some kind of felt backing. I put them on when he turned to wash his hands, and by the time he climbed out of the river himself, my legs were hidden under my skirt. We gathered everything up and began to walk. It was Walter who broke the silence. I braced myself. Now he'd want to know how my legs had got so raw and give me a lecture.

"I'm sure you know all your letters?" he said.

"My letters? Of course I do."

"My mother taught me," Walter said, "and she taught

me a game. It's called I Spy and is perfect for journeys. Do you know it?"

I shook my head.

"It works like this. I tell you that my eye spies something beginning with a particular letter and you have to guess what that something is. I'll start. So, I spy with my little eye something beginning with"—he looked about—"*g.*"

"*G?*"

"Yes, *g.*"

I swallowed. How could I have thought he was going to pry and moralize? I looked around. "Goat," I said. There was one tethered near a pile of sticks.

"No."

"Grass."

"No. Do you give up?"

"No. God."

"Glory, Belle! Can you see him?"

"No, but he's supposed to be all around."

"I've never liked that thought," Walter said, and his sunny mood momentarily vanished. "Not God."

"Goose?" I said quickly.

"No, not goose either. It's girl!" He twirled a stick. "You're it and you couldn't see it!"

"Well," I said with a certain spark, "I spy with my little eye something beginning with *h.*"

"Hair."

"No."

"Horse."

"No."

"I give up," he said.

"Horizon," I told him.

He laughed. "Ah, I see you're going to be good at this!"

We played all the way back to the inn and, quite naturally I very quickly began to spy things in threes. Walter thought this a great addition.

We reached the yard. "My turn," I said. "Can you have six letters?"

"Don't see why not."

"*K, a, t, w, d, p*," I said.

Walter frowned. "*K, a, t, w* . . ." He hummed. "No, don't know at all, but there again my spelling may not be of the best."

"Kind and thoughtful Walter de Pleasance," I said.

I thought he'd be pleased, and I think he was, though his face closed and he put up his hands to ward off the compliment. "The salve's yours," he said after a moment. "You must put it on every day and rebind your legs with new bandages. It's very important the bandages lie flat and that they don't come undone. Will you let me help you?"

I took a deep breath. "Yes," I said.

He gave the tiniest of nods, then was looking over

my shoulder. "I spy with my little eye someone beginning with *L*."

"Luke!" I cried, and Walter and I were suddenly both laughing.

We might have been able to explain our laughter and the state of our clothes had not the mountainous dame appeared and taken it upon herself to dig Luke in the ribs. "Look at them, Brother Luke, look! Love on a pilgrimage!" She wriggled a podgy fourth finger and waggled bushy eyebrows. Sir Knight also emerged. I thought he'd be shocked at seeing his noble son with a commoner like me, but he didn't seem to mind at all. Indeed, his main concern was that we were wet.

"We've been in the river, sir," Walter said in answer to his query.

"Is that what they call it nowadays?" The mountainous dame winked, digging Luke in the ribs again. "In our day, Sir Knight, we called it something quite else." Luke gave a throaty exclamation.

"Ah, yes, indeed, Dame Alison. In our day." Sir Knight waved his hand at Luke. "Now then, Master Scribe, thank you for getting Dulcie ready. My little page has not been at his most efficient this morning. Walter will need to have words with him."

"Oh, leave young Walter to his loving," boomed Dame Alison.

Luke turned his back. I tried to say something to him

on my way inside but he was closed against me. I tried again once we were all mounted and on the road, but he deliberately positioned both himself and the Master so that I couldn't get anywhere near. Eventually, after being rebuffed for the third time, I became angry. How dare Luke sulk because the Master wanted to speak to me? How dare he make assumptions because Dame Alison had a dirty mind? If he could ignore me, I could as easily ignore him. I jogged beside Walter. But somehow, the more I decided to ignore Luke, the more I couldn't stop myself glancing back. It wasn't even as though Luke was riding in silence. At that moment, he was doing his best to interest the Master in church steeples and oddly shaped clouds. It was the Master who was silent. "Would you mind, Walter?" I made a small gesture.

Walter smiled. "You want to pour your gentle balm on the Master's troubled soul," he said.

At once the nightmare gurgled up. "What do you know about the Master's soul?" I asked rather sharply.

Walter took no offense. "I imagine the soul of a man who's lost his wife is like a rose that's shed its petals," he said.

I was ashamed of my suspicion. "What a nice way you have of putting things," I said.

"Do I? Too nice, perhaps."

"No, Walter, just the right niceness."

"What a nice way *you* have of putting things," he answered softly.

I felt very warmly indeed toward him as I reined Dulcie in. I half wondered why I wanted to go to Luke when Walter offered such uncomplicated charms. Both the honey-tongued friar and an elderly barber converged on the Master, urging their mules close and pressing him with unwanted chatter. "You should rescue the Master from these dung beetles," I hissed at Luke.

Luke gave me a look. "Sir Walter Squire would pull out his sword, I suppose."

I returned his look. "You've got a pair of fists, haven't you?"

Luke's eyes darkened and quite suddenly, he issued two mighty whacks to the mules' rumps. Braying and bucking, the two creatures lumbered off.

Master Chaucer roused himself. "That's no behavior for one about to take Orders," he said, "though don't think I'm not grateful to you, boy." He saw me. "Perhaps you and Belle could ride tight to Dobs's flanks? I've had quite enough sympathy for one wife." I loved the way he could do that: make a little pun even in the midst of trouble. I tucked the end of his cloak under his saddle. At last, Luke and I were riding together, though still in silence.

Within half a minute, however, an argument flared

between Madam Prioress and a sturdy midwife over whether the day of the week on which you were born dictated your character. The midwife said it did and the prioress said it didn't. "Turn around, girl," I heard myself ordered. Mistress Midwife scrutinized me. "What day did your mother give birth?"

"Monday," I said.

"You're lying. Girls born on Monday are pure and chaste, and nobody pure and chaste would be galli-vanting around on such a"—her lip curled—"frilly pony." I interrupted but she was not to be stopped. "What's more, Monday's children have a blemish on their eyebrow or mouth. Have you such a blemish?"

"She has no blemishes." Walter appeared beside me. "Her skin's quite perfect." It was a beautiful lie.

"No, it's not," Luke said. "She's got a small mole—underneath her left eyebrow, about a third of the way along."

"She hasn't," Walter objected.

"Well, actually I have," I said crossly. Although what Luke said was true, there was no need to draw atten-tion to that particular blemish.

"Of course you have," said Luke, "because you're not a liar. If you say you were born on a Monday, you were born on a Monday."

"Bravo!" Walter raised his cap.

Luke couldn't bear that. "Don't raise your cap at me."

Walter settled his cap back on his head. "I didn't mean—"

"No," Luke said, "squires never *mean*, they just do."

"You mean I'm mean?" Walter asked.

The midwife laughed uproariously. "The squire's as good at punning as Master Chaucer!"

Luke's countenance was black. "There's no comparison between a squire and a writer."

"Quite right," said Walter. "I'm a fighter, not a writer." He said it mechanically, as though he'd said it many times before. The midwife decided to goad Luke further. "A fighter, not a writer! What do you say to that, Master Monk?"

I really thought Luke might take his knife and stab her. "Luke's not a monk," I retorted quickly.

The midwife cackled. "Ho-ho! As good as, my dear, as good as."

She pointed slyly down to Luke's crotch, then equally slyly drew a woman's shape in the air. "He may not be tonsured yet, but there'll be no wetting of the whistle for him, however charming the sugared plum on offer. Sir Squire, on the other hand, can have all the plums he wants, eh, Belle Bellfounder! I'm told he's already had a taste!"

I blushed to the roots of my hair. Luke drove Picardy straight at Arondel and tipped Walter off.

"A brawl! A brawl!" shrieked the midwife as Walter

crashed to the floor and Luke flung himself on top of him.

I couldn't think what to do, so I leaped off too and somehow took a glancing punch aimed by Walter at Luke's chin. "You've hit Belle!" cried Luke, and now they were wrestling properly, like men do at the fair. The whole cavalcade halted.

Master Chaucer was furious. "God alive, Luke!" he shouted. "This is not becoming. Sir Knight! Sir Knight! Control your son!"

But Sir Knight was gazing at the scene with some satisfaction and when at last he did speak, his tone was indulgent. "Walter. Do behave yourself." His words had precisely no effect.

"For the love of God!" Master Chaucer was outraged. He stood up in his stirrups. "STOP IT AT ONCE! I order it! It's unseemly, with my wife not yet cold."

This did have some effect. Both Walter and Luke scrambled to their feet. Walter's jerkin was torn. Luke's glasses had been knocked off. It was Walter who retrieved them. Luke snatched them from him. To need glasses was bad enough. To have them handed back by Walter was doubly humiliating.

"There, that's better," said the Master, though he could see from Luke's face that it really wasn't. "Get back into the saddle, both of you, and for goodness' sake, remember that we're on a pilgrimage. Sir Knight!

You tell them." But Sir Knight just caught Arondel and returned him to Walter. The Master raised exasperated hands. "Listen to me then. You two boys are going to ride with Belle at the front of our party, and you're going to ride like that until you can be trusted not to turn into a twist of ferrets whenever one says something the other doesn't like." Luke opened his mouth to object. The Master shook his head. "No argument. Just get on with each other. That's what pilgrims do."

Luke and Walter converged on me, each determined to help me mount Dulcie. Luke growled. "Master Wagoner!" called the Master sharply. "You help Mistress Belle to mount."

Luke turned away and vaulted on to Picardy. Not to be outdone, Walter vaulted onto Arondel. We gained the front, with me in the middle. Behind us, the whole cavalcade began to rumble. I touched my cheek. "Have we hurt you?" Both Walter and Luke spoke together.

"I've still got all my teeth," I said.

Five uncomfortable minutes passed. Walter snapped off a hazel switch and pretended it was a lance. "Shall I tell a story?" When he got no response, he started anyway. "There once was a noble king who had two sons and a daughter too beautiful for me to describe because I'm not a poet. Are you a poet, Luke?"

Luke's hackles rose. "If you want to make fun of me, don't be a coward. Do it where we can finish what we've started."

"Please, Luke," I begged.

"No, Belle," Walter said. "Men should stand up for themselves." He leaned across. "If I do want to make fun of you, I'll do just as you propose. But I'm not making fun of you."

Luke didn't look convinced, but Walter's expression was so guileless that he had to soften a little.

"It was the Ides of March." Walter settled back into his saddle. "Mars was in Aries and the birds were singing, and the sun was shining quite strongly for the time of year. Actually, it was altogether—"

"Never mind about the weather," I interrupted.

"Oh, don't you want to know about that?" Walter asked.

"Best to get to the meat of the thing."

"You're so wise. So then, the daughter, who looked much like you—"

"Really?" I gave Luke a sidelong look, inviting him to return it. He nearly did.

"The daughter who, as I say, looked much like you," Walter shook his curls, "was called Canace . . ."

I'll not repeat the story. Suffice to say that it was rather long. Eventually we got to a bit about a horse.

"What did this horse look like?" I interrupted again.

"Was it a golden-winged Pegasus or a pretty peach like Dulcie?"

Walter pursed his lips. "The best I can say is that it was a very horsely horse. Never was there a more horsely horse. It was, indeed, the horseliest of all horses."

Luke began to shift. I glanced at him, concerned. What now? Then, quite suddenly, Luke threw back his head and laughed. How my father would have loved that laugh. It was a glory of bells, all tumbling melody, perfectly pitched.

Walter, appreciating the bells, tried to remain serious. "I think horses can be horsely," he said, his own lips twitching, "just as herons can be heronly and"— we passed villagers rolling thick oak logs—"fences fencely—"

"And grass grassly and trees treely—" Luke could hardly get the words out.

"And you yoully and me meely!" I began to dissolve.

"That's it!" cried Walter. "We've cracked the great mystery of words!"

It was a miracle how Walter's flowery good nature softened everything between us. Indeed, as we pressed Walter to finish his implausible tale, Luke, his hackles not completely flat but no longer bristling, both interrupted and egged Walter on as much as I did until, finally, we were all talking as easily as if we'd been friends for years. And as I rode and chattered, I realized something very strange. For once, I didn't wish to be someone else or somewhere else. I was still conscious of my father's suffering, still conscious of my guilt, could still smell the summoner and was more than aware of Master Chaucer's troubles. Yet far from diminishing my happiness, these troubles rendered it more precious, probably because I knew it couldn't last. Extraordinary how rare it is to be happy in the here and now.

We rode long into the dusk, and though Walter kept on with his story, Luke and I were laughing so much we never learned much more about the horsely horse than I've just told you. Dinner, taken at a heavily fortified roadside inn of very few creature comforts, was eaten quickly. We were all tired. The Master ate nothing and sat quietly by himself. Everybody remarked that his wife's death weighed heavily. Just before bed, Walter was asked to sing.

"What a squirely squire he is," I whispered to Luke as Walter obediently stood on the table we had set by the fire. To mention Walter like this to Luke was still a risk, but we'd had such a happy time I thought Luke wouldn't be cross. Whether he was or not, he nudged my shoulder. I liked that.

Then a curious thing happened. Instead of the jolly tune we were expecting, Walter sang of a little bird who pressed her breast against a thorn to turn a white rose red. He sang softly, except for the part when the thorn pierced the bird's heart. At that moment his voice throbbed just like the bird's, and when he climbed off the table, he had an expression on his face I'd never seen before on anybody. Long after I was tucked up in bed with Poppet I could still see it. Try as I might, I couldn't understand what it meant.

# 6

*He knew their secrets, they did what he said.*

I rose to a murky dawn. The weather had changed. That itself should have warned me, I suppose. Despite my compulsions, sometimes I'm slow to see signs.

This inn had no inside sanitation, only a pump in the makeshift yard, and as I didn't want to wash in public, I watched from a window until the servants had done their early chores and gone to the kitchen for bread and ale. Only then did I go outside, hitch up my skirts, take off Walter's trousers and inspect my scabs. The salve was working. Since it was also four days since I'd pumiced, the rest of my scars had dulled into gray dents ridged with skin every shade of purple. "Hideous," I told the chickens who had congregated around me, hopeful of grain. I heard the inn's front door open and, for fear of the summoner, hid myself under the wall.

It was not the summoner: it was the Master, unslept, unkempt, unhappy, towel slung over his shoulder, his writing box tucked under his arm. He wandered to the pump and placed the box on the ground. When the chickens scuttled up to it, he snatched it up and placed it on the side of the well. I tutted like a chicken myself. What was he thinking? One nudge and it would tumble. He laid down his towel, cranked the well's handle, clanked the bucket onto a bench, and doused his head. Eyes tight shut, he reached for the towel. One soggy sleeve caught the box's protruding corner. I sprang forward. To stop the box from falling down the well, I had to smack it sharply. It pitched, then crashed onto the ground, spilling all its contents.

The chickens converged. "*Psh! Psh!* Get out! Get away!" I flapped my arms before snatching up plummets and cuttlefish, inkpots and oak galls, bottles and quills and all manner of enviable writing paraphernalia. "I'm sorry," I began to say, when something very bright caught the beady eye of the cockerel. He stretched his neck. "No!" I cried, and dived. Master Chaucer, all caught up in his towel, dived too. I got there first. "Here!" I held up my trophy. It was a thick gold ring, quite obviously a signet ring. Before handing it back, I inspected the engraving, hoping to make some clever remark about the Master's seal. But it wasn't a writer's seal. It was a much grander seal. The grandest seal possible. My mouth opened. "You lied!" At once, I wanted to eat my words, for surely I was mistaken. I inspected the ring again. I had made no mistake. Engraved quite clearly into the oval plate was the image of King Richard, crowned and holding orb and scepter, seated on a covered throne balanced on an angel's back. If that wasn't convincing enough, "*Ricardus Dei Gracia Rex Francie et Anglie et Dux Hibernie*" was inscribed in bold letters around the outside of the ring. I wasn't sure what some of the words meant, but even the village dunce knew the word *rex*. The ring was a king's ring, our king's ring to be exact. What was more, such a ring could have only been handed over by the king himself, and he would only hand it over for a purpose.

I held the ring as though it might bite me. The Master didn't even try to snatch it back. He just stared at it too. "I didn't lie," he said flatly. "I said I carried no document or letter and I don't. I never mentioned anything else."

The cockerel backed away, lifting his legs fastidiously high.

"Yet you've got this," I said. The Master fiddled with his sleeves as I worked out the rest for myself. "Luke. His memory. He said you gave him puzzles and he wasn't to write them down. Of course you're not carrying anything. He's going to France. He's going to take this ring and deliver a message in code." The Master began to wring drops of water from the hem of his tunic. I waited. Nothing. "Does he know?"

With false bravado, the Master shook out a few more drops, then gave up and slumped down. "Of course not."

"Shouldn't he know?"

"What he doesn't know he can't tell."

"You don't trust him?" I could hardly believe this either.

"My dear Belle, of course I trust him. I'd trust him with my life. I also care for him. He will be completely innocent if—" He didn't want to go on.

"If he's caught."

He flushed. "The likelihood is very small."

"But it could happen."

"Yes, it could happen." He leaned against the well. I held out the ring. What else was there to do? I certainly didn't want it. He took it and we both watched the cockerel tip all the ground pigment out of a leather wallet from the writing box. "Why?" I asked. "Why are you doing this?"

His voice was very low. "Weren't you listening when I said I was a trimmer?"

"Yes, but the king doesn't own you, you said that too. And that he was far from perfect."

A long and sorrowful sigh came from deep within. "He's so young," the Master said softly, "just twenty at the Epiphany, and so vulnerable. I know what I should have said when he asked for my help. But if you'd seen him, well . . ." He sighed again. "He's the same age as my eldest son, and so loaded down with cares. It's a terrible thing to be king."

"We all have cares," I said rather primly.

"But we don't have a kingdom."

I couldn't think of a suitable retort. After all, what did I actually know about kingship?

The Master perched on the side of the well and began to speak, and this time I didn't even try to stop him. Although I didn't want to know, I did want to understand. I didn't want to think him a bad man. "You guessed right," he said. "Luke will deliver the ring together with the puzzles he's memorized to the abbot of St. Denys. The abbot already knows the code and he'll do the rest. At least Luke's part will be quickly over and without him even being aware of it." If he wanted praise for this, I didn't offer any. "I did the same for Richard's grandfather," the Master continued, crushing the ring between his palms. "Not the same message, of course, and usually the message is written and delivered without the need of a code and the king's seal. But that won't do now, with England so divided. If King Charles is to help Richard, he'll need to prove that his help was sought, otherwise he'll be condemned as an invader, and he doesn't want that. The king's seal will be proof enough."

I jolted. "Once French troops have set Richard back on his throne, will they go home again?"

The Master swallowed hard. "We have to hope so, because if they don't, I'll be responsible for something terrible." He crossed himself and his tone became so fearful that my skin prickled. "The loss of England to France and a war on English soil that will last for generations," he whispered. "You've already seen the ditches and fences being erected in every village? Even this inn has barricades. At the moment, they're in case the king and the commission come to blows. It's always the ordinary people who suffer when our rulers can't get on. But if French troops come, it will be a different kind of war, a war against a conqueror such as we haven't seen since the days of William the Bastard."

I folded my arms tight. Composing himself, the Master unfolded my arms and took my hands in his. "But don't you see, Belle? I can't, *can't* have the deposition and death of God's anointed king—oh, what am I saying?" He started again. "I can't have the destruction of a mere boy on my conscience, not one who trusts me enough to give me his ring and embraces me in a way my sons have never done."

I broke away. Despite the gloomy dawn, the ring glittered on the Master's palm. There were footsteps, heavy and purposeful. A chicken squawked, booted none too gently out of the way. I didn't have to look to know who was approaching. The Master's eyes strained wide. The ring shone like a fiery stain. "Oh my Lord!" He could hardly breathe. I couldn't bear it. "On your finger," I hissed.

"What?"

"Stick the ring on your marriage finger. Didn't you ever play hunt the thimble when you were little? The best way to hide something is to hide it in plain sight."

Blindly, he obeyed. We both bent to pick up the remaining scattered writing tools.

The summoner flicked his watery eyes from the Master to me and finally to the writing box. "Well now," he said, hacking up early morning phlegm and scratching his boils, "what have we here? A little conspiracy?"

The Master cleared his throat. "Conspiracy's a long word to use before breakfast."

"Conspirators get up early." The summoner wiped away a gob of saliva. "I've been told that the contents of a writer's box reveal everything—*everything*—about the writer. All his foibles. Everything he'd prefer to conceal. Cherrywood, this one, isn't it?" He moved closer and stroked the box the way I once saw an old bargeman stroke the flesh of a drowned girl.

"Walnut," said the Master. I wished he didn't look so frightened.

"Walnut!" sneered the summoner. "Well, well. Show me all its—its *secrets*, Master Chaucer. Will you do that?"

The Master could have refused. Instead, he fiddled about, his fingers trembling round a ring that seemed determined to glow with all its might. I began to hand him the things I'd collected and he named each item as he put it in its appointed place. "Gall, er, pricket, stylus, er, er, miniver brush, swan—no—goose feather"—his voice was at least five tones higher than usual, particularly when the ring snagged on bristles or feathers or a fold of parchment. Several times the summoner frowned. He knew we were hiding something, but my hunch was right: he took no more notice of the Master's ring than he did of his own. Naturally, though, the refilling of the box took too long for his liking, so he pushed the Master aside and ran sweaty fingers round the inkwells and bottles, pressing the box here and there as though something might spring out of the wood itself. Finally, he picked the whole box up and, with a low-life smile, casually dropped it. Surprisingly, it didn't splinter, but just as he hoped, a drawer sprang out, a flat drawer with no lock or mark, a drawer whose presence was clearly supposed to be known only to the box's owner.

"Ah!" said the summoner, licking his lips. "Aaaaaah!" From the drawer he removed a fold of the thinnest Italian paper. I tried to still my breathing. The summoner wasn't interested in me. He gazed long and hard at the Master before unfolding the paper and inspecting it minutely, even wetting his forefinger and rubbing spittle over the surface. The Master didn't move. The summoner held the paper to the light. Though he turned it over half a dozen times, it remained steadfastly blank. When, finally, he had to admit that there was no message, he scrunched the paper up and tossed it down the well. There was no sound as it hit the water.

The Master, leaning heavily on the bench, tried not to hide his hands in his sleeves. "Writing boxes are not really very fascinating," he said, and I was relieved that his voice was less shaky than his legs. "I'd say they're usually not as fascinating as people think—or hope." He crouched to pick up tools scattered for the second time that morning and I crouched once again to help. The summoner crouched too. All our hands were together. We could see the summoner's thick gold bands biting into his flesh. The thumb ring was streaked with tarnish. He leaned right over so that the Master's left hand was right under his nose. A bead of sweat dropped from the Master's brow as he paused, his hand hovering over a small glass paperweight with a flat bottom and some kind of dice in the middle. He didn't dare move his hand away.

The summoner, alerted by the pause, placed his hand directly over the Master's. Though the king's ring was now hidden from view, the summoner was actually touching it. Not only that, he curled his own fat fingers around the Master's and moved the Master's hand for him. He actually moved it. I thought I might faint. The Master, ashen faced, prepared for his hand to be drawn upward and held aloft. But after a moment or two's indecision, the summoner did precisely the opposite. He looked underneath and gave a low, crowing whistle. "Ah," he said, and let go of the Master's hand. Master Chaucer moved not a muscle. There was no hesitation from the summoner now. He grasped the paperweight and his knees creaked as he straightened up, grinning broadly and rolling his prize from palm to palm.

My relief was very short-lived. The Master was following the rolling of the paperweight as though mesmerized. I scrutinised the weight more carefully. It was obviously hollow, for as the summoner rolled it the dice rattled, changing numbers: 3, 6, 2. The sequence seemed random to me. That, presumably, was the point. Code has to seem random to those not party to its key. My heart sank again. Yet another betrayal. What more secrets did the Master have? The summoner threw the paperweight up and caught it, but all the while he was as glued to the Master as the Master was to the dice. "I'll take this as a gift," the summoner said.

"I'd much rather you didn't." Master Chaucer's cheeks were twitching.

"I expect you would, but I like gifts." The summoner rolled the weight a little more and when he pretended to drop it, the Master's gasp was audible.

"Perhaps I could give you something else?" Master Chaucer knotted his hands. He seemed to have forgotten all about the ring.

"No, I'll take this." The summoner stopped rolling the weight and slipped it into his pouch. Other people began to appear. Grinning, the summoner picked up a stray goose feather. "What a productive morning," he said, and ran the feather over the back of my neck before sauntering toward his breakfast.

The Master collapsed heavily on the bench.

"What's he going to discover now?" I dreaded the answer.

"Discover?"

"The dice," I said with sharp impatience. "The dice! I saw it. Don't pretend I didn't."

"Oh, that. It means nothing. It's a time waster."

"A time waster?"

"Yes. When writers get stuck, they like to waste time. I roll the weight and guess what number'll come up. Sometimes I note the numbers down to see if there's a pattern."

"You mean," I said slowly, "that it contains no secret."

"If it does, it's beyond me."

"But you were so frightened. I could see! And so could the summoner—" I stopped. "Oh!"

"Oh, indeed, Belle." The Master managed a ghostly grin. "I certainly was frightened but my wits didn't entirely desert me. We've set the summoner nicely on the wrong track. Now he'll waste some time."

I nearly whooped. But very quickly my insides began to shrivel. It seemed so typical of me, somehow, to endanger my father when I was supposed to be helping him. The summoner would be back. I also had squarely to recognize something else: I was helping Master Chaucer not because his cause was worthy—I'd really no idea if it was worthy or not—but simply because I liked him. We walked slowly together. Before we got to the inn door, the Master set the box down and slid the secret drawer back into its place. "I'm so sorry," he said, clearly feeling the need to apologize.

"I'm frightened for my father," I said miserably. "Do you think the summoner would really hurt him?"

The Master gave a vague shake of the head. "It would be dishonest to give you false reassurance. He'll hurt him if he has to."

"Why does he hate you so much?" I asked. "It can't just be because the king likes your poetry and laughed at his singing."

"Ambition," the Master said, closing the box's lid with a snap. "If the summoner can help the king's enemies bring the king down, then money, castles, and a title will certainly follow. Nobody will dare laugh then." He picked up the box. "He believes that exposing me as a spy will increase his chances of becoming a great man because destroying my reputation will immeasurably enhance his own. And so indeed it may. He's the future, Belle. We'd better get used to it."

"I'll never get used to it," I said vehemently.

The Master put the box down again and looked at me very straight. "Listen to me, my dear girl. Despite what you've just done for me and despite what you know, you're not yet committed to the king's cause. Not at all. You're still a pilgrim and it's to your father, not to me or the king or anybody else, that you owe your primary loyalty. Think hard about what you want to do, Belle, and after you've thought you must act as you think best."

"That's not fair!" It was hard keeping my voice low. "I don't know what's best anymore. I think what you're doing's wrong, but I don't know what's right."

"Few of us really know what's right," the Master said. "We just know what we feel is right. What do you feel is right?"

"It's easier to say what I feel is wrong. It's wrong to put my father in jeopardy. It's wrong to keep secrets from Luke. It's wrong to betray you."

"Indeed. It's a hard choice you have to make." He watched me with sorrowful care.

"But I didn't choose any of this!" I cried, half angry at myself, half angry with him.

Now he looked at me more candidly. "If you could choose again, would you choose not to be here?"

I should have been able to say yes. With my father in the summoner's sights, that's what I should have said. But I couldn't, not honestly. I couldn't wish I'd never met Luke or Walter. King's spy or not, I couldn't wish I hadn't met the Master himself. A movement caught my eye. The summoner was watching us from an upper window. He was fully dressed and had the paperweight in one hand and something else in the other. I squinted. Maybe it was a trick of the light, but I was pretty sure he was also holding a baby's rattle, almost certainly the one the mother had lost at the start of our journey. In an odd flash, I saw England under the authority of a man who rejoices in stealing something of no value just because he can. I could see what my father would think of such a man. I shuddered. "I'm with you," I said to the Master.

I hadn't been aware he had been holding his breath before he let it out. "God bless you, child," he said.

"He'd better bless Luke," I said tartly. "I've made my own decision but Luke's had his made for him." The Master winced. "And no more secrets," I added. "Do you promise that I'm not going to discover something else you haven't told me?"

The Master became very still. A battle was going on inside him. "I can't promise that," he said.

"We need to trust each other!"

"Do you have secrets, Belle?"

I thought of my legs. "Yes."

"And is it necessary for me to know them?"

"No," I said.

"Nor you mine," he said. "Isn't that what trust's all about?"

Only when he was sure that I wasn't going to disagree did he pick up his box again and follow me inside.

At breakfast, I noticed that the king's ring had gone from his finger. I didn't think that wise but now I had another problem. With shy confidence generated by the previous day's happiness, Luke gestured for me to take the empty seat next to him at the table. I had to pretend I hadn't seen. I couldn't sit next to him and smile away knowing that the Master was using him as a dupe. If he ever found out, and discovered that I had known all along, he'd hate me, and I found I didn't like the thought of that. So I perched far away and watched his face fall as Walter, last night's ache apparently banished, took my place.

Half an hour later, Walter found me with Dulcie. He'd not forgotten about rebandaging my legs. We found a private corner at the back of the stables. He hummed as he worked and, as he tied the last bandage in place, I tried not to resent the fact that it was so easy being him and so difficult being me. To add to my woes, there was a fatal inevitability in Luke seeing Walter and me coming out of the stables together. When Walter asked Luke if he'd seen his little jeweled knife, Luke shook his head and quickly moved away, as though if we came too close, we might scald him.

# 7

We set off in bad order. The summoner was lurking. The franklin was bossy. Luke rode alone out in front. The mother traveling in the wagon, whose name nobody seemed to know, was unwell. Sir Knight began some long dirge about the heroism of illness. The mother was not comforted and both her children screamed throughout.

I rode by myself, one hand on the reins and the other pushing Poppet into my chin. I was upset about Luke and I was worried. If Master Chaucer chose to serve the king, that was one thing. He cared for the king and the king for him. But what did Richard care for me? If my father was in danger, would he help? I doubted it. I put Poppet away and scratched my legs through the bandages. How I missed my pumice stone.

By late afternoon, unable to stand either my own company or the chitter-chatter of Mistress Midwife and Dame Alison and the constant yapping of Madam Prioress's wretched dogs, I inevitably gravitated to the solace of Walter. It seemed unfair that everybody else should be happy, so I began to relieve my own ill temper at their expense. "Do you know what's in that fat friar's purse, Walter?"

"Not a clue." Walter smiled.

"Pins and bells for curls and girls."

"Really?"

"Yes. He makes out he's so holy but he'll give any man absolution for a silver penny. Mind you, he's not as bad as Pardoner Bernard. *He* tells people that old bit of cloth he carries around is a piece of Our Lady's veil, and he gets them to pay to touch it when actually it's a piece of linen cut from a lady's undergarment, and not a very clean one at that."

"I see," Walter said, his smile a little fixed.

"As for high-and-mighty know-it-all Merchant Beaverhat, he's just as bad as the friar and the pardoner, perhaps worse, because he's clever with it."

"Clever?" asked Walter, clearly unhappy at my spitefulness. Perhaps his sister was never spiteful. I didn't care and, to his great discomfort, spoke more loudly. "He's shortchanging all the innkeepers on the way to Canterbury because he reckons that if he compounds his sin on the journey, he'll get more salvation for his money when we arrive."

Walter's face begged me to stop. I didn't. "As for Dame Alison of the five wedding rings, I think her husbands must have all drowned themselves to get away from her; and cranky Mistress Medic," my voice was louder still, "keeps her fees low because behind those three teeth, her tongue's sharp enough to slice off even the biggest wart."

There was a snort from behind. I bristled. If anybody was going to criticize me, my tongue could match Mistress Medic's. The snort came from the Master and it wasn't altogether disapproving. Nevertheless, I did feel a tinge of shame because both Dame Alison and Mistress Medic were within hearing, something that I'd really known all along, and neither was smiling. Dame Alison was steadfastly turning her rings and Mistress Medic's faraway look was even more pronounced than usual.

Without a word to me, Walter dropped behind to speak to her. I should have done so too. I didn't.

Master Chaucer took Walter's place. "You've a proper gift for anecdote," he said, curling and uncurling a strand of Dobs's mane. "A little raw and self-conscious, but a gift nonetheless. Let me give you a tip, though." He blinked at me. "Only a fool makes enemies unnecessarily." It was the mildest of reprimands. It was enough. I hated myself. We rode in silence until we heard Sir Knight cry out, "Take care! It's not safe to ride alone!"

Luke had disappeared around a bend in the road. The Master followed my eyes. "Go to him."

"I can't."

"Don't be foolish," said the Master gently. "My business with Luke isn't yours. Look. In three days we'll be at Canterbury and after that he'll be in the cloister. Do you think it makes it better to ignore him?" He raised an eyebrow and the side of his lip kinked. "Tell him a tale or two. A monk needs something to amuse himself during the interminable chanting."

"He doesn't want me near."

"Nonsense. He's unhappy because you unsettle him. You've read enough stories to recognize the signs. Don't make him lonely as well."

After a second's pause, I spurred Dulcie on. Sir Knight shouted a warning when I cantered past. I waved.

Luke stiffened when Dulcie's nose appeared beside Picardy's. I thought he might not speak, but he spoke at once. "Shouldn't you obey your future father-in-law?"

"I don't know what you mean," I lied.

"Do you think I'm stupid as well as blind?"

"I don't think you're either blind or stupid."

"Well, you're wrong." He crashed his knuckles against his glasses. "I'm both blind *and* stupid." He forced himself to be calm. "I'm sorry," he said. "I've no business to judge, and anyway, I knew Walter was in our party when I encouraged you to come on this pilgrimage. Once he'd met you, it was inevitable that you'd fall in love."

"The stables—the river," I said quickly. "It's not what you think."

"No? What is it, then?" The gray eyes waited.

But I felt shy with Luke in a way I never felt with Walter. I couldn't tell him about my legs. "Something else," I said lamely.

"Yes," Luke said bitterly. "Something a squire can give you but a celibate monk can't."

"No. I've told you. Not that."

"A lovers' secret all the same."

I didn't want to talk about secrets. Picardy began to jog. Luke was going to leave me. I had a sudden inspiration. "You've got something to give me, something that nobody else could, something that's yours entirely."

"Oh? What's that?"

"Your memory. I mean, anybody can fight and pay compliments, but almost nobody can remember anything worthwhile. How do you do it? I want to learn."

"It's a trick," he said, after a small pause.

"Everything's a trick, Luke."

He slowed Picardy to a walk. Our knees touched. "What do you want to remember?" he asked.

"Words," I said at once. "Words in books. Can you remember those?"

"That's beginner's stuff." He polished his glasses. "You make a pattern in your head, perhaps of the first letter of every line. Setting key words to a tune can help, or making up a silly rhyme, or just allowing the shapes to press themselves into your brain."

He waited. I think he wanted to see if I was serious or not.

"Show me," I said.

He scrutinized me quite hard before drawing a thin roll of parchment from his belt. "This is what the Master was dictating earlier," he said. "We could try, I suppose."

I smiled straight into his eyes, and the smile he eventually returned was like a gift.

"In Brittany, or as it then was called, Armorica," he recited,

*Here was a knight enthralled*
*To love, who served his lady with his best*
*In many a toilsome enterprise and quest,*
*Suffering much for her ere she was won.*

"What happens to him?" I prompted.

"That's not the question a memorizer asks," Luke said, and he was still smiling. "I say '*iatis*' to myself."

I looked at the parchment and nodded. "The first letters."

"I look at the page as a picture and hear it as a song. That way, it seems to paint patterns in my head."

I concentrated very hard. "In Brittany, something something Armorica." I stopped. "I can't do it."

"Look again. Forget the words. Hear it as a painted tune: called, enthralled, best, quest, won—"

I started, then faltered, then started again. He encouraged and guided and in a few minutes, I could recite the whole thing.

"You won't recite it in front of the Master." Luke was suddenly concerned. "It's just a fragment of something and he doesn't like his work to be seen before it's finished." He put the parchment away.

"I won't. It's our secret."

He flushed. "Secrets again."

"In the great panoply of secrets, I don't think this is a big one." I had an overwhelming desire to tell him everything about the Master. I couldn't bear to be deliberately keeping him in the dark. To stifle the temptation, I went back to his text. "The end of the next line will be 'son' because that rhymes with 'won.' Then either the knight or his lovely lady will be tested by another, and their love will be stretched and almost broken, but then somebody will do something great and everything will turn out well."

"Stories are like breathing to you," Luke said, disconsolate again. "Even Walter with his horsely horse has more natural talent than I have. I'm the Master's temporary scribe and soon I'll be a monk. I'm nothing and nobody." He stopped. "I'm sorry. I don't mean to whine."

"You're not whining," I told him. The wind had dropped completely and beneath the cloudy sky, the day was hovering above a gauzy twilight. It gave me an idea. "Take off your eyeglasses."

"Why?"

"I want to try something."

Nervously, Luke did as I asked. He didn't entirely trust me and who could blame him? "Will you do exactly as I say?"

"That depends."

"First, forget everything and everybody," I ordered. "Have you done that?"

"As far as I can."

"Now, what can you see?"

He gazed ahead intently. "Nothing except the road, and it's empty."

"Yes," I said patiently, "it's empty in real life, but look again and ask yourself what you might see."

He thought hard. "I might see somebody coming along, I suppose."

"In my imagination I already see somebody," I said. "Tell me."

"I see a figure on a dark horse, and the horse's skin shimmers like water at midnight and its eyes are silver. There's a smell too, of oil and leather and a battle lately fought. Can you see it? Can you smell it?"

Luke gazed ahead even more intently. "Perhaps. Go on."

"The figure is a man, fully armed and helmeted. He

has a purpose. I'm not sure yet what it is. Can you hear the hoofbeats?"

Luke was scarcely breathing. "I can," he said, "but I think there's more than one man."

"No," I said, "only one. He's got a message for us from another world. Perhaps this is the knight of Walter's story. Perhaps he's a knight of the Round Table. In a moment he'll pass in a scattering of dust, leaving only a nosegay of flowers and a promise to return."

"He wants to leave with more than that!" Luke shouted.

"What?"

"Duck!" And when I didn't, he threw himself from Picardy onto Dulcie, who snorted and tilted away, leaving Luke clutching at air. I could now see quite clearly what I had completely failed to see before, which was that Luke was right: there was not one imaginary knight approaching; there were at least a dozen real ones. What was more, these were not chivalrous nobles scattering flowers and enigmatic promises. Their matted hair, grime-gritted skin, and rough, mismatching armor revealed them as men-at-arms gone bad, their honor blemished, their swords stained, and their iron clubs spotted with old flesh. The pilgrimage route from London to Canterbury offered rich pickings. With our baggage carts bumbling behind, we must have looked to be a particularly juicy prize.

Thin and flat-eared with misuse, the bandits' horses bared their teeth at ours. Luke squared up like a boxer. I screamed, for the bandits were whirling their clubs. In seconds, the shrill screams of the lady pilgrims echoed my own. The bandits were amongst them.

A man the shape and color of a dirty leather strap issued brisk orders, which were less briskly obeyed. When Luke had been restrained and Dulcie and Picardy seized, we were marched back to the rest of our party. With the bandits growling like dogs, we were herded off the road through the thicket into a scrubby clearing. The prioress's dogs yapped and yapped and yapped. Luke managed to stay beside Dulcie, leaving Picardy whinnying in the rear. I begged Luke to go back for him, but he wouldn't leave me, and I was so thankful for that.

Once in the clearing, we were all forced to dismount. Three of the bandits took our horses and tied them together. One tried to unwrap the prioress's arms from around her dogs, but she clutched them as hard as the mother clutched her babies. I thought the man might just club the creatures—anything to stop their infernal noise—but though he threatened, he let them be.

Walter appeared on my other side, and he and Luke squashed me between them, with Master Chaucer forming a barrier in front. Sir Knight roared as loudly as a bull as the robbers divested him of his sword.

Everybody else was forced to throw their weapons into a pile.

"If we're to die, please God make it quick," Madam Prioress sobbed. I held on to my pendant and thought of my father. I could hardly believe this was real. The dogs yapped and yapped.

The leathery leader banged two shields together. "Shut those damned animals up or I'll do it myself." He brandished a dagger. I whipped around and slapped both dogs hard on their rumps. The prioress was outraged and the dogs' yaps rose to howls. I slapped them again. Only when I threatened a third belt did they finally quiver into silence.

"That's better." Sir Leather Strap dropped the shields. For effect, he thrust his sword into the ground in front of him. Earth is not unlike flesh. It slid in with a kind of squelch. I pressed closer into Master Chaucer's back.

Sir Knight, hopping from foot to foot, objected to our treatment in the strongest possible terms. "We're holy pilgrims on our way to the tomb of St. Thomas! God won't forgive you for this." But everybody knew that without his sword and horse, he was a tuskless boar. Eventually, knowing he looked ridiculous, he fell as silent as the dogs.

"Peace at last," Sir Leather Strap said, as though we were a class of noisy children. "And now that I can get a word in, I'll tell you what I want." He leaned on his sword hilt. "I want gold."

"Gold?" repeated Sir Knight stupidly. "Why would we have gold? I've told you, we're just poor pilgrims on our way to the tomb of St. Thomas."

"No pilgrims are poor," Sir Leather Strap said. "If you were poor, St. Thomas wouldn't be interested in you."

"We've no gold," Sir Knight declared. "You can search our baggage all you like."

Sir Leather Strap pursed his lips. "As we will. I'll be sorry if it turns out to be true because then we'll have to check your teeth."

The merchant shut his mouth with a snap, as did Summoner Seekum, Master Friar, and almost everybody else. I'd inherited my mother's teeth, white and strong, but they were hardly going to take my word for that. When Sir Knight had nothing more to say, Sir Leather Strap ordered that we should be divided, men on one side and women on the other. I found I'd been holding Luke's hand. Letting go was awful.

As we were pushed about, there was argument and agitation between the robbers themselves, and it became clear that some had more on their minds than gold. There were unmistakable gesticulations. I was the youngest, so they singled me out. They formed a line. They prodded me down it like a cow at auction. It's hard to tell you what it felt like.

When I reached the end of the line, the men formed a circle. It amused them to whirl me around, and I grew dizzy as their faces flashed and disappeared, flashed and disappeared, in a grinning, pointing blur. I knew I must not fall. Once on the ground, I'd never get up again. But my feet were faltering, my legs were tangling, and I was pitching into a terrible, surging sea of arms that grasped with greedy and evil intent.

Just before the sea roared over my head, I heard Luke's voice. "You want gold?" he was hollering. "I can give you more than gold. I can give you gold that will never be spent, but touch that girl and you'll get nothing, nothing." He hollered again and again. The sea wavered.

"You said if we gave you gold, you'd let us go. I can give you gold, I tell you. As much as you like. A hill—a mountain—a whole universe."

The thieves sniggered. "What are you, some kind of a wizard?" Dirty fingers pulled at my skirt. The sea surged again. In a moment, the men would hear only the pumping of their blood.

Luke hollered louder. "Of course I'm not a wizard. I've much more power than that. I'm an alchemist. Do you understand? An alchemist. But I repeat, touch that girl and you'll never know what I could have done for you. Never. What's more, I'll use my skills to hunt you down and I'll make your skin burn and your toes rot so that you'll believe yourself already in hell. I have that power and you'd better believe me when I tell you that God himself can't stop me from using it."

My padded trousers had come undone and my skirt was above my knees. Luke's voice rang out once more. "Let the girl go and I'll provide riches beyond your wildest dreams. Touch her and you'll leave with nothing but a curse." Then his voice changed. "I have the philosopher's stone," he said, and his voice boomed like a thunderclap.

Sir Leather Strap shifted. "What did you say?"

"I said I have the philosopher's stone."

There were exclamations amongst both pilgrims and thieves. Sir Leather Strap banged his two shields. "You're telling me that you have the elixir that transforms base metal into gold?" His voice was an almost comic mix of deep mistrust and fascinated hope.

Luke paused for dramatic effect. "I don't just have it," he declared, "*I make it*," and though his voice was deliberately soft, it was as though God himself had spoken. Momentarily, even I was forgotten. Sir Leather Strap recovered first. "I don't believe you," he sneered, but couldn't disguise that Luke's words sparked like a flint against a tinderbox.

"It's because I make the elixir that I go as penitent to Canterbury," Luke said.

The spark snuffed out. "You have, at your fingertips, the gift of eternal riches and you want us to believe

that you're going to do penance for it?" Sir Leather Strap was completely disbelieving.

Luke stood very tall. "I've trespassed onto God's territory, meddling where man shouldn't meddle. So I've decided to cast my tools and all the elixir I have left onto St. Thomas's tomb and pray that God will help me forget the recipe."

Sir Leather Strap's lips dried even as his mouth watered. "But at this moment you can make gold?" The spark flickered back to life.

Luke nodded.

"If you're lying . . ."

Luke blinked and his cheek twitched. Sir Leather Strap observed him closely. The spark had now lit a fire that flared out of his belly and into his veins. He could see the gold. He could smell it. He had a terror of losing it. He gestured to one of the men. "Bring the girl here and open her mouth, because if you *are* lying, boy, I'll have everybody's teeth, whether gold, bone or plain enamel, and I'll start by plucking out this creature's little treasures one at a time with the farrier's nail pullers and have them made into a necklace."

I was dragged over and forced to kneel. I remember Sir Knight calling out "For shame!" and beating his hands together. I remember Walter surging forward and being thrust back. I remember clammy, prying fingers crushing my tongue and making my lips bleed.

Most of all, though, I remember the blankness that is a fear beyond terror, because I alone amongst this company knew that making gold was one trick Luke had refused to learn.

"Don't hurt her." Luke couldn't keep his voice even.

Sir Leather Strap shrugged. "That's up to you and you'd better hurry. We need to see gold before nightfall, and it's already beginning to get dark."

Luke swallowed, shrank, then, with a small jerk, was alive with movement. "Light every torch, every lamp there is," he ordered, moving swiftly toward the baggage carts. "I'll get what I need. You get kindling and twigs. We need a fire and a bowl of cold water."

The men looked to their leader. "Well, get on then," cried Sir Leather Strap, running after Luke. "Yes," Luke said, not slowing his step, "you stay close. I'll need an assistant." He brushed past me. It was the only comfort he could give.

By the time a fire was lit, Luke had returned with his own pack and a brown leather box big enough for a child's armor. Using two broad tree stumps as tables, he opened the box and set out two dozen unlabeled vials, half a dozen bottles, and several twists of paper. My guard, now more interested in Luke than in me, relaxed his hold. I closed my mouth. The filth on my tongue was sickening but I didn't dare spit.

"You must tell us what everything is." Sir Leather

Strap peered at the vials by lantern light. Luke took a lantern too, and without looking at the vials or bottles, slowly began to recite in a hypnotic voice: "Borax, verdigris, bullock's gall, arsenic, brimstone, sal ammoniac. I've chalk and quicklime and ashes and of course the white of eggs, and alkali, tartar, salt and saltpeter, iron for Mars, quicksilver for Mercury, lead for Saturn, and tin for Jupiter." It was a litany, just like my mother's bell litany, but though it reassured Sir Leather Strap, it did not satisfy him. "Where's the elixir?"

"Be patient!" Luke admonished. He delved into his own pack and brought out a crucible, a retort, a pan for boiling water, and a small drab bag. Sir Leather Strap tried to grab the bag but Luke raised it above his head and the thief had to make do with the crucible. "I should have been an alchemist," he said, running his hands lovingly all over it. "I've a real feel for it."

"I'm sure you have," said Luke, secreting the pouch in his sleeve. "How's the fire? I'm ready to begin." His skin gleamed. Beneath his eyeglasses his pupils were molten lapis. I think only I could sense that he didn't dare pause, even for a moment, lest he lose his nerve. "Take an ounce of mercury from this vial and place it in the crucible," he ordered Sir Leather Strap. This was done. There was utter silence now save for the grazing of the horses, the crackle of twigs, and Luke's voice. His twitch had returned. "Place the crucible in the hottest spot." Sir Leather Strap sweated and swore as he burned his fingers in his haste to obey.

With a great flourish, the small drab bag reappeared. Luke extracted a snatch of powder between finger and thumb and dropped the powder into the crucible. A puff of steam escaped as he clapped on the lid and threw the bag onto one of the tree stumps. "Poke the fire," he said. "It must be hot as hell." He seized a branch himself, pronging it purposefully amongst the embers. Flames shot up. "That's better." He let go of his stick. For several minutes, he did nothing but observe. Then suddenly he cried, "This is the moment!" and with a pair of tongs seized the crucible, withdrew it from the flames, and poured a bubbling flash of tawny liquid into a mold, which he at once dropped into a bowl of cold water. It hissed and spat. He stood back. His twitch was wild. Dropping the tongs, he put his hand into the water.

"Not so fast," Sir Leather Strap snarled. "I'll do it."

Luke shrugged. "As you like."

Without even rolling up his sleeves, Sir Leather Strap plunged both hands into the bowl, brought out the mold and tipped it over. Into his hand fell a dull-colored ball about the size of a marble. He held it up. Everybody gazed at it. It didn't glint. It didn't gleam. It looked like something you might find on the road and kick into the ditch.

Luke backed away. Sir Leather Strap's neck bulged

and his face flushed purple. He was sobbing with disappointment. "A dirty trick! Nothing but a dirty trick! Fetch the nail pullers! I'll have that girl's teeth and I'll have them now."

At once, my captor thrust both his hands back into my mouth, and seconds later I tasted the sourness of cold steel. I couldn't scream but I heard Walter shouting and Luke cursing and the prioress's dogs breaking their silence and yapping, yapping, yapping. There was blood on my tongue. Then, above the gurgle, another voice. "What are you doing, man? Let me see that!" Merchant Beaverhat thrust himself forward. He took the discolored ball. The steel in my mouth was suspended.

"Have you ever seen raw gold?" the merchant asked, and didn't wait for an answer. "Gold's my business, and believe me, I've been offered enough imitations in my time to know the difference. May I?"

Sir Leather Strap nodded dumbly. The merchant produced a magnifying glass and rolled the ball very slowly back and forth.

"Well?" Sir Leather Strap couldn't keep still.

Merchant Beaverhat continued rolling the ball, then rubbed it on his sleeve, and, as he rubbed, like a princess shedding a beggar's cloak, the ball shed its tarnish. When he held it up again, it shone like the moon. The silence that greeted it was the silence of reverence. Luke stepped toward me.

"Not so fast!" Sir Leather Strap seized his arm. "It's proper gold?" he asked the merchant. "You're absolutely sure?"

"As sure as I'm a pilgrim."

"You swear it on your life?"

"On my life."

I could have kissed the merchant. I never thought he'd lie so beautifully on our behalf. I was doubly sorry I'd ever been rude to him. "God's blood, boy!" Sir Leather Strap reclaimed the ball quickly and kissed it with awestruck amazement. "You've really done it."

Luke let out a long breath. His skin was ghost white though his pulse was racing. He had something else to say, a splash of truth as penance for the success of his deceit. "Nothing in this world is quite as it seems. Be in no doubt that what you have now will destroy you. When you're at the devil's gate, sir, don't cry out against me. Do you understand?" He stood tall and brave and slightly spooky.

"Oh, I understand all right!" crowed Sir Leather Strap. "You're trying to frighten me into not taking the elixir. You won't succeed." Backing away, he bumped against the tree stumps, and with one swift arm, he snatched up the powder bag, sealed it carefully, and dropped it into his pouch. Then he swept everything else onto the ground, stamping on the vials and containers until they and their contents were nothing but mud. The leather box itself he kicked until it split. "There'll be no elixir for anybody else." He wagged his finger at Luke. "There'll be just what I have here, and I'd say that makes me the richest man not just in England but in the world!"

"*Us*," his fellows echoed, just beginning to move again. "Makes *us* the richest men in the world."

Sir Leather Strap had quite forgotten his men and now that he had his prize was not pleased to be reminded. Quicker than a rat, he scuttled to his horse, swung himself on, and galloped off. There was an immediate outcry. The nail pullers were dropped as his men rushed for their horses, then rushed back to us, then back to their horses, until, finding the lure of the elixir too great, they also sped off, alternately begging Sir Leather Strap to wait for them and damning him to hell. Before they'd even all gone, I found myself swept up and enclosed in Luke's arms, our hearts hammering in unison, the smell of sulfur more welcome at that moment than the smell of jasmine.

Walter broke us apart. "Superbly done, Luke," he said. Forced to let go of me, Luke gave a tiny groan. I can still hear that groan. It was sweet as a song.

Master Chaucer was congratulatory but anxious. "A performance worthy of a more discerning audience than those dimwits, my boy. We shall learn in time how you did it, but now we must move along. If the men return, they mustn't find us here."

"What do you mean, a performance? The gold wasn't real?" The merchant couldn't help himself. He had been gazing at Luke with more respect than he'd ever shown any man. "But it *was* real. I felt it. I tasted it."

Luke blinked, and, like an actor stepping off the stage, became himself again. "It was real," he said simply, "but not through alchemy. Gold balls are easily secreted in an alchemist's bag. It's a trick, a sleight of hand." He reached his hand into his pouch and flicked something into the air. At once a tiny cloud appeared, a miniature of the one he had created when Dulcie bolted. "Like that," Luke said.

Everybody gaped, then laughed nervously. The merchant's face fell and my estimation of him fell correspondingly. He'd not been acting on our behalf after all. I felt less sorry that I'd been rude to him.

"Come on," Master Chaucer urged again. "We must get out of here. Sir Knight, gather your wits!" Sir Knight could not, so in the end it was Luke, Master Chaucer, and Master Reeve who chivvied us into some kind of order.

After an anxious half hour, we found shelter in a village. The inn wasn't big enough to accommodate us all, so we pitched camp in a pasture behind its back wall. As the ale flowed, we relaxed a little and Luke was pressed to reveal more alchemists' tricks. I slipped in beside him.

"Not nothing and nobody now. You're a hero."

"So it would seem," he said, and added with a slightly bitter stab, "my father would have been proud."

"You saved me from those men," I said. He raised his cup and offered it to me, and as my lips touched where his lips had been, I imagined what it would be like to kiss him.

I had only a moment to wonder, for Master Summoner, half ironically and half sincerely, chose that moment to raise his own cup in a toast, and the Master, who was holding a piece of bread in his right hand, raised his own cup with his left. It was the absence that shrieked. Where once the king's ring had sat solid, there was now only emptiness. Master Summoner's gaze fixed on this emptiness. He frowned at first, not quite comprehending why an emptiness should have caught his eye. Then suddenly he understood and his toast, when it came, was triumphant.

# 8

*I know the service of my love is vain,*
*My recompense is but a bursting heart.*

It's odd how two lives can run simultaneously. On the one hand, once you've begun to think about kissing somebody, it's quite difficult to stop. On the other, Master Chaucer, the summoner, and myself were now caught in an odd triangular standoff to which the rest of the party, whose only anxiety was to reach Canterbury as quickly as possible, was completely oblivious. I never asked Master Chaucer where the ring was. I didn't want to know.

Luke and I rode together. Making gold had blown away all the chemical pastiness from his skin, and the hint of sulfur too, leaving him smelling of ordinary things like soap and warm leather, horse and earth. But his effect on me was far from ordinary: now, his every movement and every expression began to burn itself into my soul, making it harder and harder for me to behave naturally. I knew I'd fallen in love. I found this curiously upsetting. As you may imagine, I'd been in love before, but in the past my beloved had always been a mythical hero and I was always in control. Now

I'd fallen in love with a real person, I wasn't in control at all. How my legs itched. How my heart twisted and turned. How I longed for an elegant nonchalance that completely eluded me. I wanted to speak easily; every word seemed clumsy.

Nevertheless, there was something I wanted to do. When we stopped for refreshment near a small river, I was determined. "Luke," I said, hoping my voice sounded more normal to him than it did to me.

"What?"

"Can I cut your hair?"

His eyebrows shot up. "Why?"

"It gets in your way, and look," I held up a lock, ignoring his flushes, "it's good hair really, only you've let it grow so long it's gone all lank and reedy. Let me cut it! Do!"

Though he took some persuading, I sensed he was not really unwilling. If I found a stool, he would sit down. I found one. He sat. I was used to cutting my father's hair, and Dame Alison, while winking at Walter at what she called my "youthful fickleness," lent me some scissors. I didn't look at Walter myself. I was too busy measuring and cutting until Luke's rat's tails were around his feet and he was left with a thick, tidy mop. He got up. "Wait," I said, "I haven't finished." I fetched a few things. "Follow me." He obeyed and I led him to the river, made him kneel down, and removed his eyeglasses.

"No," he said, rising. "If my hair's to be washed, I'll wash it myself."

"Don't be silly," I retorted. "You won't wash it at all well. Men never do. Come on. I always wash my father's." That was a lie. The widow washed my father's. But Luke's hesitation was his undoing. I quickly filled a bowl and he had either to bend forward or get completely drenched. He bent forward.

It was an odd experience and though conducted in full view of everybody, more intensely intimate than I had expected. Both of us felt it, which was why the silence became more and more marked as I whipped up the soap and then worked it right into his scalp, my fingers learning the shape of his head and kneading the tender knots between crown and spine. Several times, he tried to interrupt and push me away. But I would not be pushed away. Nor did I know how to stop, so after I had rinsed the soap off, I started all over again. The audience, bored now, retreated. When I couldn't draw things out any longer, I took a towel and knelt down in front of him to rub his hair more easily. He raised his head. Without his eyeglasses, with his hair tousled and his skin rosy from the chilly water, he reminded me of Lancelot before his great deceit gnawed his beauty away. I couldn't stop myself. I inclined toward him and closed my eyes. I'd no idea what it would be like to kiss a boy, since I'd never done it before, but I knew I wanted to more than anything.

A sting and my eyes snapped open. Luke was up and flying off as though I were the devil. It was the edge of the towel that had stung me. Unbalanced, I toppled over and my throat and stomach filled with something horrible. Then, just as quickly as he had departed, Luke returned. "I'm sorry," he said, and I could sense his blood fizzing. "You can't know how sorry I am, Belle. But I'm already known to some as Master Monk, and even if I wasn't, wouldn't it be the worst kind of cheating, just before I renounce the world, to behave like—" He stopped.

"Like what?" I could barely speak.

"Like the lover I can never be," he said flatly, and the fizz fizzled out.

"It was only going to be a kiss," I whispered.

He came closer and reached for his eyeglasses. "To you maybe, but not to me."

"Luke," I said.

He swallowed. "God kept his promise, Belle. He made me Master Chaucer's scribe. Don't you see? I'm honor bound to keep my side of the bargain, and kissing you, when I've already really renounced women, would be—"

"Have you kissed a girl before?" Embarrassment made me rude.

"No." He blushed.

I addressed him very coldly. "I don't count it much to give up something you don't even know you'll miss."

His hand was six inches from my cheek. His fingers hovered. He wanted to touch me. I know he did. "Believe me, I know what I'm missing," he said, and his sorrow was so heartfelt I couldn't be cold any longer.

"It's not fair. How can I compete with God?" My voice was all cracked.

"It would be better to ask how God can compete with you," Luke said, and his voice was echo deep.

I clung to the echo. Surely God wouldn't mind? But Luke stepped back, and that was the moment I ran away, wishing I'd never seen that red spark in his eyes, never felt our hearts hammering together, never felt his scalp under my palms. I bumped straight into Walter. He caught me up and twirled me around. "A dance!" he crowed. "Let's dance!"

"Yes, that's it, let's dance!" I cried, my arms wide. I would dance until I was too tired to care and too breathless to cry. I would dance until I'd danced Luke right out of my head and out my heart and out of anywhere else he was lurking.

If Walter was surprised by my crazy abandon, he didn't say so. Instead, he called for a tune, and when the skipper obliged with the buzz of a Jew's harp, swept me along. Soon, the sergeant was thumping a rhythm on a cartwheel and the wagoner was clanging two iron shoes. In the end, the skinny cleric, swelling like an angry gander, clapped two saucepans together and cried, "Enough! Enough! We're pilgrims, not peasants."

"For shame!" Dame Alison admonished, her feet tapping. "They're young. We've just had a merciful release. Let the girl be merry now, for as soon as she's hooked a husband, the dancing will be of quite a different kind."

"Shame on *you*, madam," the cleric retorted, and snatching the Jew's harp from the skipper's lips, he smashed it underfoot.

"There," said Dame Alison when the music stopped. "Now we must all be miserable."

Walter kept hold of my hand and walked me back to the river. I steered him away from the place where I'd washed Luke's hair, heading to where the bank flattened out. Here Walter knelt down, cupped his hands, and offered me a drink. His hands shook a little. Then he carefully dabbed my face with a white linen square he had tucked in his belt.

Some devil made me say it. "You can kiss me, you know." I wanted Luke to be watching. "You really can. I shan't mind at all."

Walter dropped the cloth. "You're too beautiful to kiss," he said, quickly adding, "you see, kissing's for earthly, ordinary love and my love for you is mystical and courtly."

"Oh, Walter! How can you say that? You've seen my legs!"

He stood, drew me up, and tucked my arm under his. "Beautiful Belle, your legs will soon be as perfect as the rest of you. But you must understand that though earthly love needs kisses and all that stuff, courtly love mirrors the love of God, and he doesn't go around kissing people. A kiss between us would ruin everything."

I pulled my arm away. "Just tell the truth, Walter. I'm not good enough for you."

He blushed. "That's not the truth."

"Yes, it is," I said, fighting to keep control. "I've been living in one of my stupid stories." Tears poured down my cheeks. I was an idiot. I had ruined everything.

"Belle!" Walter called as I ran away, but I didn't stop until I'd got to the baggage carts and found Poppet. And I didn't stop with her. Suddenly, I was pulling apart somebody else's luggage, I didn't care whose, and then somebody else's again as I searched and searched. When I found what I wanted, I ripped off Walter's careful bandages without even an attempt at privacy. "Perfect legs! Perfect legs! What's the use of those?" I spat at myself as I began to rub. The pain from the pumice provided instant relief. I stopped crying and concentrated. Up and down, side to side, starting on a new patch when flowing blood made the stone glide instead of scour, I did my shins first, then my knees, then my ankles—both legs. I don't know how long it took. I don't know if anybody saw, because from the first tingle to the last torment I was in the world of harm, a world I controlled, a world with no room for anybody else. As long as I could pumice, I didn't need Luke. As long as I could pumice, I didn't need Walter. As long as I could pumice, I didn't need anybody or anything except that small gray scraper. Eventually, sated, I repacked the baggage I had upset. I kept the stone. It was mine now, and as I rolled the bandages round my tattered legs, I swore that I would never be without it again.

When it was time to move off, I mounted Dulcie with difficulty and rode alone until the summoner decided to engage me in conversation. However, I heard nothing except the scolding of my own internal voice until the whole company was startled by the thunder of hooves and men crying out in distress. We faltered to a fearful halt. Flying directly toward us, and riding as though the devil was snapping at their heels, were the bandits, though this time minus their leader. Sir Knight and Walter drew their swords. Granada and Arondel reared. But the bandits had no intention of stopping. We were of no interest anymore. "The French are here! The French! England's lost!" they shrieked, then vanished in a cloud of dust.

## 9

Bright shields and trappings, headpieces and charms,
Great golden helmets, hauberks, coats of arms,
Lords on appareled coursers, squires, too,
And knights belonging to their retinue . . .

We couldn't vanish. We couldn't even run without leaving behind the mother and her children, to
say nothing of our belongings. All we could do was
speedily make for the protection of the nearest town.
I couldn't look at Master Chaucer. If he was responsible for the French arriving so soon, that would mean
he'd lied to me again. It was a dismal thought. More
than dismal: it turned him into an enemy. Nor could
I look at the summoner, for fear that he had guessed
everything. My father! My father! Nor could I look at
Luke, or ride with Walter. I was glad to concentrate on
the rush. The nearest town was half-derelict. "Plague's
been here," Dame Alison said as we hurried over the
tumbled stones. "Better the plague than the French,"
Mistress Midwife gabbled. "At least that's what I've
heard." Everybody crossed themselves madly, and I
began to count chickens, sheep, travelers, the pots on
a peddler's back, clouds, leaves, and even dewdrops,

forcing everything into multiples of three though many didn't want to go. I didn't bargain. I didn't know what bargain to make.

The townsfolk in their terror were openly hostile. They agreed to let us stay if Walter would find out for certain how many of the enemy were likely to attack. When he came to say good-bye, I was more than aloof. Even in the face of this great danger, the refused kiss rankled. But by nightfall, when he still hadn't returned and we were forced to negotiate rates at the tavern, I tortured myself. How could I not have said a warm good-bye, after all he'd done for me? Why shouldn't he refuse to kiss me? He had his position to think of. And anyway, I was only using him to get at Luke. Even on pilgrimage I was utterly selfish. I pumiced my legs again, but for the first time, it disgusted me and I threw the pumice away. Much later, I lay rigid in my bed, seeing only Walter maimed, Walter chained and tortured, Walter hanging from a tree, his legs kicking, his eyes sightless. Every time I heard a horse, I rushed to the window. It was never Arondel.

When I could lie still no longer, I went to Dulcie, tethered with the others by a crumbling barn on the edge of the town. Though it was barely dawn, I could hear the complaints of a gang of forced laborers digging a defensive ditch at double speed.

Dulcie wasn't grazing. She too was waiting for

Arondel. I folded my arms around her neck. By the time I returned to the inn, windows were being boarded up and shutters locked with iron bars. No news was bad news. The town was girding itself. Sir Knight, grim faced, was waiting by the inn door. He was fully armed and that terrified me more than anything else. "Where can Walter be?" I cried. He shook his head.

The day passed second by second, minute by minute. In the afternoon, exhausted and feverish, I went back to bed. I thought I'd lie awake, but I must have drifted off because I was awakened by a great clattering. Hope and fear erupted in equal measure. Clutching both Poppet and my locket, I peered out. Please God, *please God*, let it be Walter. There was a flash of blue leather. I hardly dared believe it. I leaned so far out of the window it was a wonder I didn't fall. Arondel was whinnying, Walter was upright, but he was making an extraordinary noise. My heart quailed. Then it came to me. The noise was—couldn't be—was—laughter. I launched myself down the stairs.

By the time I reached the yard, Walter had already flung himself out of the saddle. Everybody was crowding round. "It's all perfectly fine, perfectly fine," he was exclaiming, and as though to illustrate just how fine everything was, he hitched one of the town's urchins onto Arondel and allowed him to hold his sword. The boy swung it about. Walter grinned, though the grin

was strained. "Hey now! Take care with that thing! It's sharp and Arondel's head is quite valuable."

"Never mind Arondel's head!" Sir Knight, who had sweated in fear and impatience all day, couldn't even pretend to be calm. "How many French knights?"

Walter retrieved his sword before Arondel lost his ears. "Quite a few, Father, quite a few." The townsfolk groaned. Walter waved his arms. "Wait! Wait till you hear the best of it! These knights aren't enemies at all! Well, they are," he corrected himself, "but not at the moment. They've been captured and brought over here to wait until their ransoms are paid. There'll be no battle! There'll be a tournament to keep the knights amused. The jousting field's only a few miles away and they've invited us to go. Isn't that fun!" I was overwhelmed with relief. This was not the Master's doing. I thanked God most sincerely for that.

Luke, however, was up in arms. "Fun?" He confronted Walter directly, hands on hips. "You think we should be having *fun* with Frenchmen?"

Walter spun round and round. He began to laugh again, and though I didn't want to admit it, something about his laughter didn't ring at all true. I glanced at Sir Knight. He was chuckling. "Stop spinning for a moment, Walter, and tell me who's to fight," he said, happily divesting himself of his armor.

"Sir John Savage"—Walter continued to spin—"and

for the French"—the spinning jerked a little—"Sir Jean d'Aubricourt."

Sir Knight's chuckles were cut off at their source. "Sir Jean d'Aubricourt?"

"Yes. He was captured by Sir John Savage and the tournament's really to celebrate his release. His ransom's paid and he's about to go home."

Sir Knight stood quite still. "Did you speak to him?"

"I did."

Father and son exchanged glances. My nerves shredded. I ran to Walter. "What's the matter?"

But Luke had already seized Walter's shoulders. "Wait! I can hardly believe it. Everybody's been up all night frantic with worry about you and all the time you've been discussing plans for a tournament?"

"Were you worried about me? Really?" Walter seemed oddly taken aback.

"Of course we were worried!" Luke was exasperated.

"I'm sorry for that," Walter said, "very sorry." He gave a small shake. "I really am. Still, the tournament will make a perfect end to our pilgrimage." Luke was not satisfied, and he and Walter began to argue until at last the Master had to intervene. Master Summoner observed Master Chaucer with the unblinking gaze of a viper.

Walter took Arondel to the stables. I followed and, just as I suspected, found a very different, much graver

Walter. When he saw me, he tried to smile again. I shook my head. "Don't pretend. There's something wrong."

He removed Arondel's bridle and handed it to a page. "You notice too much, Belle."

"Don't brush me off."

He sighed. "Remember I told you about my sister?"

"Yes."

"Well, the French knight she ran away with is Sir Jean d'Aubricourt's son."

"So your sister's here?"

Walter shook his head slowly. "No. That's not it."

"What then?"

He suddenly lost all his bloom. "It means there's a feud between our families that can only be settled by blood."

I was aghast. "But you said the tournament was to be fun!"

He gave a pale smile. "Some people think that a blood feud is the most fun of all." He would say nothing else, and from the moment we returned to the inn, he and his father kept to themselves.

Just before dinner, I took the salve and slipped down to the river to do my bandages myself. I closed my eyes. Why couldn't the world stand still in a nice place? When I opened them, the summoner was sitting beside me and I cursed. I should have hidden myself better. Before I could move, he crushed my right hand under his left, those dreadful rings making dents in my fingers. He stared at my legs with open disgust. "You really aren't a good girl, Belle. Those scabs! I never noticed them before. What a punishment!"

I didn't speak.

"The Master's ring," he said, continuing to stare at my legs. "Do you know, now that he's not wearing it, I can see it much more clearly in my mind's eye. Perhaps I've caught some of the alchemist's powers! And I find myself thinking it strange indeed that an indifferent poet should have *such* a ring." He shuffled a bit closer. "Don't you agree?" Since the evening of the thieves' attack, I was quite cold inside. I suppose I really knew that he'd understood the significance of the ring, but to have him say it so boldly was like being struck. He delighted in drawing out the torture. "I think I know that ring."

He was enjoying himself. He took hold of my shoulders and forced me around. "A few questions spring up. I'm sure they're puzzling you too. Why should the Master stop wearing such a very important ring when it must have been given to him by a very important person?" He raised greasy eyebrows. "And where is it now? Has he hidden it somewhere amid these girlish curves?" Four fat and dirty fingers thrust themselves down the front of my shift. He spread his fingers, grunting his appreciation at what he found. "Come now," he hissed when I tried to pull away, "a girl with legs like yours can't afford to be fastidious." Then he drew his hand up, pulled out my pendant, and snapped the strap.

"Give that back!" I tried to snatch it.

He held it high and opened it. "Ah, this will be more useful than that time waster." He removed the lock of my father's hair. "I'll return it as soon as I've got the king's ring and your promise to give evidence against Master Chaucer. You see, you haven't been quite as helpful as you should have been."

"You're the devil." My father's hair in his horrible hand!

"Master Chaucer's a traitor."

"Look," I begged, "please. I'm nothing and nobody. I just want to pray for my father at Canterbury. Keep the pendant, but give me back my father's hair."

"When I have the ring and your promise." He let go of me. For one awful moment I thought he was going to scatter Father's hair into the river, but he squashed it back into the pendant and tied the strap around his own neck. He watched as I rebandaged my legs. Occasionally he licked his lips, no longer a viper, but a stoat.

# 10

This stranger-knight so suddenly presented,
Bareheaded . . .

The sun wasn't even risen when people began to stream
out of the town. Nobody wanted to miss the tournament. News of the blood feud had somehow trickled
out and, just as Walter predicted, this added an edge to
the excitement. Some people walked, others squashed
themselves into carts. We pilgrims rode, all except the
prioress, who was carried in a chair, her dogs on her
lap, and Sir Knight and Walter, who sat in the blue
wagon. Sir Knight's page walked Arondel and Granada
to the jousting ground to keep them fresh. Walter was
pale. His father seemed to be praying.

Riding just in front of me, the Master was trying to
cheer a silent Luke. "You can use Dobs as a packhorse for
the journey to St. Denys. A man with a packhorse somehow commands more respect than a man loaded down
like a tinker's mule." Luke tried to be grateful. The Master
waved the thanks away. Luke fidgeted. "Why don't you
go ahead," the Master said kindly. "Picardy could do with
a gallop." Luke sped off at once, head down, spurs glinting. I began to follow. A gallop might ease the terrible

gnaw of worry in my stomach, and what would I feel if Luke vanished with that bungled kiss his last memory of me? The Master caught Dulcie's rein. "Luke has a temper to conquer," he said, half-sympathetic, half-disapproving, "and you won't help."

"What's going to happen?" I whispered, nodding at the blue cart. Walter and his father were now in deep discussion. "The feud's between Sir Jean d'Aubricourt and Sir Knight, isn't it? I mean, Walter won't have to fight?"

"I don't know," the Master said shortly, "but we shall shortly find out."

I held Poppet to my chin. I couldn't look at the summoner. My pendant round his neck was an abomination. But as we rounded the final hill and the jousting ground was spread before us, the spectacle took even my breath away. This was to be no halfhearted affair. From tent to pennant, from tunic to trappings, from sky to grass, the place was awash with more colors than a tapestry. And the noise! It was like a fairground.

Master Chaucer took in the scene slowly, from left to right, then from right to left. "Sometimes I wish I were an illustrator," he said, his eyes alight. "To capture such a scene in a drawing or to paint it on a wall; to capture it exactly in one split second, like the blink of an eye—now, there would be a skill. Am I wasting my time writing black marks on a page, Belle? Given a choice, wouldn't you choose one picture over even the most well-chosen words?"

I couldn't answer that. I just wanted the day to be over.

The broad, grassy turf where the jousting would take place had been pitched so that only one set of stands had to be constructed. A daisy-dotted bank served very well for both us pilgrims and the townsfolk. The tents of the knights, some grand and some not so grand, speckled the other side of the valley like decorated biscuits, and emerging from them, ready to take their seats under the stand's striped canopy, were a variety of rich and high-born ladies, shimmering in silks and satins. Many had already attached fluttering favor ribbons to shoulders and breasts. With no threat of rain, jeweled slippers were on show, sparkling like diamond dewdrops amid the green. It was a scene from King Arthur, except that the blood would be real. I shuddered.

When the ladies spotted Dulcie, they waved, obviously thinking that only a lady like them could be riding such a pretty pony. However, when they took in my loose hair, my clothes, and, of course, the lumpy bandages peeping out from under my skirt, they whispered behind their hands. Despite my preoccupations, my face flamed.

We dismounted, tethered the horses, and found places to sit. The summoner, half gossiping with the pardoner, made sure he could see the Master at all times, and at every opportunity, he winked and touched my

pendant. "Where could Luke have gone to?" My temper was fraying.

"Probably best he isn't here," the Master replied. "It's hard for him to watch others fight when he can't fight himself." Luke jealous of men fighting. Jealous! Men are strange creatures.

The noise rose to a pitch: the hiss of steel; the persistent patter of the hog-roast sellers; the hawkers' wheedling cries. Overhead, a couple of curious buzzards hovered, hoping for flesh. A trumpet sounded. At once, scores of squires hurried to set up their lords' shields under a large crimson awning set beside the stand. It was clear at once that most of the knights were English, with only a dozen or so French captives. Chief of these was Sir Jean d'Aubricourt, whose shield was set a little apart from the others.

After some delay, another trumpet sounded. There was an expectant hush. "Now it begins," said the Master.

The first contestants emerged, and such was the weight and thickness of their armor that they rolled rather than walked to the mounting ladders, their pages close behind lest they toppled backward. Some of the townsfolk began to laugh.

"Never mock men dressed for war," the Master reprimanded. "Fully armed knights aren't made for walking." The laughter subsided.

Two contestants settled at either end of the arena,

their shields buckled to their breasts, and after fastening their helmets, they took up their lances—wooden headed in their case, for theirs was not a blood feud but fearsome nonetheless. The next thing I knew, splinters were flying as, with a terrible crack, the point of one lance went through a shield and shattered. The knights turned, ready to charge again, only one horse balked and refused to move. That was the end of the first contest.

Four more contests followed, filled with spurrings, gallopings, crashings, crossings, and refusings. Some women lost interest and began to gossip. Children squabbled and stole. Lovers grew intimate under blankets, and the very old fell asleep. There was still no sign of Luke, and Sir Jean d'Aubricourt's shield swung unattended. At midday, I was struck by a very happy thought. "Perhaps Sir Jean's gone home already," I said to the Master. The Master shook his head and pointed.

A squire in the d'Aubricourt livery had just emerged, and he held high above his head a lance, the end of which glistened silver. The squire shook the lance: this was the blood-feud lance. The crowd sang like hounds on the scent. This was what they had been waiting for.

Walter appeared, bearing his father's shield and a lance that matched his opponent's. He walked stiffly, shouting some kind of war cry. The Walter of the horsely horse seemed very far away. I clutched at the Master. "He's just doing what he has to do," the Master said grimly.

When Walter had finished shouting, he retreated to the crimson awning, where he stood quite alone. "I'm going to him," I said, and was gone before the Master could stop me.

Walter blinked when I arrived at his side. "Tell me you're not going to fight," I begged. "Please tell me it's just your father."

"My father's to fight first and . . . and . . . and if he falls, I'll fight after," Walter said in a flat, bloodless voice. "And I'm glad to. The fight may be over my sister, but I can carry your favor."

"Don't, Walter."

Something in him began to melt. "Belle—" We were interrupted.

"Ho there! It's time." It was Sir Jean d'Aubricourt's squire. "I hope your father's in good jousting form, Walter. Sir Jean's never been in better."

Walter hardened again and, bidding me go back to the Master, went stolidly about his squirely business.

All the spectators were awake now. The old men dug each other in the ribs. The children's eyes were round.

Walter settled his father on Granada, then stepped back to stand at his designated mark. Both he and his father moved like wooden soldiers. Sir Jean, on the other hand, mounted with a flourish and his squire strutted like a peacock. Only when the two knights settled their lances, the tips polished to deadly points, was

Sir Jean's squire still. Even a peacock fears the unpredictability of the tournament.

And what followed was unpredictable indeed. First, Granada galloped wide because Sir Knight's helmet slipped and he had no idea where he was going. The crowd howled their derision. They did not appreciate a circus. Then, Sir Knight's chain hauberk got hooked onto the end of Sir Jean's lance and he was dumped like a pile of silver laundry in front of the stand. Sir Jean leaped off his horse and pulled out a sword as sharp as his lance. They would finish this off on foot. But when Sir Knight tried to stand, he crumpled. One ankle had twisted. When he did rise and pull out his sword, he was obliged to hop. Disgusted, Sir Jean sheathed his sword and stamped back to his tent.

Walter threw Granada's reins to a page and hurried to help his father. I ran down again, and the Master followed, with the summoner close behind. "We're disgraced," Sir Knight moaned, trying and failing to walk properly, "and it's my fault. How could I have thought to pursue a blood feud during a pilgrimage?" He ground his teeth. I'd never seen him so upset. "This is God's punishment: public humiliation to add to the shame of my daughter's elopement." He was utterly crushed.

"We're not finished yet," Walter said.

"Yes! Yes! It's finished," I cried. "Please, Walter."

But nobody took any notice of me. Sir Jean, still

fully armed, then lumbered over. "Will you publicly crave mercy, Sir Knight? Will you go down on your knees in front of the stand? If you do that, we'll forget this feud."

"Impossible," Walter said.

"What else can we do?" Sir Knight wrung his hands in some despair. "We've offended God by swapping the pilgrim staff for the lance when we're just two days short of Canterbury. Without God's favor we can never win. Oh, why of all people did we have to bump into you, Sir Jean?"

Sir Jean snorted. "If you're fearful, sir, just say so."

"I'm fearful of God," Sir Knight said, trying to regain some dignity, "as any wise man is."

Sir Jean turned to Walter. "Well, Sir Squire," he said. "Are you less fearful than your father? Mount up! His horse is still fresh enough."

"Walter will do as I do," said Sir Knight at once. "As his father and lord, I forbid him to fight. I forbid it utterly. He's a pilgrim too."

Walter went red, then white, then red again as Sir Jean's ardor cooled to contempt. "You English . . ." The insult hung unfinished.

"I'll fight," came a voice from outside. Luke pushed through.

My hand flew to my mouth. This was too much.

"No," I heard Walter say loudly. "He's not a knight,

Sir Jean, and he doesn't approve of tournaments like this." Luke tried to interrupt. "You said so," Walter said to him directly. "Everybody heard."

"I don't deny it. But no Frenchman should go away disappointed," Luke said, his eyes glinting dangerously.

The Master quickly intervened. "Walter's right, Luke. You can't fight." He turned to Sir Jean. "The boy's not even a squire: he's my scribe," he said.

"And who might you be?"

"Geoffrey Chaucer."

"Master Chaucer?" Sir Jean started. "Well, I never. One of the few Englishmen I admire. I write poetry myself. We might engage in some wordplay later." The atmosphere lightened a little. Sir Jean looked from Sir Knight to Walter and back to Sir Knight. "Very well. I'll go and disarm, but I warn you, I consider our business unfinished. We'll cross lances again, and when we do I'll show no mercy." He found Luke in his way. "Move, boy," he said. Luke didn't move.

"Don't, Luke," said Walter quietly. "It's over."

"Is it?" Luke said, and making two hard fists, he punched Sir Jean's breastplate as though it were a boxer's bag.

Sir Jean lurched backward.

"Come on," Luke said, and a bright red spot appeared in each cheek. "You seemed very keen just a moment ago."

"You're a scribe."

"Then the joust shouldn't be very long."

"Don't be a fool. You've nothing to do with this blood feud."

"I've knocked on your shield."

"Luke," remonstrated the Master, "what are you thinking?"

"I'm thinking," said Luke slowly, but with clear intent, "that I don't care about any blood feud, but if I win, I want the whole of Sir Jean's ransom."

At this, Sir Jean began to laugh, and from behind the Master, the summoner laughed too. Luke glared at him, which made the summoner laugh louder.

Sir Jean waited for the laughter to die down. "And what would you do with my ransom, boy?"

"I'd give it to somebody who needs it to care for her father."

I almost stopped breathing. "Oh, Luke," I said. "I don't want the ransom money. I don't want your charity."

"It wouldn't be charity," Luke said, "it would be a miracle."

I couldn't allow it. "You have to refuse, Sir Jean. It wouldn't be fair at all. As you say, Luke has nothing to do with any feud. He's had no training, and anyway, nobody can joust in eyeglasses."

"It's true." Walter piled in. "Eyeglasses are no good under a helmet. They'd steam up. He'd be fighting in a fog."

But Sir Jean was regarding Luke with some speculation. "A half-blind scribe fighting for a miracle," he remarked. "It's almost better than a blood feud."

"Do you accept my challenge?" Luke looked at nobody but Sir Jean.

"You'll be hurt."

"Perhaps you'll be hurt."

Sir Jean spread his legs like oak stumps. "You verge on the insolent."

"Master Chaucer!" I beseeched. "Stop this!"

"I accept," said Sir Jean quickly, before the Master had time to intervene again.

And that was it. There was no going back. Suddenly Sir Jean was hurrying to his horse and Luke was asking Sir Knight for his armor. Sir Knight flapped his arms vaguely up and down. "That was silly, very silly. Do you know at all what to do? I mean, it takes years, but perhaps we could start with how to hold—"

"I've been watching," Luke said shortly. "I know enough."

It took ten minutes to get Luke ready, and with all the padding, the armor was clearly much heavier than he expected. But when he moved toward me with that ungainly roll, I was not even tempted to laugh. In what odd ways our dreams come true. "I want to carry your favor," he said. "It'll be the one and only time. I'll carry the pendant you wear." My reply was a choke. He didn't hear it because he had already thrust me aside and plucked my pendant from the summoner's neck. I should have known he would have noticed. Walter gasped. Luke himself was wordless as he returned the pendant to me and I, equally wordlessly, fastened it under his collar. Luke nodded, then climbed up the mounting ladder and onto Granada.

By the time the two horses reached the open ground, the crowd, deprived of any blood, had grown impatient, and when they saw Luke's spectacles, some of the ladies in the stand sniggered. Luke's cheeks turned crimson although he kept his eyes firmly ahead. At least the pilgrims and townsfolk applauded. An underdog is always popular. When the townsfolk began to whistle, Granada threatened to bolt. I bargained furiously. "If I see three swallows—no, three birds of any sort—if I see three purple shoes, if I hear three people say Luke's name . . ." I saw no birds or shoes and heard nothing.

Only when Luke reached his place at the far end of the arena did he cram the helmet over his head. It was obvious at once that the arms of his glasses were too thick for comfort, for Sir Knight's helmet was quite close fitting. Nevertheless, he grasped a lance. When the cuff of his gauntlet snagged on the end, the ladies laughed openly, and Luke had no choice but to allow Walter to hold Granada until the lance was safely under his arm. He was hardly prepared when the trumpet sounded for the contest to begin. Sir Jean was waiting, visor closed.

Luke pulled down his own visor, pushed it back up, then pulled it down again. Walter let go of Granada. The horse, not used to Luke, spun in reverse, then bolted forward so that Luke had to hike up his lance when already going full tilt. To underline his superiority and confidence, Sir Jean was deliberately slower off the mark and asked his horse only for an idle canter. As they approached each other, Luke was struggling to keep the lance straight, but a lucky strike had him catch Sir Jean's shoulder and jolt the opposing lance away. There were a few splinters. The crowd booed. I could sense Luke's relief. He had survived at least one encounter. He pulled Granada around and galloped in the vague direction of his mark.

As Walter feared, in the tin oven of his helmet, Luke's spectacles clouded up and he became hopelessly disoriented. In the end, Walter had to run and lead Granada back to the proper place. There was general laughter now, even from the pilgrims. I couldn't bear it.

Perhaps because of the laughter, once back at the mark Luke wrenched off the helmet and threw it away. Grasping a new lance, he raised it to show that he was ready. "You've forgotten your helmet," shouted the steward. Luke raised his lance again. Sir Jean frowned. "Does a knight have to wear a helmet?" he called.

The steward consulted his superior. "It's up to each man what he wears or doesn't wear." Luke shook his head at Walter, who was clearly begging him to put the helmet back on, and raised the lance a third time. Sir Jean shrugged. "So be it."

"God in Heaven," Master Chaucer expostulated. "He can't really be going to joust without a helmet." In the stand, the ladies were suddenly silent.

In seconds, both horses were galloping. This time, Sir Jean treated Luke with more respect, setting his lance early and low. In response, remembering jousts he'd seen earlier, Luke set his later and higher, leaving Sir Jean no time to alter his grip. They clashed. The heads of the lances shattered but both riders stayed in the saddle. The ladies murmured and a few began to chant Luke's name. This made Sir Jean angry. He should have floored this scribe by now. Though he had no doubt he'd win, it was beginning to look like a proper contest, and mindful that he'd been deprived of a bloody end to the blood feud, he kicked his horse unnecessarily hard.

Allowed to gallop freely, Granada was enjoying himself, and so, indisputably, was Luke. He dumped the broken lance and raised a jubilant arm. This pleased one lady, who called out, "Well done, Helmetless Knight!" Almost at once, as sometimes happens, the name began to rumble through the whole stand and across the jousting field. Now that Luke's spectacles were his only protection, far from being a focus of hilarity, they'd become a badge of courage. "A helmet-less English scribe's going to beat a fully armed French knight!" one of the pilgrims declared. There was cheering from the daisy-strewn bank.

At this, Sir Jean clearly decided enough was enough. For this third challenge, he set his horse on a direct collision course, hoping to terrify. Luke kept his nerve and so did Granada. Two more lances were shattered. "God and his saints!" the Master kept exclaiming, elated and horrified.

The fourth challenge saw Sir Jean at his most determined. He picked up a heavier lance. Luke turned to Walter. Walter shook his head. It was clear to us that he was trying to persuade Luke to call a truce. It was also clear that Luke was refusing. He snatched up the only lance left in Sir Knight's armory and spurred Granada on.

Everything seemed to slow: the bounce of Luke's hair, the thrust of Granada's haunches, the lances veering across both horses' withers. I could hear cataclysmic music in my head. I could smell steel and sweat. I could sense Sir Jean suddenly truly nervous of his ransom money. I knew then that this would be the last challenge. Sir Jean bent low and yelling, "*Dieu, Charles de France, et mon droit!*" scored a hammer blow square in the middle of Luke's chest.

In armor the weight of a coffin, Luke hit the ground

like a stone, his unprotected head and Granada's hooves muddled together. I stuffed my knuckles into my mouth as the ladies shrieked and Granada galloped off, reins trailing. Luke didn't get up. Before I was even aware of standing, I was racing down the bank, but by the time I got to Luke, Walter was already crouched over him.

Walter said nothing, not a word, but sometimes you don't need words. It was how he held Luke, the tender curve of his elbow, the way he felt for a pulse, the delicacy of his forefinger as he wiped the blood from Luke's lip, his complete disregard for where we were or who was looking. It was only then that I understood something I should have understood all along.

I dropped to my knees and removed Luke's spectacles, miraculously unbroken. "Walter," I whispered. I touched his arm. Two pools of misery were raised to me. It was the deepest exchange I'd ever had with anybody. At that moment, Walter's soul was quite naked, and a naked soul is far more naked than a naked body. How could I have thought it easy being him? How could I have reckoned his life enviably uncomplicated? How could I, who prided myself on observing so much, have observed so little? Of course Walter didn't want to kiss me. Of course he didn't want to see Luke holding me. How could he, when he himself was in love with Luke? I knew now from where the melancholy song about the bird had sprung.

I had no idea how to react. Love like Walter's was beyond my experience. Was it wrong? Certainly, the priests thought so and warned of hellish punishments. I wondered what my father would say—or Walter's father for that matter, or, indeed, Luke himself. But in the middle of that jousting field, when I didn't know whether Luke was living or dead, I had to decide for myself. I was sure about three things: first, Walter was my friend; second, I never wanted to lose him; and third, honest love, which was the only love a man like Walter could ever feel, could never be wrong. I brushed his cheek. "Love's a surprise, isn't it," I said. It wasn't profound. It didn't solve anything. But Walter breathed out. This whole exchange had taken less than a second.

A gurgle from Luke's throat. "Don't speak," I begged.

"If he dies, I'll never forgive myself." Walter was holding Luke as tight as he dared. "I should have fought. How I hate tournaments." He was desolate.

"He's not going to die," I declared with great energy. "God wouldn't dare. Now put his head on my lap. People are coming."

"I don't care," Walter said.

"You must care," I said.

"Belle—"

"It's all right, Walter. It's all right."

When the steward and Master Chaucer arrived, I

was holding Luke and Walter was busy taking off the armor. Master Chaucer was gray.

"No, he's not dead." Walter gave a bland smile. "But he's hit his head hard. I don't think he'll ride again today, and we'll have to hope his famous memory's not impaired."

When the stretcher came, it was Master Chaucer who held Luke's hand. I think only I noticed that Walter had to turn away.

We continued on to Sir Jean's tent. With his ransom saved, the French knight was generosity itself. No expense was to be spared to repair his gallant opponent's injuries. Naturally enough, as Master Chaucer and Walter disappeared with the stretcher, the summoner was watching. There was one awful cry as Luke was stripped and checked for broken bones. I clutched the tent pole. Then there was nothing to do but wait.

# 11

The fiery dart of love so burningly
Thrusts through my faithful heart with deadly hurt!

It was the padding that saved Luke. Apart from bruising and mild concussion, he had suffered no lasting damage. Still, Sir Knight insisted on transporting him back to the town in the blue armor cart. I'd never seen Master Chaucer so thrilled. Not only was Luke a hero, but, so he whispered to me, the king's ring could be sent with Sir Jean! Luke need have nothing to do with it anymore. "God works in mysterious ways," he murmured as he climbed into the cart beside Luke. "So mysterious I doubt even he can follow all the twists and turns."

I watched the cart lumber off. Walter was riding Arondel and leading Picardy. I mounted Dulcie and volunteered to lead Dobs. As good fortune had it, Sir Knight had cornered the summoner to discuss the nature of pilgrimage. Master Summoner would find it hard to escape. Walter and I rode side by side and the two led horses flanked us. That way we took up the whole road. For the first time since we'd met, Walter couldn't look at me. I really didn't know how to start, so I waded straight in. "Are you ashamed?"

He stared straight ahead. "Yes," he said.

"Does your father know?"

"He knows and doesn't know, if that makes any sense. Mostly, he blocks it out." He paused. "It's why my sister ran off. She guessed—I don't know how because I swear to you, Belle, I've never touched anybody, man, boy, or girl, except once." His face hardened, then softened unhappily. "But she seemed to know and one day asked me outright and I wasn't quick enough to deny it. It was she who told my father. He'd never have guessed on his own. Whoa there, Picardy." The horse snatched at a branch. "We lied, my father and I, about going to Canterbury to pray for my sister's return. We're going to Canterbury to pray for a cure for me. My father insisted on bringing Dulcie. I think she's supposed to remind me that she's the kind of pony people like me end up riding and also, of course, that because I'm not—well—not normal I drove my sister into the arms of our enemy."

"How monstrous."

Now he looked at me. "No, not monstrous," he said. "What I feel's a sin. It's led to a blood feud."

"Love's never a sin," I said stoutly. "What you do with love can be a sin, I suppose, but love itself can never be any such thing."

Walter shook his head. "It makes me dishonest. I laugh and sing and flirt and eat and drink and serve and joust, but all the time it's as if I'm a character in a story."

I knew that feeling. It made me want to hug him. We had to part momentarily to allow a trail of pack-horses through. The peddler hailed Walter, with side-long glances at me. "Flaming hair, flaming passion," he chortled. "Send her my way when you've finished!" Walter responded as he always did, with a laugh and a posy of words. When we came together again, he was flushed. "You see," he said. "When you're like me, deceit becomes second nature. I even deceived you."

"No, you didn't."

"Yes, Belle, I did. When I saw you in the Tabard yard and learned you'd had no horse, I thought it would please my father to see a pretty girl in Dulcie's saddle at my request. And it worked. He thought the cure had started already. He still thinks so."

"That's why he doesn't mind me being a bell founder's daughter?"

"Better a bell founder's daughter than another knight's son."

"Oh, Walter."

"Yes. You won't want to ride with me now."

"On the contrary," I said, "I want to ride with you very much."

There was silence for a little while. I broke it again, this time without a question. I began to talk about myself. I told him about my mother, how my father's accident haunted me, about my life-in-the-head, my

hopeless housekeeping, my three-figured compulsion—
"Ah, the three-skip mounting bounce, the threefold I
Spy," he said—and my pumicing—"Ah, the legs," he
said. I nodded. I really felt I could tell him anything.
No, more than that. I wanted to tell him everything.
I drew the line only at Master Chaucer's secret. Now
wasn't the right time.

"You must be very lonely," he said unexpectedly
when my words trickled away.

I considered. "I've never thought I was lonely, but I
suppose I am," I said. "You get used to it."

"Yes, that's true."

"But you must have lots of friends," I said.

"Do you?"

"No."

Dulcie and Arondel skipped simultaneously over a
pile of dung.

"It's quite odd how similar we are," I said. "We've
both injured our fathers and we both love Luke. We
were bound to be friends."

"Or enemies," Walter said.

"Dear Walter," I said warmly, "you could no more
be my enemy than . . . than . . . Poppet."

He steered Picardy past a trio of drunken masons. "I
wish I could do something to make my father proud,
or do something to make me proud of myself."

"Weren't you with him in France?"

"Yes, but we never fought a real battle. Remember the bloodstain in his book?"

I nodded.

"It's from his thumb. He cut it on a meat knife when we were sitting comfortably at our own table. It's true we've been to France, and, two years ago, we did go on campaign to Scotland. But the only blood we saw was when villagers tried to stop us from taking food without paying. They were barely even armed. Perhaps if I fought in a real battle, I'd be different. I don't know because I never have."

I sat very still. Perhaps now was the right time after all. "Well," I said tentatively, because I had no idea what he might think, "I can't offer you a battle with swords and blood, but I can offer you this." Before I could have second thoughts, I told him about Master Chaucer, the king, the ring, and the summoner. He listened intently. "You see we're all deceitful in our ways," I said nervously when I'd finished.

"Except for Luke," he answered at once.

"Except for Luke," I said. "Turns out an alchemist is the most honest of us all."

He gave the ghost of a smile. Then the full import of what I had told him sank in. "Where's the king's ring at this moment?"

"I don't know," I said, and the sense of relief at not carrying all this stuff alone made me a little light-headed.

"I don't even know if the Master still has it. He might have given it to Sir Jean when they took Luke into the tent."

"If he didn't, we can't let Luke be sent on some errand for King Richard. Not when it could condemn him to death." He was horrified, but also glad to think about something else. "We'll find the ring. If Sir Jean does have it, he won't be leaving for home at least until the morning, and he'll be in the town tonight."

"To inquire after Luke?"

"No, because there's always a feast after a tournament, and if Sir Jean's got anything to do with it, this tournament will be no exception."

"Have you met him?" I asked.

"Who?"

"The king."

"I have," said Walter shortly. There was another pause. "We were together quite a bit when he was a boy. He only arrived in England when he was four, you know, and my father's lands lay next to those of the royal manor at Berkhamsted, where Richard lived with his mother. We shared a tutor. Not the two of us alone," he added hastily, "there were others. We all had special places in the coronation procession. Some are still his friends."

"Do you think he deserves to be king?" I asked.

"Deserves? That's not the right word. Nobody deserves

to be king. He certainly wasn't meant to be king. His brother Edward was, but he died, so Richard just *is* king, and if people go pitching kings off their thrones, I'm not sure where we'll end up. But to ask for help from the king of France! It's not—it's not—"

"Not kingly," I said, and was relieved when Walter laughed.

"Absolutely right, Belle. It's not what a properly kingly king would do."

"What shall *we* do?"

He became very serious again. "Are you sure you want to do anything with me?"

"Very much," I said.

"I'm not the kind of friend your father would want you to have."

I wanted to say that Walter was exactly the kind of friend my father would want me to have, but I couldn't. In truth, I had no idea what my father would make of Walter. "I choose my own friends," I said in the end.

Walter gave a half smile. He understood perfectly. We explored various harebrained plans, from kidnapping Sir Jean, or Luke, or the summoner, or all three. Then suddenly Walter struck his saddle. "I know just what to do."

"What?"

"We'll find the ring and simply return it to the king."

"Just like that?"

"No, not just like that. When we return it, we'll make him see that if he asks the king of France for help, he'll lose his throne, not keep it."

"He thinks he's going to lose it anyway."

"And he might," said Walter, "but if he asks for foreign help, no Englishman would ever forgive him, so he'll never be safe. He must understand that."

I was thoroughly skeptical. "Even assuming we find the ring, why on earth should the king see us, let alone listen to anything we have to say?"

There was a long pause. "He'll see us," said Walter, and looked away.

I swallowed. I couldn't ask more. I didn't want to know more. I rushed on. "What happens if he doesn't like what we tell him?"

"Then I'll be executed for guessing a truth Richard doesn't want anybody except for Master Chaucer to know," Walter said. "I mean, Richard can't allow me to live if I know that he's asked the king of France to send soldiers over here to kill Englishmen, can he? I expect my execution will be long and slow."

"Jesus Mary, don't!"

"It would be in a good cause, and you'd be safe. I'd say I led you astray." He gave a hollow laugh. "That at least would please my father."

I'd never heard him sound bitter before. It didn't suit him.

"If the Master's still got the ring, where might he have hidden it, do you think?" Walter mused.

"It's not in his writing box," I said, "or at least it wasn't. It's possible he's put it back in there, thinking that the summoner wouldn't look in there again."

"It's possible," Walter said. "Can you look when we get back?" I nodded. "And can you look in his baggage and in his ordinary clothes when he changes for the feast? Of course he could have it around his neck or in his pouch. You'll have to get close to him. We really need the services of a pickpocket." I grimaced. "Yes, I know," Walter said, "it's not nice, but remember if we find it, he can't give it to Luke. If the Master hasn't given the ring to Sir Jean, that's what he'll do." He pursed his lips. "If you can't find it, though, I'll have to find a way of searching Sir Jean and his belongings. I'm not sure how I'll do that but the ring mustn't go to France. It absolutely mustn't."

"What about the summoner?" I reminded him anxiously. "His threats are quite real and if he guesses what we're doing, my father . . ."

Walter frowned. "Whatever we do, we need to be quick."

The road filled up as we neared the town walls and we had to ride in single file. Dulcie blew hard through her nose as we passed a slaughtered pig. The smell of baking bread rose even above the smell of the sewers. Sir Jean had sent word already. A feast was being prepared.

I dismounted and patted Dobs. Walter and I began to walk toward the inn. Then something echoed. "Wait," I said, and ran back to Dobs. "Head up for a moment," I ordered, and ran my hand over the top of his crest, pressing down. All I could feel was hair.

"What on earth are you doing?" Walter had followed me.

"Just wait," I said. I began at Dobs's withers, parting the hair, my fingers searching. I moved methodically up his neck, to where the hair tangled further into a veritable thicket of knots and braids. *You could hide a library of stories in there and nobody would ever find it.* Wasn't that what I'd said the first day of the pilgrimage? *I'll remember that*, the Master had replied. And perhaps he had. He was always with Dobs and hadn't I heard him give the horse to Luke to take with him? It wasn't impossible. I squeezed and parted, forcing myself to go slowly. Just below where the bridle's headpiece sat, inside a knot that was really no different from any of the others, I found what I was looking for. "No need to riffle through the baggage," I said to Walter, and guided his hand.

He was thunderstruck. "How on earth . . . ?"

"A lucky guess," I said.

"The luckiest," Walter agreed. The page returned. It was too difficult to get the ring out now. Walter and I looked at each other. "At least it's safe," Walter murmured.

"Do you think he'll give it to Sir Jean this evening?" I was anxious.

Walter considered. "Actually, no. If I know Sir Jean, and I do, he'll be drunk, so it would be too dangerous. He might forget or repeat very loudly whatever Master Chaucer says to him." He frowned. "Perhaps he won't hand it over at all."

"If he doesn't, can we be sure he'll wait until we get to Canterbury to send Luke on his way? I mean, he knows the summoner suspects." I began to panic. "Even if you and I stole the ring tonight, I can't not go to St. Thomas's tomb. I can't break that promise to my father."

Walter was quick to reassure me. "I think he'll wait. It would look too suspicious, wouldn't it, Luke disappearing early, particularly with the Master's horse. If he doesn't hand it to Sir Jean, nothing will be done until after Canterbury."

"It's such a relief to share a secret."

Walter gave a half smile. "Particularly when you live a lie."

Now I hugged him. It seemed the most natural thing in the world to do.

Though Sir Jean had won his joust, the French knight decreed that Luke should be given a place of honor at the feast. Not to be outdone, Sir Knight declared that Luke should keep Granada. Upright again, though not yet completely steady on his feet, Luke declined.

What would a monk want with a warhorse? Sir Knight was insistent. Warhorses were valuable. Luke could give Granada to the abbot of St. Denys. Such a gift would ensure a most generous welcome. Eventually, when Sir Knight wouldn't give up, Luke accepted and, to reciprocate, gave Picardy to Sir Knight. "He's not much to look at," Luke said, "but he's solid." He paused. "And his temper is more even than mine."

Everybody laughed and applauded, especially the Master. All the while Luke was looking around. When he saw Walter and me standing close, his lips tightened. He touched my pendant, seemed undecided, then chose to keep it. My heart rose. So long as he had my favor, he was still the Helmetless Knight, and a Helmetless Knight might do many things a monk might not.

It took me only a moment to wash my face and shake out my dress. I had nothing else to wear. I couldn't sit still, though, so to stop myself brooding, I walked about the town. Smoke was rising high above the spits in the square, and every householder was busily placing color-shaded candles in their windows. Such a simple device. Such a magical transformation. The streets were rumbling with barrels of wine and ale rolled by boys standing aloft, feet slithering. Three rolled past me, followed by three girls spinning hoops. The visiting knights and ladies were also trickling in, their baggage trundling after them. One of the French ladies, exotically plumed, recognized me as Dulcie's rider. "You! Mistress Firehair! Aren't you going to dress for the feast?"

"I've no other clothes," I called back regretfully.

She put her hands on her hips. "Ladies!" she cried, "our redheaded pilgrim has no feasting clothes!"

Three of the ladies circled me. I remarked that they seemed to have a lot of baggage for the wives of prisoners. Did they leave nothing at home? They smiled at my naivety. "Oh yes," they said, "plenty." There was a general consultation. "We can spare something, if you'd like."

It seemed odd, being offered clothes by the enemy, but with my pendant still around Luke's neck, I felt a sudden, wild surge of vanity. "I would like that," I said. "I'd like it very much."

They flocked to the tavern with me in their midst, fussing and bickering half in French and half in quaint, heavily accented English. They wanted to give me a bath in rosewater. That I did decline. I don't know what they made of my silk-covered legs. I expect they thought I'd been burned. As they squeezed and buttoned and gathered and sewed, I was asked many questions about the Helmetless Knight, and I obliged as the occasion demanded, constructing a whole knightly persona for Luke, most of which I lifted from stories of the Round Table. He had jousted, so I declared, with Black Knights and Green; he had consorted with enchantresses; he had once saved a damsel from a boiling cauldron. By the time my hair was dressed as fancily as my feet, Luke was a complete work of fiction.

But then I was too, for the ladies had turned me into a creature of Parisian refinement. In a dark green, close-fitting gown of green velvet, with a sea-green underskirt of fine-meshed gauze peeping through a slit up to my waist, I was both sylph-thin and softly rounded. My sleeves were tight to the elbow where the velvet widened to reveal an inner sleeve of gauze the same color as the skirt. This gauze tapered into a cuff at the wrist and into it, as well as into a sea-green ribbon tied round my neck, were stuck tiny diamonds of glass. There were diamonds too, in the soft green calfskin shoes bottomed out with a small heel that showed off my ankles. The effect would have been greater without my silk bandages, but at least they were better than Walter's woolen hose or multicolored scars.

After various discussions, the ladies piled my hair high, securing it with threads and bows and small steel clips. My neck felt very bare and my head so heavy that I dared not even nod. Chalk for my cheeks, kohl for my eyes, and pale salve for my lips finished their work and when they showed me my reflection, quite unexpectedly I caught a glimpse of my mother. It was the first time I realized she'd been beautiful.

My fellow pilgrims were gathered together, drinking. Summoner Seekum was in an evil mood. I didn't care.

Walter knew everything. We'd found the ring, and from the gossip of the ladies, I learned that Sir Jean would certainly be in no fit state to receive either it or Master Chaucer's confidences. My clothes meant that I was both myself and not myself. Tonight I could live a fairy tale rather than make one up. Morning would come soon enough.

The moment I saw Luke, I knew that probably through the Master's contrivance, Walter had had a hand in dressing him, because only Walter could have chosen clothes for a Helmetless Knight and only Walter would have chosen like a lover. Over a clean white undershift, cuffs and collar billowing like drifted snow, Luke wore a russet jacket, tailored at the waist and speckled with gold embroidery. His usual workman's trousers had been exchanged for woolen hose of the same russet hue, and he wore them inside his own black boots, cleaned and expertly patched. His hair was washed. That gave me a pang, but only momentarily. Through the glass of his spectacles Luke's eyes shone like two burnished shields, and when I moved forward to greet him, they looked straight into mine without any confusion or uncertainty. Just like me, tonight he too was both himself and not himself. I don't know whether he even noticed what I was wearing. All I know is that we were both exactly where we wanted to be.

I can't, or perhaps don't want to, describe the details of

that evening. If you've ever been in love, and been loved, and had an evening when you both feel suspended an inch above the ground, you'll understand that descriptions either flatten or exaggerate. The evening did have details, of course, such as the moments when dances ended and Luke would raise his palms and I would raise mine and he would press his whole weight against them. And the moments when we shared tumblers of wine and he deliberately placed his lips where mine had been. I don't remember anything we said, though I suppose we must have spoken. I do remember that Luke didn't cling to me, nor I to him. Some of the magic, you see, was in seeing him paired with gowns of dawn red and rose pink, daffodil yellow, and deepest damson, yet knowing all the time that he was only really conscious of sea green. And I think some of the magic for him was seeing me dance, even with Sir Jean d'Aubricourt himself, all the while knowing that I was longing to return to him. I had imagined many times how such love would feel: like strong mead on an empty stomach or a shiver of lightning. It was like neither of those. It was simply a feeling of utter wholeness. That's all.

When the minstrels stopped for bread and beef, different entertainment was called for, and Luke and I formed part of a cozy circle round a small brazier near the middle of the square. Master Chaucer sat nearby with Walter on one side and the ever-vigilant summoner on the other. The summoner was trying to speak to the Master and the Master was irritated. He turned to Walter. "Sing for us," he said.

"What song would you like to hear?"

"The first that comes to mind."

Obediently, Walter stood, looked about, and saw his father. Quiet fell. He blinked, and then, with his eyes fixed on Luke and me, he began:

> *Your two eyes will slay me suddenly*
> *I see their beauty but cannot play my part*
> *So I must travel with a wounded heart.*
> *Unless I can perform a hasty healing*
> *My heart will open and be too revealing,*
> *Your two eyes will slay me suddenly.*
> *Upon my word, I say this in good faith,*
> *That you are of life and death the king*
> *One day the real truth shall be what I sayeth*
> *Until that time I am content to sing.*

The Master, who I don't think had intended to pay much attention, was transfixed. The song's form, at least to start with, was his, but by changing some of the words and supplanting the major with a minor key, Walter had turned a lightweight tease into something quite else. I was terrified at the risk Walter had taken. What would happen if everybody realized to whom

this song was really directed? I tried to catch his eye, but Walter was in his own world. I saw that Luke's face was full of shadows. He had guessed, but guessed entirely wrongly. "Walter loves you," he said to me. "Don't deny it. And Sir Knight approves." It was true that Sir Knight was nodding.

That was the moment we bumped back to earth. Clothes or no clothes, after Walter's song Luke couldn't stop himself thinking about the time, very soon to come, when he would be Brother Luke, while Walter would be Sir Knight's heir and free to marry. I ached for him but I also ached for Walter, though I didn't know how to tell Luke why. "He does love," I whispered in the end, "but he doesn't love me." It was probably a good thing that Sir Knight chose this moment to ask Luke if he'd seen his book. He'd brought it out to show Sir Jean and put it down somewhere. Luke hadn't heard a word I'd said. When the minstrels started up again, though, Luke didn't ask me to dance. Instead, he walked to one of the bonfires and gazed into it. I found Walter behind me, grasping my shoulders unusually firmly. "You haven't told Luke. Please say you haven't."

"He wouldn't—"

"You mustn't. Please, Belle. I'm begging you."

"All right, Walter, I won't, I won't."

When I turned back to the fire, Luke had vanished. He still had my pendant, though.

At midnight, my hair finally tumbled down, and by the time I heard a distant bell for morning prayers, I had to admit that the feast was over. Now everything was as it had been, only somehow worse because the evening had started so perfectly and ended so cloudily. I calculated the number of dances I danced with Luke. Nine. Then I found I had three hairpins left. Even with these good omens and even dividing the stairs into three equal sets of three, I was very downhearted when I finally took off my green gown. Tomorrow we would be at Canterbury.

Not wanting to sleep, I wandered out. The roads were littered with congealing pig bones, heels of bread, and snoring revelers. With the colored lanterns extinguished and rats fighting in the rubbish carts, the town was dismal.

Luke was standing by the well, his arms crossed, still wearing the russet jacket. My stomach knotted. He moved forward when he saw me but expressed no surprise that I should have appeared. "I want to return this," he said, and held out the pendant.

I didn't take it at once. "Don't go to St. Denys."

"I promised," he said, and held the pendant out again. A little magic flickered as our fingers touched.

"The feast," Luke said, closing my fingers into a fist and keeping hold of it for a moment.

"Yes?"

He hesitated. "You looked so different in those clothes."

"In what way different? Nicer?"

"Nicer?" He seemed puzzled. "I don't know."

"You didn't think I looked nice?" I was upset. I wondered if I had misunderstood everything. My legs itched.

"No—I mean yes." His old confusions returned. "What I mean to say," he said, recovering a little, "is that I don't know how to describe how you looked." He thought. "You looked like a song," he said finally.

"The Helmetless Knight and a song," I said softly. He took the pendant back and I bent my head as he fastened it round my neck. I could feel his breath in my ruined hair.

"There." He touched the pendant for a last time as it swung. "We had an evening, didn't we? Just the sort of evening people dream about. I'll remember it all my life." The muscles in his cheeks were working very hard. "And if I have to think about you with anybody, I shall be easiest thinking about you with Walter. He and Sir Knight have security and money. They don't need to try and win a ransom to help your father. And Walter's a good man, I think."

"Break your promise!" I urged. "Stay with me!"

He shook his head. "No, Belle. I won't be a promise breaker. What kind of person would that make me? A charlatan, like my father. Just the sort of person I don't want to be."

"I wouldn't care," I said.

"Yes, you would," he said flatly. "You'd not break a promise. You're like the Master. You may make things up for stories, but I'd trust you with my life."

"Oh, Luke . . ." I was half crying for his perfect faith. "Don't! The Master and I, we're just like everybody else. We do what we must to get by." He wasn't listening. He was fighting something in himself. "What is it?" I asked, half-hopeful, half-fearful.

"I want to kiss you right this moment," he said without any confusion at all. "I want it more than anything I've ever wanted in my life. I want to kiss you and for you to kiss me. I've been thinking about nothing else for hours."

"Don't think about it, Luke, just do it," I whispered.

He put both hands on my shoulders. I could feel each finger pressing tight. He hurt me, though he never knew it. He was trembling. Then he let go, one finger at a time.

"I can't!" The words dragged themselves out. "If I kiss you, I'll be lost. Don't you see that?" The last finger pressed, then rose.

"I wish I'd never met you," I sobbed.

He let go of me entirely. "I don't wish the same," he said, his voice hard and tense. "When I'm lonely in my

cell, I'll recall every conversation, every swing of your waist, every tint in your hair. I'll forget nothing."

"I hope it's torture!"

"Torture?" His smile was a grimace as he stepped back too far for his arms to reach me or mine to reach him. "It'll certainly be that. But I know—I'll always know—that it was worth it."

I only just caught the last bit, and I don't think I was meant to. "Luke!"

I raised my hand, palm out, just as in the dance. He raised his hand, palm out. Then he made it into a fist, spun around, and strode quite violently away.

# 12

Blessed St. Thomas answer to your need!

The worst of it now, far worse than wondering how Walter and I would get to the king, was that I didn't know whether Luke would say a proper good-bye to me or whether that meeting by the well was the last time I'd see him. To some people, it must seem selfish and even silly that something so personal could be more important than the future of a monarch or even a nation. I can't apologize for that. The lives of monarchs and the fates of nations are the concern of many. My life is of concern only, or at least mainly, to me. Of course I would be sorry if Richard was deposed or murdered, but another Richard would be along directly. There would never be another Luke, though, so it was he who was still uppermost in my mind when, toward evening the following day, we saw the outskirts of Canterbury.

Most of the pilgrims raised a cheer, though when we got closer the cheers turned to groans at the dreadful state of the road. Soon, the horses were fetlock-deep in mud. Closer still, we could see that the great cathedral was caged by thick bars of scaffolding swarming with workmen. "Why do cathedrals always have to be bigger and taller?" Dame Alison complained. "Can God really be impressed?"

"Everything's so very dirty." Madam Prioress sighed, and Dulcie, splashed all the way to her tummy, snorted her agreement.

Despite knowing it would upset Luke, I was riding with Walter. How could I not? Walter needed me. And anyway, Luke and the Master were a long way behind, with the summoner, naturally, behind them. As soon as we saw the cathedral I tried to reorganize my thoughts so that at least until we'd visited St. Thomas's tomb my father, and only my father, would be in my head. But my thoughts were slippery as a bog in the rain.

Mistress Midwife, because she knew it would upset people, bellowed a new concern. "Perhaps St. Thomas's body has been removed because of all the work, in which case our journey will be quite wasted." The prioress began to cry and I almost joined her. If St. Thomas's body wasn't in the cathedral, what sort of a sign was that? But Dame Alison was having none of it. "St. Thomas hasn't moved for nearly two hundred years. Why on earth would he move now?"

The mud got worse as we entered the town proper, and I could hear the mother in the wagon shrieking as she and her children were hurled from side to side. It couldn't be helped, particularly as it wasn't only the mud the wagoner had to contend with, it was the sheer volume of traffic. I know it was the time of year for pilgrimage, but it was hard to believe that a town could hold so many people, let alone so many sick and disfigured. The whole place limped and groaned, even the physically intact crippled by their burden of sin. Men whose complexion and girth declared them professional people of means adopted rough sackcloth, some rendered deliberately ragged. And overlying all the sweaty stink, the cloying stench of competitive piety.

My heart missed a beat when I saw a huddle of young monks under the direction of a novice master pushing their way through the crowds. A vision of Luke, tonsured and tripping over the hem of a shapeless habit, burned itself onto my brain. I knew then that however much I was tempted, I would never visit him at St. Denys. It would kill me.

After some unsuccessful forays, we found, set right on the river, a hostel from which a group of similar size to ours was departing. We were glad to have found it, despite the lice-ridden fleeces that were to serve as blankets. And we wouldn't be here long, since, just as Dame Alison predicted, Mistress Midwife's fears about the removal of St. Thomas's bones were entirely unfounded, and it was arranged that we should file into the cathedral at noon the following day to make our offerings.

Once settled, we were at the mercy of the priest and the friar, praying and confessing. Naturally, since my sins would include lust and deceit, I couldn't confess to a priest I knew, so I rather shamefacedly asked Walter for three pennies and found a very elderly priest hearing confessions under an awning on a side street. Not only was he more interested in the pennies than me, but he was deaf, so it was quite easy to confess honestly.

At supper, as things turned out, Walter sat next to Luke and I sat next to Walter. The summoner seated himself opposite Master Chaucer, and after we'd eaten what passed for food, he followed the Master and Luke out. This, for once, was more relief than worry. If the Master had decided to remove the ring from Dobs, he couldn't do it with the summoner watching.

"We'll get the ring when Luke's setting off," I said to Walter as he redid my bandages.

"Perhaps I could offer to hold Dobs?"

"Best not. He already thinks you're just waiting for him to go to sweep me up," I said, blushing a little.

Walter gave a bleak smile. "I wish it were true."

"So do I," I said impulsively.

"Dearest Belle," Walter said. "You'll fall in love with somebody else eventually, and even if you don't, you'll want to marry a man who'll love you properly. Anyway," he shook himself, "now's not the time for all that. You must concentrate on your father."

After supper, we were given rolled-up mattresses of thin and moth-eaten horsehair for which, so Dame

Alison grumbled, we'd paid as handsomely as for greater comforts in other towns. Austerity, not luxury, carried a premium here.

I folded my pendant into my palm. Luke was just behind the wall at which I was staring. Perhaps he was staring at it too, thinking about me. I became very angry with myself. There would be plenty of time to mope. Tonight was my father's night and I must make my preparations for tomorrow properly. There'd be no second chance for a miracle. I shifted onto my side and forced myself back in time until I was once again in that bell tower, once again dizzy, once again making that fateful sideways dip, once again hearing the boom of the bell and the crunch of the bone, once again seeing the stunned shock on my father's face and, worst of all, watching him confront each day utterly dependent on a widow he didn't like. I tried to pray for some abatement of the pain and despair my father suffered. I reiterated my promise that if God would restore my father's legs, I would make bells of which both God and my father could be proud.

Once I got going, I did quite well, but as the night dragged sleeplessly on, not so well. The desire to slip away from my father and into dreams of Luke was irresistible, and by the time a peal summoned the monks to Matins, I was in the kind of fever of temptation and torment that I knew only a pumice could assuage. I got up more than once, thinking to search for one, and each time I forced myself back down. Several times I touched my legs with my nails. The urge to scratch was overwhelming but I lay rigid. This was my penance. I must bear it. I did.

We gathered midmorning, shoeless and wearing no adornment of any kind. I still held my father's pendant in my palm and had Poppet hidden up my sleeve. Sir Knight and Walter carried small boxes of coins. The mother carried one daughter and held the other by the hand. She had no other offering. Getting here was enough. Summoner Seekum swung a heavy purse bearing the archdeacon's crest, the pardoner something he swore was St. Joseph's toe, and the old reeve a vine. Master Chaucer carried a small framed icon of his wife, though, when I admired it, he said it looked nothing like her, so he hoped God would not mistake her for somebody else. I wasn't sure if he joked or not. Luke carried nothing because the bandits had left him nothing, though his gift was actually the greatest of them all: he was giving himself.

We were delayed by Dame Alison, who wanted to offer up her wedding rings but found them vanished. Muttering about witches and thieves, she fetched a large pearl instead. I thought I'd tell her afterward where I suspected the rings were.

It was hard to get a proper view of the cathedral

through the masses and we were in it before I'd taken stock of it. Despite the throng, once under the portals, I shivered. I couldn't forget that murder had been done in here.

The day was cloudy, so we couldn't appreciate the glories of light streaming through the colored windows. In the glow of the sconces, however, I could see how diminished we all looked in our shifts. Even Summoner Seekum's coarse self-congratulation had shrunk to faltering smugness. Without his belt and pouch, his stomach sagged like an old sack, and Dame Alison, unbolstered and flat-footed, was just an elderly lady searching for forgiveness and peace.

Luke's voice made me jump. "After you've prayed for your father, will you pray for me?"

I wanted to say no, that I wouldn't pray for him, not here, not anywhere, because he was going to leave me. But he was so nervous and sad that I couldn't be cruel. I nodded. "Will you pray for me too?"

"Always," he said.

We moved forward. A sudden draft around our ankles had us huddling together and I knew that Luke was also remembering the draft Archbishop Thomas Becket must have felt before he heard the scrape of the swords that sliced into his head and elevated him to sainthood. I pressed against Luke's side. He didn't move away. Had Archbishop Becket been frightened at the end, I wondered, as we inched toward the Chapel of the Trinity. Or had he braced himself and met immortality without blinking? Had he imagined that, two centuries later, his bodily remains would be venerated by silly girls like me? I pressed harder against Luke. "I'm not thinking of my father! I can't keep my mind where it should be!" I panicked.

He took my hand. In the crush, nobody could see. We reached the chapel and stepped inside.

Then we gasped in unison. I don't know what I'd expected, but the chapel containing the bones of the saintly archbishop and martyr was no gloomy charnel house. Rather, it was a dazzling treasury more suited to one of the Master's exotic tales of the East. There must have been a king's ransom of jewels piled up, topped with a golden crown an emperor would have coveted. Nor was this a place of quiet contemplation. An army of deacons, all armed with steel-tipped sticks, prodded us into line. To them, we were not pilgrims but potential thieves and to be treated as such. When I finally reached the bank of prie-dieux, though I was ordered to kneel in a most peremptory fashion, I stood stupidly and gawked. If Luke hadn't pressed me down, I'd have missed my chance to kneel at all.

The casket, long as an armor chest and with one hinged side open, was set high. The sconces were all smoking badly, but it was possible to see half a dozen gray bones within. To tell the truth, after more than two centuries, the bones could have been gnarled bits of wood for all I could tell, but I wanted so hard to believe in them that had the casket been completely empty I could have seen in it whatever anybody suggested. Though my lips prayed for my father, I couldn't help thinking of my mother. She was buried in a casket too. Was this what was left of her? Perhaps, since she'd only been buried five years before, there would be other parts, horrible parts, *soft parts*, still decaying. Would I recognize her? My skin grew cold.

I began to pray properly just before I was forced by the prodders to rise, so my prayer was completely garbled. "Dear St. Thomas, intercede with God for me and make my father's legs like new. If that's not possible, could he live without pain? I mean, please let him walk without pain."

It was all the time I had and I'd not even mentioned Luke. I tried to kneel for longer but was forced up and, along with all those others with offerings not valuable enough for display at the front of the tomb, was ushered toward the back. I deposited my pendant reluctantly, and watched it slither away. In amongst all these riches, why would St. Thomas care about such a thing? I immediately wanted it back. Then I was frightened. Even to think such a thought was an insult to St. Thomas.

One of the deacons poked me in the ribs. It was time to leave. Luke was already vanishing into the crowd, as was everybody else in our party. I tried to follow, but an anxious mother holding up a sickly baby was in my way. "Help my baby," she pleaded loudly and frantically. "No more vomiting, no more fits. Help him!" She repeated herself again and again, stretching higher and higher, her arms too thin to manage the weight of even such a tiny burden. When the strain became intolerable, she carefully lowered the baby and hugged him to the side of her face the way I often hugged Poppet to mine. A deacon tried to hurry her. She took no notice. He shook her. The baby's head lolled, and both the mother and the deacon peered at it. I saw the mother freeze. The deacon summoned a priest who peered also, then snatched the baby from the mother's arms. "A miracle!" he shouted. "We have a veritable miracle. This lady prayed for relief of her baby's suffering and St. Thomas has taken the poor mite to himself. The babe suffers no more. He's in a better place!"

The mother began to scream and I wanted to scream too. Was this how miracles were made, by twisting the words of the desperate? I fled as best I could, trying to remember the exact words of my own prayer. Had I stressed enough that when I asked for my father to be without pain, I didn't mean that he should die? Had I specified that he should be able to walk *on earth*?

Had I used the word *live*? I thought I had but the more I thought, the less sure I was. I became as frantic as the mother. If my careless action had caused my father's injuries, would my careless words now cause his death? *What if God twisted my prayer too?* And because I hadn't prayed for Luke, did that mean something terrible would happen to him?

I knew what I needed to do. I needed to make my offering and my prayer all over again, this time removing any ambiguities. I tried to return to the tomb. I pleaded with the ushers. But no matter how I struggled, I was shoved down the long side aisle toward the door. Then I was back in the square, shaking.

Pilgrims who had already been absolved were milling about, some talking excitedly about their experience, others standing stunned. I saw nobody familiar until I spotted the Master waiting on a side street. Beside him was a groom holding Dobs and Granada, Granada fully saddled and Dobs irritable under half a dozen saddlebags. Luke had already reached them and Master Chaucer was urging him to mount Granada. "Luke!" I cried. "Luke!"

He heard me. Master Chaucer, though, shook his head. Luke looked uncertain, then mounted. I shoved and pushed my way through. Luke couldn't go, not now, not like this. I reached him just in time and clung to Granada's stirrup.

Master Chaucer was more flustered than I'd ever

seen him. "Let go, Belle. If he rides hard, he can catch the tide. His job with me is over. He must go." He had to stop himself glancing constantly over his shoulder. Luke took up Dobs's reins. "It's best not to drag out our good-byes," he said tightly, looking down at me. "I hope you prayed that I'd be a good monk."

I was mad with fear. "All my prayers went wrong. A baby died. The mother's words were all distorted. Now I don't know—do you think—how can God—?"

"No time for this, Belle," interrupted the Master. "We've said our good-byes and Luke's *got* to go *now*." His eyes were gimlets boring into me. Behind his head, I saw Master Summoner accompanied by two armed men at the opening of the street. The time for games was over.

I dug my nails into my arms. Where was Walter? We must get the ring from Dobs. But Walter was nowhere to be seen. Perhaps he already had the ring. I'd no idea. I began to babble. "Granada doesn't like to be crowded and you'll manage him better on his own. I'll take Dobs. Please let me do that." I took Dobs's reins to lead him.

"Just get on," Master Chaucer said, pushing Dobs and I both away, "go, go. Give my best regards to the abbot. Don't forget to tell him you've been my mainstay. A real mainstay. Tell him that exactly."

"I'll tell him," said Luke, "and the rest. Thank you, Master Chaucer."

Master Chaucer waved his arms. I think Luke could hardly believe he was being bundled off so unceremoniously. "It all seems to have gone so quickly—"

"Yes, yes, now go." The Master's urgings were verging on rudeness. From up on Granada, Luke could see beyond us. He could see the approaching summoner who, back in his usual clothes, was back to his evil self. "I'm begging you, Luke," the Master pleaded. "As you love me, go."

"Come on," I said, grabbing Granada's reins and tugging. Granada balked, then jogged. Somehow we rounded the corner. Luke, straining backward for a last glimpse of the Master, left Granada to me. I urged both horses into a trot, veered up another side street, then darted down an alley and around another corner until, between the circumlocution and the crowd, it would have been hard for anybody to follow our trail. Luke didn't pick up the reins himself until we reached the boundary wall and began to follow it toward the eastern gate. "What's going on, Belle?"

"I've just done everything wrong." A huge lump formed in my throat. I was going to cry—no, not cry—I was going to sob with those great racking sobs that take you over and which you think will never stop.

"Belle! Belle! You've done nothing wrong except to love me," Luke said. His face was very gray. "And you'll stop doing that."

"I won't, I won't."

He was half concentrating on me and half still looking backward. "But that's not everything, is it? I saw the summoner. He had armed men with him. Is the Master in some kind of trouble? You've got to tell me."

I shook my head.

"Belle! Don't lie. If you know, you must tell me!"

I gripped Granada's reins and forced myself to be calmer. "The summoner wanted to take you into Archdeacon Dunmow's service." It was the first thing that came into my head. "Those men were supposed to escort you."

"Me in the service of an archdeacon?"

"Yes." Now that I'd started talking, it seemed easier to keep going than to stop. "The summoner was very impressed with all the things you did over the cloud and the gold and he told the Master you'd be more useful to the Church in England than to a monastery in France, so he'd decided to force you to go with him and become a priest."

"Force me? He has nothing to force me with."

"Yes, yes, he does." How my legs prickled under the silk bandages. "Blackmail," I said. "Something to do with the Master, not you, and the Master didn't tell you because he didn't want you to be worried. That's why he sent you off so quickly. Once you're on board a ship, you'll be safe." A little truth always makes a stronger lie.

"What? How do you know all this?"

"I guessed from something the summoner said. You know how he was with me. He tried to draw me in but I refused."

Luke was frowning. He had myriad more questions, but we'd reached the gate. This was it. This was where we would have to say good-bye. My breath stuck in my throat at the sight of the road down which Luke would ride away. How would I actually be able to watch? And I still hadn't checked Dobs for the ring. We were through the gate, and, as the road cleared, Granada lengthened his stride. Now I had to run. Dobs, ears back, resented the pace and I was thrown about and bruised. Luke, grim faced, slowed Granada and took Dobs's reins from me. "You can't run all the way to the coast," he said, and those gray eyes were very dark.

"You must hurry," I said, panting. "You mustn't let the summoner's men catch you." But I clung on.

"They mustn't," Luke said, but didn't speed up.

"Give me your knife," I said.

Luke's eyes flew wide. "For God's sake, Belle—"

"No, no! I'm not going to harm myself," I babbled. "I just thought—I just thought—I just thought that the Master's been so fond of Dobs, he should have a hank of hair as a remembrance."

"Of course." Luke fumbled to pull out his knife. "Trust you to think of something like that."

I reached up and took the knife from him. Trust? What did that mean anymore? "I'll cut it from underneath," I said, "so as not to spoil Dobs's natural beauty." I don't know how I actually made a joke. I delved deep into the thicket of mane. The ring was still exactly where the Master had fastened it. It was hard to get the hank away. I had to saw, and all the while Granada was trying to speed up and Dobs to slow down. It seemed ages before I had the hank in my hand. I let go of Dobs and knotted it with the ring safely in the middle. "There," I said. "Dobs won't miss this and the Master will like to have it." Only now did I come to a halt. "You must go as fast as you can." I tried to be matter-of-fact, but it was too hard. Above me, his face tilted and the sun casting a halo around his hair, Luke was the Helmetless Knight again. I held on to his knee. "Luke . . ."

"Belle . . ."

There was shouting. We both glanced behind. The summoner's men were through the gate. "Don't let them catch you."

He hesitated only a moment longer, leaned down, tried to say something, breathed against my cheek, then dug his heels into Granada's sides. The horse leaped forward. Dobs got spooked and leaped too. "Watch out, you clumsy oaf!" shouted a muleteer swerving to avoid them.

That's how Luke and I parted. Without any grand gesture, without any tears, without even a sigh and a final embrace, he disappeared into a river of traffic, and I was left with a knife, a hank of hair, and the king's ring and no idea what would happen next.

# 13

*For he had subtly formed a gang of spies*
*Who taught him where his profit might arise,*
*And he would spare one lecher from his store*
*To teach the way to four-and-twenty more.*

What did happen next happened very quickly. Indeed, by the time I got back to the inn, some of it had already happened. With Luke gone and the pilgrimage over, the summoner had had the Master marched back to the hostel, and there, directly and openly, with the horses milling about and the baggage carts being filled, accused him of sending messages to the French king on behalf of King Richard and of using King Richard's ring as his authority. The last proof needed, so the summoner declared, was that Luke had been sent off at suspicious speed. Not that this mattered, since he would be arrested any moment now and brought back to face the commission to answer charges of his own. And of course, as if this wasn't enough, the summoner knew just how to twist the knife. The Master had been clever, he said. He might survive because of his fame and his name, but Luke wouldn't. Luke would be arraigned for treason and receive the traitor's reward.

This, so the summoner heavily implied, had all been part of the Master's calculation.

During the stunned silence that greeted this extraordinary news I stumbled back into the yard, retaining enough presence of mind to stuff the hank of hair down the front of my dress. This was a mistake, since it gave me a lumpy look in the summoner's favorite place on a woman. I crossed my arms, then uncrossed them and wished I'd stuffed the hank somewhere else.

"Luke knows nothing and carries nothing. He's just anxious to start God's work," the Master began to protest, though he was unconvincing. The other pilgrims were either blankly incredulous or wouldn't look at Master Chaucer at all. Walter was standing by Arondel's head, biting his lip and with no sparkle in his eyes. When he saw me, his face expressed, by turns, relief, sympathy, and alarm. He'd no idea whether or not I had the ring. The summoner saw me too and squinted to see if Luke was being brought in behind me. When he saw he was not, he glared and made his noose gesture. "The boy'll be found before the tide turns," he said.

This made Master Chaucer bluster. "The abbot at St. Denys will take a very poor view of your malicious arrest of one of his young novices." Under his hat, his face was red and sweat beaded his forehead.

"He's not a novice yet," the summoner said. At a gesture, his men closed in around the Master.

Master Chaucer took a step forward. "Are you arresting me?" he asked.

The summoner hesitated and his men, seeing this, hesitated too.

"If you've anything more than the cock-and-bull story you've dreamed up, you'd better produce it now," Master Chaucer said, wiping his forehead. There was a pause. "Well, Master Summoner? Isn't it the truth that you can't arrest me because there's nothing to arrest me for?" The Master's confidence began to return.

The summoner's face set in fleshy ridges, his boils round red stones. "We'll see just how clever you are, Master Chaucer, when we have the boy." But he was forced to draw his men back. I could still feel Luke's breath on my cheek but I could also feel the king's ring burning against my chest and see my belongings stowed as usual in the blue armor wagon, Poppet sticking haphazardly out of the top. Dulcie and Arondel, saddled and ready, stood together. Picardy stood separately, restless and neighing for Dobs.

The other pilgrims, very uncomfortable, began to mount their horses. The very mention of treason silenced them. Despite their liking for the Master and their dislike of the summoner, this was dangerous territory. Not even Dame Alison made any remark. Walter moved forward a little. I knew he wanted to signal that he didn't have the ring, but any movement might alert Master Summoner.

I struggled to think. One thing was obvious: the summoner must abandon his pursuit of Luke. More than that, he must forget about Luke. It must be made abundantly obvious that Luke was of no interest to him.

The mind really is a curious thing. It sometimes makes decisions that take you quite unaware. I, for example, was quite unaware that my hand was shooting down my front, my fingers scrabbling. When I had hold of Dobs's hair, I ran to Walter and made my three-skip mounting bounce. He was alert and ready and without hesitation pitched me onto Dulcie and catapulted himself onto Arondel. Then I held up the ring. I was quite aware now. "Let all of you see this!" I shouted. "I've got the ring that Master Summoner's so anxious about. I repeat: it's me who has the king's ring. Me, do you hear? I've got it. Master Summoner, if you want it, come and get it."

The summoner gave a roar. "Master Chaucer gave it to you!"

"He didn't!" I yelled back. "Look at his face!"

The Master's face was, indeed, a picture. Nobody could have faked such amazement—well, horror really—but it seemed like amazement to those who didn't know his guilty secret.

"Now," I cried, "forget Master Chaucer and forget Luke. You've no proof against them. None whatever."

The summoner recovered himself and laughed.

"You think you can just say that and be believed?" He began to move toward me at the same moment as I moved toward him. I don't think he knew what was coming until the second before it actually happened. Only when I was right on him, Luke's knife and surprise on my side, did his hands fly to his waist. By then it was too late. I'd already slit his leather belt, seized the pouch, and, for good measure, slit his tunic so that the audience could appreciate the full hairy sag of his stomach. The red of his spots purpled and his eyes bulged. One hand shot up, the other he slapped over his stomach. "Give that pouch back. Give it back at once or I'll have you for a common thief."

I dangled the pouch above his head. "A common thief? That cap fits you better." I tossed the pouch to Walter. He opened it, exclaimed loudly, and threw each item back to its rightful owner: the rattle, the crucifix, Sir Knight's book, Dame Alison's wedding rings—it was quite a hoard. Finally, Walter drew out his own jeweled dagger and Master Host's horn spoon. It was the last that caused the greatest gasp. "How—how—how *ridiculous!*" Dame Alison said, outraged.

The summoner was beyond caring about Dame Alison's outrage. He lunged at me and Walter just as I dug my heels into Dulcie, and Walter, stuffing his dagger and the horn spoon back into the pouch, dug his spurs into Arondel. Scattering our fellow pilgrims, we galloped out of the yard, and as we passed the blue armor wagon, in a lovely gesture, Walter leaned down and scooped up Poppet. We could hear the summoner yelling for his horse and then spewing out a stream of invective when he found it to be as yet unsaddled. I caught a fleeting glimpse of Master Chaucer's face as I sped away. Relief? Bemusement? Anger that I'd upset his plans? I'd no idea. I also heard Sir Knight roaring for his son to return to him at once. It was odd, hearing him raise his voice. Walter blinked, but though I believe it was the first time he'd ever disobeyed his father, he didn't hesitate, and in moments we were in the street, barging past new arrivals at the inn. "Don't go in there!" some devilment made me yell. "There's flies in the soup and piss in the porridge!" Their faces! I laughed, though it wasn't a nice sound.

The traffic slowed our mad dash. Dodging knots of flagellants and squeezing past wagonloads of the infirm, Walter and I almost lost sight of each other. At the city's west gate, the throng trying to enter was so dense that we were brought to a complete halt. Several times, Dulcie and Arondel were almost bodily lifted and forced back the way we had just come. We did get through in the end, though, and at once pushed the horses into a brisk canter. By this time, the adrenaline had stopped pumping and I was already whithering inside. Had I made Luke any safer, or Master Chaucer? Certainly, my father would suffer. But there was no going back. "Which direction?" I was not even tempted to smile at Walter.

"The king's in the north," Walter said, not even tempted to smile back.

"How do you know?"

"Squires' gossip at the tournament. We'll have to hurry, though. You made the summoner a laughing stock. He'll never forgive that."

"Oh God! What have I done?" I kicked Dulcie hard and her stride lengthened. "Never mind the king, I've got to get to Southwark." I turned south.

Walter caught up with me. "Listen to me, Belle. You can't protect your father after what you've just done. Only the king can do that, and only if his writ still runs. For your father's sake, and Master Chaucer's, we must get to the king before the commission removes yet more of his powers. Don't you see?"

"I see only that I'm a disaster. I've ruined my father's legs, I didn't pray properly for him, and now I'm going to see him executed!" I couldn't stop myself. The hanging boy was on my back in all his creaking horror. I made Dulcie gallop faster.

Arondel matched Dulcie, stride for stride. "Listen to me, Belle," Walter urged, edging Arondel slightly in front. "The summoner can arrest your father but he can't arrange a hanging without a trial, and for a trial he'll have to concoct a better charge than gossip. That will take a little time. If we can find the king, and, as I say, if he still has authority in London, your father will be safe."

"If—if!" I cried wildly. "Too many ifs!"

"Your father's a good man. You've been on pilgrimage. St. Thomas will help him."

"Oh, Walter! Do you really believe that?"

Walter swallowed very hard. "Luke would."

I bent my head. He was right. It was the only thing to cling to. I shivered closer into my saddle. "Northward, then," I said, "and let's hope the squires were right."

We traveled very fast, the horses glad to do so. Ten miles on, Walter insisted on buying pies and loaves from a roadside vendor. He bought three of each, which made me want to hug him, and shoved them into the summoner's pouch. "Supper," he said. We stuck to the main roads because they were the quickest and it was on these that we'd be most likely to hear news of the king. We had to hope that we could simply outrun the summoner if he gave chase, though a more subtle pursuit was more his style. However, even we couldn't gallop in the dark, so when night fell we tethered the horses at the back of an abandoned shelter and went inside. The floor was filthy and Walter laid out his cloak for me to sit on. I unpacked the food. Walter took out the spoon and the dagger. The latter he wiped carefully before sticking it back in his belt.

The former, he contemplated. "What a strange man the summoner is," he said. "I can understand stealing my dagger or Dame Alison's rings. Those things are worth something. But this spoon? Or the child's rattle? Or the wooden dog?"

"I pumice my legs and count to three," I said. "There's no accounting for peculiarities."

"You *used* to pumice your legs, Belle."

I gave him a long look. We chewed in silence, both avoiding the subject of Luke. It was too painful. When I couldn't swallow any more, I turned my attention back to the pouch. "There's something else in here," I said.

"Oh?"

I pulled out a little soft-backed book.

"Ah," Walter said, also giving up trying to eat. "Our summoner's poetry book, perhaps? Or a book of songs? Remember him singing on the very first day of our journey? Not the songliest of songs, but a song nonetheless."

I did give a half smile now, though it would have looked more like a grimace to an onlooker. The book, barely the size of my palm, was horribly sticky. I made a face. "It smells," I said. I opened it. "It's too dark. I can't see what's in it."

"We'll have to wait until morning." Walter took the book and put it on a jutting stone shelf. "Lie down now, Belle, and get some sleep." He found some leaves to shove under the cloak for a mattress, salved my legs, wrapped me up with Poppet, and then settled himself on the other side of the shelter. "Walter," I said, after a while.

"Yes?"

"It's cold. We can share the cloak."

"I don't think that would be very seemly."

"There's nobody here, and, well, anyway . . ." I couldn't go on because I didn't know what words to use.

"There's no danger to your virtue?" His voice was low in the dark.

"Anyway, you're the squireliest of squires," I said. There was silence. "Please. I can't sleep knowing you're so uncomfortable. Sharing the cloak would be the chivalrous thing to do."

I heard him move, and then he was next to me, knowing just how to pillow my head on his arm, just how to nestle Poppet between us and just how to position himself so that I got the best of the cloak. It was the first time I'd ever slept so close to a man, and with Walter it was so easy, so comforting, and so beautifully pure that despite everything, I lay happy for a moment in the joy of it.

When I woke, light was creeping in and I was alone. I could see the horses already saddled. Walter was sitting bolt upright by the far wall, the summoner's book open between his hands.

I began to pull leaves from my hair and shake out the cloak. "So, what is it? Songs or poems?"

He looked up. "Neither."

"Oh?" I took the cloak to him.

He snapped the book shut and threw it down. "You mustn't read it."

I was taken aback. "Why not?"

"It's a tally book," he said, his face full of disgust, anger, and all manner of inexpressible feelings.

"He's a summoner," I countered, "so he would have a tally book to note down the people he's summoning to the bishop and make a list of their sins." I bent down.

"Don't! There are things in there nobody should see." He was very distressed.

"I'm not a child, Walter. If Archdeacon Dunmow can read it and survive, I expect I can manage."

"I don't think the archdeacon's going to read it."

"Why ever not?"

Walter's hands shook. "He's in it."

"He's in the summoner's tally book? I don't understand."

"He and almost every other powerful churchman, in London and beyond. And their sins!" He stood. "It's a list of perversions I'd never dreamed of." I stared at the book. Walter stood above me. "There's sins," he said, "and next to them there's figures. Money. The bigger the sin, the larger the amount."

Silence followed. I broke it. "Little jars of poison," I said slowly.

"What?"

"Just something I said to the Master." I shook

myself. "What you're telling me is that it's a blackmail book, not a tally book: that the summoner, or his spies, root out people's worst secrets then charge for keeping quiet." The sun sent its first rays across the floor and illuminated the greasy fingermarks on the book's cover. It had evidently been pored over many times, usually during a meal, for the spine was crusted with crumbs. I touched it gingerly with my toe.

"We must destroy it," Walter said, and moved to pick it up.

"No," I said at once. "We'll keep it. It's a weapon."

Walter thought for a moment. "Yes," he said tightly, "I suppose it is." He stuffed the book back into the pouch and attached the pouch to Arondel's saddle. He couldn't bear to attach it to himself. Before we mounted, he went to the roadside ditch and scrubbed his hands. Only when we were some way along the road did I realize that I hadn't done my triple bounce. I thought of getting off, but there wasn't time. Instead, I reassured myself by seeing three silver birches in the corner of a faraway field. In truth there were lots of silver birches, so it was actually no reassurance at all.

# 14

Even going as fast as we could, it took us more than a week to find the king. His whereabouts were not secret but he didn't stay still for long, so we were always having to alter our direction. Some days I panicked, wondering what was happening elsewhere. Would the summoner have already arrested my father? Would Master Chaucer be cursing me?

After that first day, Luke did creep into the conversation: neither of us could keep him out. Walter was reticent to start with, but then, just the way it is with somebody you love, he couldn't help himself. He told me where he'd first set eyes on him, at least a month before I had, at prayers at Westminster. It was there that the pilgrimage had first been planned and the meeting at the Tabard arranged. "I noticed him at once," Walter said, "because he was fighting with a man who'd insulted the Master. It must've been just after the Master had given him his job. I went to separate them. We weren't introduced. Luke probably forgot he ever saw me. But I didn't forget him. There was something about—"

"His eyes," I said. "A kind of lightning fork in that goose gray."

Walter nodded. "And his hands. Have you noticed his hands? If I could draw, I'd draw them. They're fine hands, yet when they're fists, they could crack a man's jaw."

"When did you know you loved him?"

He stared through Arondel's ears. "It just crept up on me. Perhaps for certain after the horsely horse day. When he laughed." His lips thinned. This was not easy for him. He turned to face me, suddenly filled with passionate intensity. "I meant what I said the night of the feast. You'll never ever tell him, will you, Belle? Please promise me. No, don't just promise, swear it."

"He wouldn't mind."

"You don't know that and anyway, it's not the point. I don't want him to know. There'd be either revulsion or pity and I couldn't bear either. You must swear."

I put one hand over the top of his and our reins got muddled. "I'm never going to see him again, Walter." My chin was trembling.

"Swear anyway."

"I swear."

"Thank you," Walter said. We didn't speak much again that day, and after he'd salved my legs that night and we lay together, I found his cheeks were wet. I wiped them gently dry with Poppet, then held him against me until morning.

We pushed on. Never have I been so tired. Indeed, I was so tired that some days I noticed nothing at all and this frightened me. What if a magpie had crossed my path and I hadn't saluted? What if things kept coming at me in fours? At night I would have worried myself sick except that I had Walter, and whenever I began to toss and fret, he'd stroke my hair and count all manner of nonsense in threes like a mother crooning a lullaby. During the day, he himself was often very preoccupied. One morning when I woke, he and Arondel had vanished. I stood uselessly by Dulcie, faintly alarmed. After ten minutes, I was terrified. Two mules ambled by. I waited in vain for a third. There was no third. Just when I was beginning to despair, there were hoofbeats and Dulcie whinnied a welcome. I ran to Arondel and beat Walter's foot. "I thought you'd gone. I thought you'd left me."

He leaped off. "Darling Belle! Of course I hadn't. How could you think such a thing? I just went to get news and more food. You were sleeping so soundly I didn't want to wake you."

I was ashamed of myself. "I'm sorry." I tried a shaky grin. "I saw two mules."

He shook his head in the most gentle of reprimands. "Two mules or two thousand, I'll never desert you while you need me," he said.

"Is that your promise?"

"It's my promise."

I couldn't forget the twisted Canterbury "miracle" words. "And by 'desert' I mean you have to be alive, not a spirit like my mother. A flesh and blood Walter, a breathing—"

Though gray with exhaustion, Walter began to laugh and his eyes twinkled. "Flesh and blood, living and breathing, cross my heart three times, click my thumbs three times, stamp my feet three times." He took my hands. "Dear Belle. You don't need to bargain for me. You've got me. As much as I'm any woman's, I'm yours. Now, let's eat as we ride. The king's only twenty miles away. If we hurry, we can reach him before he moves off again."

We hurried, and after we'd overtaken two companies of mounted archers flying the king's pennant, we hurried more, and it was still well before midday when at last we saw a small company of knights, some of whose badges and coats of arms Walter recognized. "We'll follow them," Walter said. "Our journey's nearly over." Though our blood was pumping, as we grew closer to the king's camp, Walter turned nearly as white as Luke. This was a difficult moment for him. We were soon accosted by armed men. "Let me speak," Walter murmured. I felt for the king's ring in my wallet and nodded.

I don't know what Walter said, but nobody really challenged us until we reached a large circle of nearly two dozen tents, some plain, some striped, pitched defensively

round a multicolored pavilion. Under an awning, three scribes seated on three stools were busy taking down names from a line of knights and men-at-arms. As each individual gave his name, he was handed a gold-colored badge and an embroidered white stag by a young man with a smile that didn't quite reach his eyes. At the badge giver's touch, each knight fell to his knees as though brushed by the finger of God. I didn't need Walter to tell me that the young man was the king.

We dismounted and handed the horses to two pages. Before we got into the line, however, Walter's arm was seized by a burly baron who squinted at him as though he knew him but couldn't quite place him. "Name."

"Walter de Pleasance, son of Sir Lawrence de Pleasance."

The man's face cleared. "Walter de Pleasance! Of course. We haven't seen you for a while, though I should have recognized the horse's blue trappings. Now then." He looked Walter up and down. "You're hardly dressed for combat."

"I've been on pilgrimage," Walter explained.

"On the king's behalf, I hope." Walter inclined his head in a way that could have meant anything. The man squinted at me. "I see you've picked up a pretty 'blessing' on the way."

Walter blushed. "This is Belle."

"Indeed." The man gave a rough bow.

"We need to see the—"

"WALTER!"

Walter's face split into a huge smile, half of relief, half of genuine pleasure, as the king, dropping all the badges, launched himself toward us. "My lord!"

"None of that! Richard, just Richard to you. Where've you been? I've missed you!" The king's boyish enthusiasm added luster to a flat but pretty face, which few lines had yet marred.

Walter responded to the embrace. "I've missed you too. Can I introduce you to Belle?"

Richard took a step back. "Belle?"

I curtsied. He eyed me with some curiosity and a smile of welcome that was a little more distant. He looked at Walter again, his pleasure clouding. "Is there something you want, Walter?"

"Want, sir? No, nothing."

"Everybody wants something these days."

"I want nothing except a moment or two of your time."

The king threw back his head and his laugh was a little too loud. "Hear that, Robert?"

A tall man, only a little older than the king but with an air of calculation about him, stepped forward. He nodded at Walter with neither dislike nor warmth. "I do, my lord."

"Remember Robert de Vere, Earl of Oxford, now Duke of Ireland?" the king said. "He's had more than

a few moments of my time." The earl just stood. "But you're worth every grant of land and every privilege," the king added hastily, then dismissed the earl, who bowed, picked up the scattered badges, and, without seeking permission, gave them out himself. Richard watched him for a moment, clearly unsure whether or not to take umbrage at this breech of etiquette. He decided not. Instead, he linked arms with Walter and drew him along, leaving me trailing behind. "Well, here I am. Have a moment of time and then dine with me, though we may have to get you some clean clothes, and Belle too." He tossed my name over his shoulder.

"I've been on pilgrimage," Walter said, then added, as if it were a matter of no importance, "with Master Geoffrey Chaucer."

The arm tucked into Walter's involuntarily tightened. "Indeed! Come. We'll speak in my tent where you can sit in comfort."

I think he'd have happily forgotten about me, but I wasn't going to let him.

As soon as the tent flap was shut behind us and we were alone, the king was urgent. "You've a message for me from the Master?" He was almost whispering, his eyes never leaving Walter's. He was trying to gauge how much Walter knew. He gave up. "Give me the message quickly."

Walter coughed, gestured backward to me, and I came forward holding the king's ring. The king took it, at first with some bemusement, then with increasing excitement. "The King of France has sent this back already? He's coming to help me?"

"Not exactly."

"Not exactly?"

"King Charles never received either the message or the ring."

The king froze. "But Master Chaucer promised." His face contorted. "*He promised.*"

"He—"

The king wasn't interested in listening. "He promised and he's let me down. There's a word for people like that."

"Richard!"

"My lord, to you."

Walter winced. "Please listen to me, my lord. Master Chaucer hasn't let you down. There were complications. I learned of your message—it doesn't matter how—I learned of it and took it on myself to bring the ring back."

"But, you idiot, without the ring, my message has no authority, and without my message I'm likely to lose my throne." The king spoke slowly, every word iced with fury.

"The interference of the King of France will lose you your throne." Walter's voice trembled. "Listen, sire. You're the King of England. You must look to Englishmen to help you."

"But they don't help me, Walter." He spoke as if

Walter were a half-wit. "They conspire against me. The commission! My loving uncles! All those so-called faithful nobles." He almost spat. "I can rely on nobody except those like the Earl of Oxford, who owe everything they are and are ever likely to be to me." His face dissolved like a small child's. "I thought Master Chaucer was on my side."

"My lord, it's not a question of sides. It's a question of what's right."

"My throne's my right! Now get out! Get out! I'll find another courier, send another message, and this time I'll choose somebody more competent than a dull-witted old poet."

Walter gestured helplessly and began to retreat. To annoy the king further would only make things worse. I felt faint. This couldn't be how everything ended.

The king suddenly shifted. "Where are you going?"

"I've nothing else to say, my lord." Walter looked beaten.

"So you think I'll let you spread the word that I've been looking for support over the sea?"

"I'll say nothing, my lord."

"'I'll say nothing, my lord,'" the king mocked. "No, indeed you won't. Robert!" He moved purposefully toward the tent flap.

I put my hand on his arm as he passed. He flinched, as though I'd hit him. "Take your hands off the king!"

I removed my hand. "Sir," I said quickly. "Your throne *is* your right and we can help you secure it."

"You?" He didn't even look at me.

"Yes," I said. "Walter and I. We can deliver the support of Londoners to you."

Walter gave a small exclamation. The king made no noise at all. I thought he hadn't heard. He was almost out of the tent when he stopped. "How?"

I was careful not to step toward him because even now he could barely look at me, and he was so near the tent flap he could have slipped through in an instant. "I can't tell you, sir. You'll have to trust me." He turned away. "But it can be done!" I said more loudly. "It can be done."

He hesitated, took hold of the flap, then let go. Now he scrutinized me from top to bottom. "Why should you want to deliver London's support? What have I ever done for you?"

He was so close that I could see something of what Master Chaucer had seen. King or no king, Richard was just a boy, and though care and worry had left no outward lines, anxiety bit at him like the midge. He seemed less unkind than slightly unhinged. Hemmed in by his position, his character, his advisers, and his youth, the most powerful man in the country held less mastery over his own fate than I over mine. Had he been me, of course, he'd have used a pumice stone. As

it was, he just floundered, complete control over anything, even his own person, always out of reach. I felt
sorry for him.

"You're the king," I said, and looked at him candidly.
"You should be in control." I knew instinctively that I
shouldn't mention my father. Richard must believe that
everything we did was for him.

There was a long pause. "What did you say your
name was?"

"Belle."

He stepped back. "Well, Belle," he said, in uncon-
scious imitation of my father's rhyme, "deliver London
to me. With the support of the capital, I'd have no
need of Charles of France. It's September. I'll give you
until November. I want to be king of my own country
in more than just name well before Christmas. Can
you make sure of that?"

He expected me at least to gulp. I didn't. "November,
then, sir."

"A triumphant return."

My heart quailed slightly. "A triumphant return."

"And what surety do I have?"

"My life," said Walter at once.

"Walter—no . . ." I couldn't say more. I had to exude
confidence.

The king rocked on his heels. "Your life, Walter de
Pleasance? Are you sure?"

"Quite sure, sir," Walter said.

"Shouldn't Master Chaucer suffer for his failures?"

"Master Chaucer is a great man, sir."

I watched the king digest this. Then he said, "You're quite right, Walter. He is a great man. He'll be remembered long after either of us. Now go."

Walter bowed, and after all the outbursts and tantrums, we left the king lost in thought. If I hadn't before known the meaning of mercurial, I knew it now.

# 15

To give the man his due and not to skimp,
He was a thief, a summoner, and a pimp

Walter and I set off directly to London, and this time
our journey wasn't filled with either Luke or silence. It
was filled with something disgusting: the summoner's
book. I knew that if we were to deliver London to the
king, blackmail was our best hope. Walter argued against
it, but in the end he gave in and took Dulcie's reins as
I digested the long lists of depravities, immoralities,
obscenities, gross indulgences, and deviations, both
sexual and financial, all unpardonable and inexcus-
able, and all with the names of archbishops, bishops,
priests, judges, franklins, deacons, knights, magistrates,
and guild masters attached. Nobody, not even fellow
summoners, had escaped Seekum's repulsive attentions,
and everything, including dates and circumstances, was
marked down, mostly with sums of money attached,
some paid, most still due.

A few of the expressions the summoner used I didn't
understand and didn't want to. Some I did understand and also didn't want to. Children in charitable
institutions were mentioned in connection with clerics

and judges. Also other men's wives. Nuns. Mistresses. Prostitutes. Animals. And of course boys. The book was a hellish portal to an underworld whose joining fee was the trappings of worldly power. Most damning of all were the witnesses, who had signed their names clearly and, so they had attested, willingly.

I didn't want to read more than I had to, so I read only the pages under the heading "London." Nor do I want to tell you the next bit, but I must. There was a charge against Master Chaucer. It was rape. There were dates and a name. Cecilia Champain, 1380. I couldn't believe it. I wouldn't believe it. But I knew this was the reason, that morning by the well, that the Master wouldn't tell me he had no more secrets. I dreaded seeing his name again. Fortunately I didn't.

Walter and I didn't cling together on these nights. When he salved my legs I couldn't look at him. This was nothing to do with the boys in the book and the endless lubricious descriptions of what men did with them. Walter was not like these men. Never. Never. It was me who was rank as an unwashed pot.

We did speak, of course, but only of practical matters. For a start, we had to calculate the best way to go about the dirty duties we must perform. Walter insisted that when we made our visits, he would do the talking. If I, a young and supposedly pure girl, articulated the sins, I would open myself up to accusations of debauchery.

Just having said the words would be enough to convict me. I didn't want to agree but knew Walter was right. Yet if Walter was to speak, he must memorize the sins, because we couldn't have the book in our hands in case it was seized and destroyed. He tried to learn the memory tricks Luke had taught me, but though he practiced and practiced, he always forgot something; either the date or the amount or the name itself. In the end, I had to take over. We'd only get one chance. We couldn't risk a sudden lapse. It was vile. "We're as bad as the summoner," Walter said sadly as London grew nearer and my memorizings more fluent.

"We're saving the king," I said fiercely, "and the king will save my father." Neither he nor I asked whether the king was worth saving. His value was a matter for others.

Luke would now be at St. Denys. The abbot would have heard the coded message but when he didn't find the king's ring where he was expecting it, he would have discounted it. *Better safe than sorry*, he would have thought. If King Richard was serious, another message would come. I wondered if Luke was tonsured yet, all that lovely hair shorn into a ruffle around a hideous bald circle. I saw his eyes reflected in his spectacles. I saw them looking at me. I blotted them out. Thinking of him would cause madness . . . or pumicing. The pilgrimage already seemed like another life.

As soon as we reached London's straggling outskirts, I hid the book in the one place I thought nobody would look. Borrowing a needle and thread from a tinker, I sewed it inside Poppet. It was an unimaginable thing to do but I couldn't think of anywhere safer. After I'd sewn her up again, she looked much the same, only slightly fatter, but a lump arose in my throat. It was like filling her with excrement.

We entered the city proper on a wet afternoon and Walter insisted that our first job was to purchase clean clothes, and richer ones for me than I'd ever had before. I protested. This was extravagant nonsense, but he knew what he was doing. Appearances count for a great deal, as was evident as soon as we began our visitations. When we arrived at a palace, an abbey, or a house and asked to see the named man, it was our clothes and the horses that secured us entry. Even though I was a girl, if I adopted my haughtiest expression, we looked just the kind of affluent and influential people the archbishop, abbot, priest, or guild master would want to see. The named man always greeted us quite warmly—Walter's whole demeanor encouraged that. But the warmth lasted only a moment, for we didn't indulge in small talk. I would first name the place listed in the tally book, or sometimes the amount of money. That alone was enough for a rapid cooling. A pattern emerged. The man would carry on smiling, but blink and usually raise his hand. I would stop. Any retainers or servants would be dismissed. Walter and I would wait patiently and then, in a flat voice, I'd continue. The man would keep blinking, then bluster denials, expostulate about my wickedness, and threaten us both. We would listen. Eventually proof would be demanded. Walter would say that we had proof, written proof, but it was hidden. The man would begin to grin, sensing an advantage. His tone would become patronizing. I would then repeat the name of a sworn witness, sometimes two. After that, though it might take a little time, there would be a general collapse. Blustering would tail into silence. Curses would erupt, then dissolve. Less often, there would be tears and pleading. All of the named, from greatest to least, asked us how we had come across the information. We didn't answer that. All of them wanted to murder us, but without first finding and destroying the proof, we knew they wouldn't dare.

Then Walter would offer a proposition. You have influence over the city, he would say. You have at your command armed men. You could do your bit to ensure the king's safe and, indeed, triumphal return to London. If you do that, our proof may well vanish, though if we hear of any reprisals against the witnesses we've revealed, our proof will mysteriously reappear. We didn't wait to hear their agreement. We knew we'd won when we left their yards unmolested.

After our third visitation, we were followed. At first it was easy to get lost in the crowds, but after four days and ten visitations, we had to part with the horses. Walter left them with a cobbler and paid him well to keep them safe. I hated leaving them, Dulcie whinnying after us.

Now we did our visitations in the dark, like thieves, and slept in a different hostel every night. Our reputation preceded us. Nobody refused to see us. The visitations became vile in a way I hadn't expected. Wielding power over people is chillingly seductive. Watching those big men quail and quiver, as squalid in their pleading as they were in their depravities, excited and sickened me simultaneously. I, a girl of no account, held these men's reputations, indeed their very lives, in the palm of my hand. I felt like God. When you have power like this, you don't have to count to three or pumice your legs. You are invincible. Afterward, I was filled with self-loathing. Perhaps I was no better than these men after all.

It was a relief when, in the end, we were simply met at the door with a nod. But I insisted we continue to visit. Richard's return to London must be more than a passing triumph. It must be solid and unshakable. If I was making myself the summoner's deadly enemy, the king's writ must run so completely that my father would be safer than the Tower of London.

We heard of my father's arrest from a laundress. She was full of gossip, as laundresses are. London was turning

against the commission, she said, because God was leaving messages in churches that he was on the king's side and London never wanted to be on the wrong side of God. I forced myself to hear her out. There were those who said that the messages had been planted by a bell founder who pretended to be crippled and then flew about at night, disguised as a crow. Now I cried aloud. "There, there, dear," the laundress said, completely misunderstanding. "They've got him in Archdeacon Dunmow's dungeons, so he'll not be flying anymore. He's to be tried and he'll be condemned. Pretending to be crippled, indeed! The cowardice of it!"

I grabbed Poppet and struggled into my clothes, wet as they were. "I've got to go to him. He won't know what on earth's going on, although he'll guess it has something to do with me. What happens if he's tried and condemned before the king comes to London? What happens if our blackmail doesn't work or it's all too late?" I rushed blindly into the street. Walter flung coins at the astonished laundress and rushed out behind me. "We'll go straight to Archdeacon Dunmow's house," I shouted. "We haven't visited him yet. Now's the moment."

"Wait!" Walter cried. "That may not be the wisest thing to do."

I wouldn't wait and Walter could do nothing but follow me.

It was roughly two miles, I reckoned, to the Dunmow residence. We wound through the streets, half running, half walking, dodging the throng until I ran slap bang into Sir Leather Strap. I hardly recognized him at first, he looked so disheveled. His nose had been broken. He knew me, though. "Ha! I knew I was right," he cried. "I saw you yesterday and I've been following you. Where's your bespectacled friend? I've a bone to pick with him! Several, in fact."

"I don't know what you mean. Get out of my way." I couldn't bear a moment's delay.

"You know full well what I mean. I was duped. Base metal into gold! That elixir was nothing but dog dirt and dust. Look at me! It's been my ruin and somebody should pay."

"You're mistaken," I shouted at him. "I don't know who you are."

He pointed at my hair. "Oh, you're unmistakable, and I'll be paid well for your miserable carcass because I know somebody who wants it. But I don't care about you. I want that white-faced, lying alchemist."

"He's where you can't find him." I tried to push past.

"Well then, you'll have to do." He grabbed my hair.

"Walter!" I couldn't help shrieking.

But Sir Leather Strap had a knife. "Get away, squire. I'll not be done out of my dues twice," he said. "I got into big trouble because of your friend. He kept the real elixir for himself and palmed me off with rub-bish. I know he did. But my men, cretins all of them, wouldn't believe it. Not at all. They beat me within an inch of my life and called me a liar and a thief. I only managed to stop them murdering me by saying that I'd find that damned alchemist and get that elixir if it was the last thing I did. I was on my way to Canterbury to find him but guess who I met journeying home? Your very own party! Your father's very angry with you"—he stabbed the knife momentarily at Walter—"and Summoner Seekum's very angry with you." He jabbed the point of the dagger into my neck. I felt the ooze of blood. This seemed to alarm Sir Leather Strap, who spat on his thumb and dabbed. "They said the boy had gone overseas. I didn't believe them. Then the sum-moner said if I brought you to him unharmed, he'd give me gold. And here you are." He began to shove me forward, holding me so close I could barely breathe.

"Let go. I won't run away," I said. "I want to go to the archdeacon's house."

"Oh, don't think I'll be fooled twice. I know your sort. Tricksters all." He held me closer, as though he thought I might use some magic spell to evaporate. Walter followed helplessly as I was pushed up and down streets both familiar and unfamiliar. At last we arrived at an extensive stone building with a new front door of thick oak and thicker iron bars. Half palace, half hovel, the archdeacon had obviously taken it over from somebody rather grander than himself who'd fallen on hard times. Sir Leather Strap kicked at the door, which was opened eventually by a servant in a stained apron.

"Get Seekum," Sir Leather Strap said.

The servant had barely stepped back into the dark when the summoner himself appeared. I think he'd been waiting. He scarcely looked at me to start with, just chewed on a chicken leg as Sir Leather Strap made his demands. Then he gestured with his head to the servant, who brought a bag. The summoner crunched the chicken bone and weighed the bag in either hand before tossing it to Sir Leather Strap. "I'll hold on to her until I've counted it," Sir Leather Strap said, when he had the bag secure.

The summoner didn't bother to answer. He had no more interest in Sir Leather Strap: his eyes were fixed on me. I didn't know how to appear: defiant? submissive? terrified? bold? "I want to see my father," I said, in a mixture of all four emotions.

With exaggerated courtesy, the summoner opened the door wide. I pulled away from Sir Leather Strap, held my head up, pressed Poppet to my side, and went in. There was a kerfuffle behind me. "Not you," I heard the summoner say. Walter was frantic. "I'm going with her."

"You're going nowhere, squire. If you want to see her

again, you'll need to come to Westminster Hall. That's where treason trials take place."

"Belle! Belle!"

The door was slammed in Walter's face.

The summoner neither touched me nor spoke to me as I was hurried along damp corridors. At last we came to a line of cells, most of which were empty, though the smell told me they had recently been full. A fat-legged, sunken-cheeked woman was sitting on a stool right at the end of the line, supping from a tankard. When she saw the summoner, she wiped her mouth on her hand and, with some difficulty, got up. The summoner gestured with his head and she opened one of the wooden doors. I walked swiftly inside. I didn't want to be pushed. "Father?" It was empty. The summoner filled the doorway. "Give me my book and I'll put you in with your father," he said.

I shook my head.

"Tell me where it is, and once I've fetched it, I'll let your father go."

I shook my head again. Without the book I had no weapon at all. "I couldn't give you the book even if I wanted to," I said. "We saw Master Chaucer's name in it, so we destroyed it. Please. Leave my father be."

The summoner froze. "Destroyed it? All that work! God's work! Gone?" He could scarcely absorb the enormity of his loss. "I make few mistakes," he said, cracking his knuckles, "but I made a mistake with you. I thought you cared for your father. I thought you were loyal to England. No matter. You see, you think you've been clever." He came very close. "The truth is, when bumptious girls like you take on somebody like me, they never win." Those eyes raked me up and down, lingering where men's eyes linger. He was tempted to take a very personal revenge. Sweat prickled my back. He touched my breast with the flat of his hand. The woman jailer coughed. His hand turned into a fist and I thought he was going to hit me. Instead, with a wily twist, he jerked Poppet away. I screamed. "Give her back! Give her back!" He dangled her by one leg upside down. I couldn't bear it. "Give her to me!"

"People who play at politics can't play with dolls." He twirled Poppet around. She looked so helpless. I lurched forward and tried to rescue her. "What a poppet it is," he said, and, with a ghastly smile, lumbered backward, bidding the woman lock the door behind him.

I tried everything with that woman: kicking and shouting; bribery (though I had nothing with which to bribe her); praying softly as though I were a saint; crying; pretending I was ill; declaring I was dying; threats and pleading, sometimes on my knees. I begged for news of my father. I begged for Poppet back. In the end, there was nothing to do but curse God that

I'd ever got involved with a pilgrimage that had led to this disaster.

I was not ill-treated. Food and water were passed through a flap and the small bucket left in the cell for my waste was removed three times a day. Though the cell was windowless, I always had a candle. Three blankets were left so I wasn't cold. Nor did the summoner come back to taunt me, though since I didn't know he wasn't returning, I hardly dared sleep.

Yet it was awful. It wasn't just that I was terrified for my father. It wasn't just that I missed the physical warmth of Walter or the comfort of Poppet. It wasn't even that I thought the summoner would find the book, or that, despite our efforts, London would not rise for the king, though both those things were likely. The worst was that as the days dragged on, everything became unreal in the extraordinary silence of the place. There was literally nothing to see, nothing to hear, nothing to do. Nothing dripped. Nothing rustled. Nothing sighed. The woman didn't sit outside my cell. She came and went and I couldn't even count her footsteps because I never heard them. It was like being buried alive. After the first two days, I tried to fire my imagination. I closed my eyes and was in a cloud, whirling through time. I held the candle close and was a fire-breathing witch. I even stood straight, arms by my sides, and tried to be Excalibur again. That, surely, would at least provoke guilt-ridden remembrance. But I remained only me, in this place, with nothing. After a while, the urge to count in threes became almost overwhelming, even though there was nothing to count. I fought against it. If I started to count, I'd never stop.

Sometime during what I think was the fourth night, I unwrapped my legs. I missed the salve but it had done its work. In the soft glow, you might have thought I'd just had some bad scrape, perhaps falling off a horse. A horse! I thought of Dulcie. And then I thought of Arondel and of Granada and then, by association, of Luke, who was never far from my thoughts anyway. I made myself breathe very slowly and deeply until I was dizzy, then, swaying and humming, tried to relive our dances. That worked until I crashed into the wall and fell, almost extinguishing the candle. I didn't dance after that.

Only later did I learn that I was imprisoned for twenty-one days. If somebody had said a week or a year I'd have believed them, since I lost all sense of everything. Had I been left much longer, I expect my willpower would have crumbled and I would have started on the one, two, three; one, two, three. They'd have got a surprise, when they came for me, if I'd emerged jibbering. As it was, I learned something in that cell that I never forgot. Fear, hope, and despair can all be banished if you simply retreat so far into yourself that you no longer really exist. After I'd failed to turn myself into a cloud or a witch or Excalibur, I turned myself into nothing. I was just a shell. Nothing could hurt me because there was nothing to hurt, and if there was nothing to hurt, there was no need to count. It was, in its way, a release.

It was not the summoner, but two smartly dressed upper servants who eventually unlocked the door and told me to follow them. They were armed and marched on either side of me. In the corridor, we met another man. He was carrying parchments: clearly a clerk. I asked no questions; nobody volunteered information. I gestured that I'd like to wash. That wasn't allowed. We proceeded to the door through which I'd entered, and, squinting in the sudden sun, my world quickly darkened again as I was lifted bodily into a closed cart. I heard a peal of bells. It was a triple peal but somehow this didn't reassure me. Indeed, after the silence it was loud enough to break my shell. Though I fought against them, feelings started to creep in. I could hear people talking when the cart stopped at crossroads and wondered if anybody was concerned for the wretch inside. Most would give the cart a cursory glance and forget it. That was the best policy until the cart came for you.

We traveled for about an hour. We didn't cross the river. I would have heard the echo of the steel-rimmed wheels. I told myself that my father would be dead, Walter would have fled, and Master Chaucer would have disappeared.

Wherever we were going, there would just be me, and if there was just me, I could tie myself in a knot so tight that whatever the summoner did or said couldn't hurt me. That was the only way to keep my fear contained.

When we halted, I was bundled into the closed courtyard of a grand palace with glass windows, thin as a cathedral's. Westminster. I tightened the knot. Somebody was waiting, holding the salve bag in one hand and a purse stuffed with coins in the other. Walter! The clerk glanced inquiringly at the doorkeeper, who took the coin, slipped it under his tunic, and shrugged.

Walter ran to me, frowning at the guards until they moved away. He forced me to sit on the cart's running board. His cheeks had lost their bloom but he was not gloomy. "I bribed my way down here. It wasn't hard. I said you might die without the salve and they didn't seem keen on that." He opened the bag and took out the jar. His hands were shaking. "I've tried to get in every day to see you. They wouldn't arrest me because my father begged them not to." He swallowed his mortification and shook his head. "Never mind about that. You're to be taken to the hall. Your father's already in there. It's a show trial, Belle, but you've got the book in your poppet." I stared only at my legs. "There's something else." He put his hands on my shoulders. "Luke's in there too." He went back to my legs and rubbed the salve in hard. I couldn't speak. "Yes," Walter said.

He was the babbler now. "When the Master was sure the summoner had lost all interest in Luke, he went to St. Denys himself. He wrote a song and left it in the guesthouse. It was a rather naughty song about a spectacled youth who followed the Rule of St. Benedict so closely he dried up, like parchment. Of course it was found, just as Master Chaucer meant it to be, and the monks teased Luke mercilessly. Guess what happened next?" Walter answered for me. "That's right. There was a fight, and then another and another, until the abbot told Luke to leave, and when Luke said that God would never forgive him if he broke his vow, the abbot said that God would never forgive *him* if he kept it. At least that's how Master Chaucer tells it. So Luke was sent back to England. Master Chaucer never told Luke of course. Luke just thinks that somehow God intervened on his behalf, though he's not sure exactly how. The Master's a genius. I'd never have thought of such a trick." He wiped his hands. As he pulled my skirt back over my ankles his expression became very dark. "Did that man hurt you, Belle?"

"I haven't got Poppet." I hadn't used my voice for so long that it came out as a frog's croak. Walter paled a little. "The summoner took her on the first day."

"Oh lord." Walter sat down heavily and put an arm around me.

"None of that." The gatekeeper, anxious now, came

between us. "Get back to the hall. You've had your time." The two servants pulled me to my feet. Walter tried to stand beside me but was forcibly prevented, so he had to follow behind as we went through the door and into the place where my fate would be decided.

# 16

*So it befell that on a certain day*
*This summoner rode forth to catch his prey . . .*

The corridor was of undecorated stone, but we soon climbed a set of steps into an enormous painted hall with four large chairs on a dais straight in front of me and wooden benches on either side. The first person I saw was my father, and my heart almost shot out of my chest. In all this mess, a miracle. *He was standing.* It would have taken more than two guards to hold me. I was away and in his arms before they realized I'd gone. He held me close. "Well, Belle," he said into my hair, "so this is where your pilgrimage has led."

I hugged him harder. He unpeeled my arms and regarded me, his beard quite gray and his face so drawn, yet so full of love and concern, that I just wanted to cry. I didn't, though. I held his hands. "You're standing."

The ghost of a smile. "Yes. I'm not going to be tried for some unknown crime sitting down. Peter Joiner made me some calipers and brought them to me after my arrest. His wife stitched these trousers, to hide them. I want justice, not pity."

"I didn't mean this to happen."

"No, Belle. You never mean anything to happen, not my accident, not the bread burning or the eggs going rotten. But happen things always do." He gripped me. "None of that matters now. Just listen. I don't know what any of this is about, but if there's blame or condemnation, I'll take it. Do you understand me? I forgive you everything, but I'll not forgive you sacrificing yourself to save me. If I hang, it'll only mean that I join your mother more quickly. I'll welcome it." My chin quivered. My father shook me. "Belle! Do you hear me?" I nodded. "And do you promise?"

"I can't," I began to sob. "I can't promise that."

"You've got to promise," he said harshly. "If you don't, you're no daughter of mine."

"Father!"

"Promise. Say, 'I promise!'"

Why didn't the guards drag me away right now, before I had to speak? They didn't, so I said the words my father wanted to hear and his grim smile was no consolation, no consolation at all.

People filed in to sit on the side benches. There was hardly a crowd. My father and I were too unimportant for that. Walter, Master Chaucer, and Luke came in together. Behind his spectacles, Luke had two black eyes and his right cheek was purple. In the poor light from the sconces, he had an unworldly air about him, as though he were just a mirage, like the clouds he had produced on the journey.

Alongside Luke, to my surprise, sat some of the other pilgrims: the prioress, Madam Medic, Dame Alison, Sir Knight, and even the skinny cleric. I couldn't think why they'd come. On the opposite benches was a huddle of other people. I didn't want to look at them. I imagined they'd come to crow. Last to arrive was Widow Chegwin, puffing. My father's face was impassive.

The judges took their seats amid great fanfare: "My lords Gloucester, Warwick, Beauchamp, and Arundel," called the clerk.

Master Summoner appeared as if from nowhere, along with a mousey man who identified himself to the judges as Archdeacon Dunmow. Silence fell. A clerk came forward and read out the charge against my father: that he, John Bellfounder, had consorted with treasonable men intent on the destruction of the realm; and that he had used his daughter, Belle Bellfounder, to send secret messages between King Richard and the King of France.

My father stiffened. The summoner never looked at him at all.

A gaggle of witnesses was called, only two of whom I recognized: the manciple in charge of buying provisions for the Inner Temple and the doctor who had attended my mother. The manciple was called first and made great show of reading out an account he'd written of a treasonable exchange he'd overheard at the Tabard, which was strange, since he could neither read nor write. The doctor just repeated everything the summoner said, nodding his head all the while. After him, all the witnesses, most of whom were complete strangers, did likewise. After half an hour of this, the judges wearily asked if there were any witnesses to speak on the accused's behalf. I leaped up and shouted, "Yes!" but my father pinned me with a glare of steel. "You promised," he said coldly. "For once in your life, keep your word." I sank down.

The summoner coughed and shuffled his documents. "My lords, my last witness is the Widow Chegwin," he said.

My father jolted and for one awful moment I thought he was going to fall. A traitor from his own hearth. I prayed that the widow might die before she took to the floor. I prayed so hard that I didn't notice my nails had dug right into my palms. The widow seemed amazed. She kept bowing.

"Are you the Widow Chegwin, who has lived with"—the summoner gave a dirty laugh—"I'm sorry, *cared for*, this cripple of a man for the last several years?"

The widow was flustered. "Cared for, not lived with, my lords. There was an accident. He needed help."

My father's head was bent. This was worse than hanging.

"And did this man, even after he was crippled and couldn't walk, insist on going to the Tabard?"

"Well, he went to the—"

"He had a chair made specially, so that he could take himself. Isn't that right?"

"A chair was made—"

"So that he could go to the Tabard. Has he been anywhere else in this chair?"

"I suppose not . . ."

The summoner stuck his thumbs into his belt, a new one, thick, with a shining buckle. "As I say, my lords, even after he was crippled, this man continued to plot. The Tabard is a well-known haunt of French merchants. I don't think we need trouble ourselves further. Go and sit down," he commanded the widow.

She began to retreat, then stopped. "But if he's so wicked, how do you account for the miracle?" she asked.

"What miracle?" sneered the summoner.

"He's standing," the widow said. "His daughter went to Canterbury to pray to St. Thomas for a cure, and her prayers have been answered. How do you account for that? St. Thomas would never cure a wicked man, or so I've heard."

The summoner spun round, registering for the first time that my father was indeed standing. He sucked violently on his teeth.

For the first time, too, the judges showed some interest. They looked at my father properly. "Is this true?" the Duke of Gloucester asked.

The widow answered promptly on my father's behalf, as she was wont to do. How could I ever have cursed her for that? "It's as true as I'm standing here." She clutched her hands together. "God be praised!"

There was a pause and then I heard, from the bench, Master Chaucer take up the chant. "God be praised! God be praised!" He encouraged the others. The whole hall resounded.

The judges whispered to each other. Eventually, Gloucester put up his hand and after some little time, the chant died away. "John Bellfounder," Gloucester said when he could be heard, "do you swear that after your accident, you couldn't walk? Do you swear that there was no pretense?"

Again the widow interrupted. "He couldn't even piss on his own, sir! What man would make a pretense about that?"

"Silence, woman!" snapped Gloucester. "John Bellfounder must swear himself." My father said nothing. He was shaking with humiliation. Gloucester turned impatiently to the summoner. "Master Summoner! Did you ever see this man walk?"

The summoner's face was contorted in a hideous internal struggle. He wanted to lie, but without having primed a witness to back up his lie, and with so many to deny his account, he didn't dare. Yet he couldn't bring himself to say no. His head simply shivered a denial.

"Well indeed, if the blessed St. Thomas of Canterbury has seen fit to bestow God's favor on a man, he will not look kindly on those who seek to take it away," Gloucester said. His fellow judges looked nervous. "I mean, if he can make a cripple walk, he could just as easily turn us all into cripples." They huddled together. After what seemed like an age, Gloucester stood up. "We are agreed. John Bellfounder! If you can walk over to me, you're a free man because then we'll really see if a miracle has taken place. If you can't, well . . ." It was clear what he meant.

My father raised his head. "Walk," I prayed, "*walk!*"

But he just stood in front of his chair. It wasn't that he wouldn't walk, it was as though he had forgotten how to walk. When he'd asked Peter Joiner about calipers, he'd only thought to stand. I could see this plain as plain. I moved forward, wanting to take his hand. I was prevented, so there was nothing for him to hold on to, and he looked so lonely standing there, with every eye on him. Minutes passed. The summoner began to grin. He sat down, placed his papers ostentatiously on the table, and twiddled his thumbs. His rings flashed in the candlelight. I could see sweat trickling from under my father's hair. I longed to shout instructions—one foot first, then the other—but what good would that have done? I moved one of my own legs, trying to identify the right muscle.

How did people walk? They just did. And my father just didn't.

Master Summoner rose. Slowly, and with purpose, he rolled the charge sheet into a ball, called out my father's name, and threw it. The ball curved through the air. Just as the summoner intended, it was going to land short. When the ball hit the floor, my father's fate would be sealed. I heard a small groan arise from the benches where the witnesses were seated. I buried my head in my hands. Then the groan broadened into something else, and broadened again. I peeped through splayed fingers. My father was not where he had been. He was holding the parchment ball and now he was throwing it back to the summoner; a good throw, a strong throw. It was Master Summoner who missed the catch. When the parchment ball flew over his head, some of the witnesses laughed out loud.

My father's face was set. He had responded quite automatically to the throwing of the parchment ball, and he had Master Host to thank for that. Months of throwing bags of beans at the bottles had kept the memory of movement in his muscles. If he just thought about catching, he could move. It was thinking about moving that made him freeze. Now he raised his arms and took a step; raised his arms, took a step; raised his arms, took a step; and in this stilted way, made it to the judges' dais. I held my breath, dreading that they would ask him to climb the stairs. I doubt if he could have done that and I could tell from the angle of his back that the pain was already excruciating. One of the judges crooked a finger. He was going to beckon, but before he could, Master Chaucer set up a new chant: "Blessed Thomas of Canterbury, intercede for all of us sinners." It was a clever chant, a brilliant chant. It didn't exonerate my father, but since nobody was without sin, it joined us all to him. The judge had little choice. He bowed his head and joined in with the Master's prayer, and the Master didn't choose to finish his prayer until my father had jerked his way back to stand by his chair and the Duke of Gloucester was ready to deliver his pardon. Then the Master called for quiet. The words must be heard by everybody so that there could be no future doubt. As soon as the pardon was spoken, the widow ran to my father, and it was lucky she did, for he needed a shoulder to lean on.

The summoner shot dagger looks and whispered to the archdeacon, who was sitting with his hands in his lap like a small dog waiting for his dinner. I was so busy gazing at my father that I jumped when the clerk prodded me toward the middle of the hall. Just being forced to stand there, like a scarecrow in a field, was hard. I imagined myself back in my cell. I was a shell, a nothing. I wouldn't move. I wouldn't speak. I wouldn't do anything.

The summoner's charges were carefully chosen, as was the order in which he placed them. Like my father, I had also been at the Tabard and had been friendly with the French merchants who drank there. Only a month ago, in plain sight of a group of pilgrims, whose number included the summoner himself, I had danced with Sir Jean d'Aubricourt, a captured French knight whose ransom had been paid and who was on his way home. Soon after that, I had shown off the king's ring, which I had obviously been using to add authority to the messages I was sending to France. In addition, the summoner had it on good authority that I'd recently been to see the king himself. Lastly, he said, his voice dripping with mock horror, I'd been spreading scurrilous rumors about some of God's servants, who also happened to be London's finest citizens. "My lords," he added with a final flourish, "amongst those who find themselves the objects of the prisoner's wild imaginings are some of the good men in this hall."

The judges murmured between themselves. "Look up, girl," ordered one of them.

I thought it best to do as I was told. I focused on the dais and could see that two of the judges had received a visitation from Walter and myself and these two were leaning forward. The Duke of Gloucester, who had not had a visit, was leaning back. I could not think that any of this was good.

The summoner called Master Pardoner as a witness against me; the rest were strangers or almost strangers. The laundress said she had known I was bad the moment she set eyes on me, although since she admitted she'd only met me once, this was poor testimony. However, several other people testified to my demonic character. A blind man told the story of my father's crippling as though I'd cast a spell on the bell. An apprentice boy who my father had sacked said that I turned milk sour. A mute girl made peculiar mouthings, which the summoner interpreted in some nonsensical way or other. After she'd sat down, much to my surprise, my fellow pilgrims lined up in my defense. Madame Prioress, in a voice high and shrill, swore that I was a simple girl who loved animals, not treachery. She produced one of her dogs and said I'd saved its life. Dame Alison attested in lengthy detail to my spiritual devotion, citing that she'd seen me on my knees every night without fail, and that I'd always prayed aloud, and exhorted my fellow pilgrims to pray with me "for the good of the realm, my lords, *the good of the realm.*" The skinny cleric, who had been so appalled by my repeating of the miller's story, said that I'd been a model of girlish decorum and added that the summoner probably imagined he'd seen me with the king's ring because of an alchemist's trick with gold he'd witnessed. Certainly, said the cleric, he himself had seen no such ring. Sir Knight also put himself out on my behalf, gushing that I'd been so like a daughter to him on the journey that he'd willingly lent me his own daughter's pony. "Girls don't plot, my lords," he said. "They marry and have babies." Mistress Medic, still staring into the distance, said that I never spoke a word out of place. I bowed my head in shame. When the franklin and the plowman extolled my virtues, I couldn't help looking at Master Chaucer. He was fiddling with his sleeves, watching the result of his coaching with some anxiety. Nobody must fluff their lines. When my defenders had finished, he knitted his fingers and unknitted his brow. He'd done all he could.

There was muttering amongst the judges. Because of my age and the character witnesses, they seemed inclined to leniency.

The summoner piped up at once. "That's all well and good," he said, "except, my lords, that this evidence changes nothing. Nobody denies that the defendant says her prayers and is kind to dogs. But she danced with Sir Jean." He addressed the pilgrims directly. "Can you deny that?" Silence. The summoner walked to and fro. "As for Master Cleric," he said, "*he* may have been duped by the alchemist, but I most certainly was not, not for a moment and if necessary, I can produce witnesses who saw the accused with the king. Can you deny you saw the king?" he suddenly barked at me. I said nothing. "No, I didn't think so." He stopped walking.

"But, my lords," he said importantly, "even if we disregard all of these incriminating acts, the last charge I read out is by far the worst. Now, I'm a fair man and a reasonable one. I'll not point to the accused's red hair, or the fact that she summoned down a cloud when her horse—the horse that Sir Knight so kindly provided—bolted for no reason—"

My defenders rose as one. "Shame on you for tainting her with witchery!" called Dame Alison. "The cloud was alchemy. The alchemist told us himself, and he'll tell you if you'll hear him." Luke got up. *No, I* thought, *no. Luke must have nothing to do with this.*

Happily, Gloucester intervened. "Silence!" he barked. "We want nothing about clouds here. Enough of this foolery or I'll clear the court."

To my great relief, Master Chaucer made Luke sit down.

"Of course, my lord," said the summoner unctuously. "As I said, discounting everything else, it's really what the girl has done since she came to London that proves beyond doubt that she's the spawn of Satan." He coughed portentously and waited until he had the complete attention of the whole hall. My father had no idea what was coming next, nor did Master Chaucer or Luke or any of the pilgrims. But the people sitting opposite did. I knew from the nervous hum amongst them that they were people Walter and I had visited.

"I can hardly go on," the summoner said. "I will because I must. Her fellow pilgrims attest to this girl's sanctity, kindness, and purity, but let me tell you that this witch has lodged in her imagination sexual deviances unknown to Lucifer himself." There was a bubble of noise. "Yes," said the summoner, "and she's seen fit to repeat her filthy imaginings to many of the people in this hall, usually not in daylight hours, no, in the dark, when the devil can ride unnoticed on her shoulder."

I could hear my father's breath rasping. I was glad he was sitting again.

"Let me tell of one," the summoner said, "just as an illustration." He crooked a finger at a man sitting on the edge of a bench. Reluctantly, the man stepped forward. I recognized him as a guild master, the benefactor of a home for orphaned children on whom he practiced his particular vice on a weekly basis. The summoner began his description. The Duke of Gloucester shifted uncomfortably. "Do we really need to hear the details, Master Summoner?"

The summoner stopped mid-sentence. "Perhaps not, my lord. Suffice for me, perhaps, to name all those the girl has tainted with her lurid allegations." He proceeded to list everybody Walter and I had visited. When he had finished, nobody knew where to look.

The Duke of Gloucester was clearly appalled—not

by the names but by me. "Do you deny this accusation?" he asked. "You'd better if you can."

I said nothing.

The summoner tapped his foot, was it three times or four? I didn't count. I was trying to think, but my brain had turned to porridge. "Let's not prolong this horror," the summoner said. "All the judges need to know is this: did you visit these people and accuse them of these repulsive practices? Remember, God is watching."

I was silent.

"You must speak, girl," said Gloucester.

I waited as long as I dared. Then I said, "I did." What else could I say? My father groaned. Master Chaucer was gripping the bench. Behind his glasses, Luke's expression was unfathomable. Now I'd broken my silence, I wanted to say more. "My lords, I didn't make up the sins and nor did the devil."

"No?" asked Gloucester. "Then where did you find them?"

"In the summoner's tally book," I said.

The summoner gave a harsh laugh. "Indeed I have a book, my lords." He fumbled in his pouch and produced one. "Every summoner has a book." He flicked it open. "James Burrows, priest, to be brought before the archdeacon on the charge of keeping a concubine. Anne Fuller, to be brought before the archdeacon on a charge of falling asleep during Mass." He looked up. "Shall I go on?"

"No," said Gloucester. He wanted this case to be over. "Never mind about the treachery. The girl's a liar of extraordinary depravity and also clearly a witch. No decent girl would be able to concoct such viciousness as we've heard today without the devil's help. Nor does she convincingly deny the charge. Only her sentence remains." He and the other judges drew close to confer.

The summoner planted himself in front of me. He was bubbling with triumph and I saw, with a kind of idiotic clarity considering my position, three boils on his nose, three buttons straining over his stomach, and three tassles on the flap of his new pouch. His pouch. I suddenly rose. "My lords, I *can* prove that I didn't make up these sins. I can."

Four pairs of hands were raised in reproof. "I can," I cried with all the conviction of hope. "I can."

There was a muttering from the pilgrims' benches. "If she can, you must allow it. That's the law." It was Master Chaucer's voice.

The judges did look up then. There was a pause. "Very well," said Gloucester. Neither he nor the others bothered to draw their chairs back into line. They weren't expecting anything.

I walked toward the dais. The two judges who had been visited retreated. Oh, how fastidious are the truly

repellent! "The proof's right in this room," I said. "Tell Master Summoner to turn out his pouch." The summoner looked embarrassed but not alarmed. "Tell him to turn it out," I repeated.

"My lords—"

"Oh, Master Summoner, for God's sake, just turn it out." Gloucester had had enough.

The summoner opened his pouch. He was too slow for me. I ran to him and plunged both hands in. It was filled with little things he couldn't resist: a doctor's pestle, a twist of salt, a woman's brooch, a pair of baby's shoes, a shepherd's whistle, a pony's bit, an odd goose-feather hat. Right at the bottom was Poppet: squashed, damp, but Poppet nonetheless. I pulled her out.

"A doll," said Gloucester, in tones of disgust.

I went to the clerk's table and picked up the little paper knife. I flourished it, then cut Poppet's stitches. As I tugged out the stuffing I heard the summoner begin to hiss, but I never stopped until I had that vile book in my hand, the crumbs still lodged in the spine and the cover speckled white where some of Poppet's stuffing stuck to it. I didn't give it to the judges: I took it straight to Archdeacon Dunmow. "Whose writing is this?" I asked.

"Why, it's Master Summoner's!" he exclaimed without thinking.

"Are you sure?"

"Do you think I'm stupid, child? I see his writing every day. I'd not mistake it."

"And what's next to the names and the crimes?"

"Why, amounts of money—quite large amounts. Oh dear." He sank back, a dog whose dinner has made him queasy.

Now I approached the judges and gave Gloucester the book. He took it rather unwillingly, read the first page and the second and the third. At first all the color drained from his face, then he blushed red, then scarlet. He snapped the book shut and regarded one of his fellow judges with stark dismay. "You? How could you? And for a silver crown?"

The summoner was frozen. Only when Gloucester spoke did he leap onto the dais with the agility of desperation and snatch the book back. At the sudden violence, Gloucester felt for his sword. The summoner didn't care, his only thought now was to destroy the book, with all that carefully collected information and all those witnesses' names. If he didn't, he'd not be alive very long: two tainted judges would make sure of that. They might make sure of it anyway. He began to tear out the pages, fluttering them into the flame of one of the sconces until they caught and flew about like ashy birds. Nobody tried to seize them. Both the sinner and the collector of sins wanted these transgressions forgotten.

However, the summoner didn't burn all of the book.

He kept two pages. His eyes were blazing. "I'll read these out because they'll interest you, my lords," he declared, "if I may." He was not seeking permission. If this was to be his end, he'd perform one last act of malice. I guessed what was coming, so was not surprised when he began: "Master Geoffrey Chaucer, the crime of rape against Cecily Champain, dated—"

"You know that came to nothing," interrupted Gloucester. "The Master was officially acquitted years ago. The lady herself acknowledged a document releasing him from all further actions." The judges began to get up.

The summoner coughed. "Try this then, my lord." He spoke very clearly and very loudly. "Walter de Pleasance, unnatural relations with two fellow squires, 15 May 1386: crime witnessed by Edward Farrier, who was shoeing the squire's horse, and Agnes, laundress. Here's her thumbprint."

There was an awful gasp. I think it came from Sir Knight. The judges sat down again. I had to hold on to the table.

"As everybody knows," the summoner continued, "this is a crime not just against God but against nature. In Italy, such men burn. Are we less moral in England?"

I was as paralyzed as my father. I'd no idea Walter was in the book *because I hadn't read it all.* I felt sicker than sick. Yet again, my carelessness was going to cost a man his life. I was the shadow of death. I looked into

the benches where my fellow travelers sat. Sir Knight was sagging. Luke looked utterly bemused. He'd not guessed at all. To him, Walter was still his rival for me. Everybody else, including Master Chaucer, had their hands over their mouths.

I balled my skirt in my palms. "That's a lie," I said.

"How on earth would you know?" The summoner was holding the pages high so that everybody could read them.

"My lords, I was alone with Walter for at least three weeks after the pilgrimage. We were together during the day, and—" I stopped. My voice must be strong and true. "And we were together during the night."

"Together?"

"We shared a bed," I said. "We were—close. As close as two people of different sexes can be."

"You're saying you had sexual relations with Walter de Pleasance?"

I had to go the whole way now. "I am," I said.

"That's no proof at all," cried the summoner.

"Silence, Master Summoner!" The Duke of Gloucester addressed me carefully. "Is this true? Do you swear it, on God's oath?"

"I swear on God's oath that we love each other," I said, "and that we are as close as two lovers can get."

Gloucester made me repeat this. I did so.

Luke had taken off his spectacles and was staring

straight ahead. Master Chaucer was watching, to see if I was believed. He knew everything. Of course he did. He wasn't the Master for nothing.

The four judges stood up. Gloucester took in the whole scene, with the pilgrims and the Londoners, then struck his sword against the table. "These trials have been a shambles and must be struck from the record," he said. He glared at the summoner, as though wondering whether to arrest him instead, then decided against it. "Come, my lords," he said, curling his lip, "we have wasted enough time here already. I, for one, have better things to do. Usher! Open the doors!"

The widow and I helped my father out of the hall. I wanted to explain to Luke. I wanted to reassure Walter. I wanted to thank the Master. But I knew what, above everything else, I had to do at this moment. Without hesitation, I got into the cart that the widow had commandeered and sat close to my father. As we set off for Southwark, I did allow myself a last look back. I didn't see Walter or Luke or the Master. All I saw was a man with a brush. Under the clerk's direction, he was sweeping the remains of the summoner's tally book out of the hall and into the gutter, where it floated, sewage on sewage, before being slowly washed into the river.

## 17

And thus she kept her father's heart aloft
With all the obedience, all the diligence
By which a child can show her reverence . . .

Being home was strange, and not just for me. My father must also have found it difficult. I'd been away about two months, he imprisoned for a fortnight, and during our absence, Widow Chegwin had scrubbed and cleaned and mended. The house we had always known was disconcertingly spotless and unnaturally tidy. When she learned that God had performed less of a miracle on my father than Peter Joiner, the widow expressed no disappointment. "God works in mysterious ways," she cooed as she inspected the hinged calipers Peter had so cleverly constructed. Nor was she resentful that it was Peter's wife rather than herself who'd been commissioned to create my father's concealing trousers. She admired the workmanship as she folded them, only pointing out one fault in the stitching.

There are, perhaps, lots of women like the widow: irritating, unlovable and unlovely, provoking gratitude and dislike in equal measure. I knew my father would never marry her, and so did she. If she minded, we never knew. For the most part, she carried on as if nothing had happened. She still managed my father, answering questions for him in her nervously interfering way and dealing with his intimate necessities. She didn't know what to make of me anymore, though, now I knew things that no child should know and had admitted freely in open court that I'd slept with Walter. This last, at least, she greeted with some cheer. The dashing squire would have to marry me. I would be Lady de Pleasance. All was well that ended well. My father made no comment. She took Poppet to clean and mend too and I didn't stop her, although, just as I suspected, when I got Poppet back, she seemed to have no connection left with my mother. I contemplated giving her a martyr's end and burning her. In the end, I couldn't do that, so I put her in a chest. She's there still.

I couldn't reveal to anybody, not even to my father, that not everything was over. Indeed, since Walter had pledged his life against Londoners rising in support of the king, he was in more mortal danger. Perhaps, now that the summoner's book was destroyed, all those creatures we had visited would feel safe enough to ignore our threats. Perhaps they'd tell their supporters to forget the king and line up behind the commission. Perhaps the Duke of Gloucester would bring pressure of his own. As October drifted toward November, I became very tense, particularly as I had no idea where

Walter even was, or Luke, for that matter, whose expression, when I'd said so boldly that I'd been Walter's lover, haunted me.

You may ask why I didn't go to find them. Obviously, it wasn't because I no longer cared. Nor was it because my father forbade me to leave the house. The plain truth is that on the first evening after the trial, my father asked me, seriously and kindly, to remain at home. Forced to accept the widow's help in many things, he wanted me to help him perfect his walking. How could I refuse? And somehow, as we moved to and fro in the house, him leaning ever less heavily on my shoulder, we never spoke about the pilgrimage: he asked nothing and I told him nothing.

One evening, when he could walk around the kitchen on his own, we opened up his old workshop for more space, and the next morning, before I opened my eyes, I heard a muffled grating sound and a gentle musical echo. For one perfect second, I was transported back to a time when my father testing a bell was as familiar a sound as my mother calling his name. I dressed and went to him. The widow was baking. As I passed, she handed me some fresh bread. I thanked her.

My father was sitting in his wheeled chair, his legs sticking out to the side. He had dusted the bell with his sleeve, making a million motes dance. The bell was a very small one. Before the accident, it had been waiting for its tone to be refined. Now, hunched in concentration, my father was fixing the clapper with a piece of leather. He didn't acknowledge me until he was finished, and when he sat back, though the room was cold, he was sweating. "I'm going to give it to Master Host," he said, "to thank him for everything. I'll inscribe his name on the inside. He can ring it when it's time for people to go home."

I ran my finger round the bell's crown. My father regarded me candidly. "Don't be worried," he said. "There was no miracle about my walking, so nobody's going to hold you to the promise you made before you disappeared. You're not cut out for bell founding. We both know that."

I rang the bell. The clapper didn't hit true at once. It needed to settle on its thong. I rang it again. The sound it made was pretty as a stream in summer. I rang it again. "I just said walking, I didn't say how. I swore before God and St. Thomas."

"Indeed," my father agreed. There was a certain irony in his voice. "But St. Thomas, like all other priests, held that we're all made in God's image, and if we're made in his image we must have some of God within us. I'm using my bit of God to release you from your promise. Is that convoluted enough for you?"

"It's not so easy, Father," I said, and knelt down, avoiding his legs.

He took my hands, though the angle was awkward.

"I think it's something else that's not so easy. Am I right, sweetheart?"

He hadn't called me that since the accident. Tears pricked my eyes. "Life's just one terrible bargain after another," I whispered. "I've said things—done things—I don't know how things will end."

He stroked my hair. "You think God keeps a tally like the summoner?"

"Or the devil does."

He drew my hands to his heart. "Belle, Belle, Belle. You think you're so important that there's a tally book just for you?"

I felt his palms for the calluses that my mother used to count with pride. "I've never thought of it like that."

He removed one of his hands and rang the little bell again. He was pleased with it. "Well, Belle," he said, blowing away the last of the dust, "it's time you did."

We remained together, my father and I, until he grew chilly and uncomfortable and my knees began to hurt. Then I got up, opened the workshop shutters, raked out the fire, and fetched a broom. My father made no comment as the widow and I worked together. By midday the room was clean.

It was 9 November when my father strode into the Tabard. His upright appearance was not, of course, a complete surprise, because it was impossible to keep things secret on our street. Peter Joiner, perhaps with the widow's connivance, had organized a party of people to welcome him. Everybody was there: the miller, six prostitutes, a bargeman or two; the usual crowd. They shook his hand. Some brought their children for him to touch, convinced of a miracle despite my father showing off his calipers and calling Peter "God's joiner."

"You'll never persuade them it wasn't a miracle," I said, and only then told him about Luke and the cloud. My father supped his ale. "Luke, not Walter," he commented.

I blushed. "He's gone."

"That's hard."

I nodded.

Master Host was, as usual, full of gossip, and a casual inquiry elicited a torrent. "Didn't want to say, with your father just on his feet and that, but I've been to the fish market this morning and the place is awash with rumors. They say the king's returning to take his rightful place at Westminster. He's less than ten miles away. He could be here tomorrow."

"What kind of welcome will he get?" I poked the fire, trying to keep my voice light.

"Who knows!" Master Host said. "The fishmen couldn't decide if they wanted him back or not, nor the butchers neither."

"What about the guildsmen?" I asked.

Master Host laughed. "Your pilgrimage whetted your appetite for a career in the city, eh?"

I tried to toss my head in my old style. "Why not? Or even at court. Powerful men make things up. I make things up. Where's the difference?"

This delighted him. "Belle for Lord Chancellor! What do you think of that, John Bellfounder?"

"I'll ring her in myself," my father said.

"You're going to reopen the business?"

"I am."

"With Belle as partner?"

"I thought you said she was going to be Lord Chancellor."

Master Host guffawed. "Drinks on the house! Whatever London decides tomorrow, we'll celebrate tonight."

It was late when we got home. After the widow and I had helped my father to bed, I paced my room until a gray dawn broke. When I got downstairs, the widow had already lit the fires and gone to buy milk. My father, too, was up. He was sitting with a drawing board on his knees, his legs neatly bent today and the caliper prongs sticking through his trousers like small horns. "It's a good thing I sat in the dark at the trial," he said, "or they'd have seen at once how the 'miracle' worked. I'm going to get Peter to make a higher table."

I nodded and crouched by the hearth. We waited, my father drawing and me staring into the flames. I don't know how long it was before the widow burst in, gesticulating backward. She'd left the front door wide open. And then we heard them, the bells: "St. Martin Vintry, St. Jude's, St. Mary's on the Wharf, St. James Garlickhythe, St. Michael at Paternoster, White Friars, St. Mary Overie." It was my father who did the reciting. "Where's—"

A huge peal burst like a thunderclap. "St. Paul's," my father said, and he began to rise. "St. Paul's!"

The bells were wild. "Who are they pealing for?" I cried. "The king or the commission?"

The widow didn't know.

"Can I go, Father? Please? I've got to know!"

He hugged me. His eyes were alight. "My bells," he said, "my bells, welcoming me back to their world. Yes, go, Belle. But be careful."

I rushed passed the widow and down the street. Everybody was outside, pulling on shawls and boots against the clammy dew. The sun was struggling in vain through the clouds. I never felt the cold. I just ran. I counted madly. Four pigeons, seven gaping children, two old men with red hats, eight barrels—surely there'd be a ninth? There wasn't. I counted one knife-grinder, seven chickens, five goats. I tried to divide my steps but kept losing my place. I didn't know where I was going. I didn't know what I had counted. I ran in a circle and found myself near the oculist's shop, and there were three people standing there. I paused, midstep, and counted them carefully. One, two, three. They turned at my cry. Luke, Walter, and Master

Chaucer. And they were shouting the words that everybody was shouting: "God save the King!"

We stood, strangely awkward, while the city erupted around us. Walter, as always, tried to make things easy. "You see, Belle, those who didn't see the summoner's book destroyed were reluctant to believe it really had been and, in the end, the momentum we created couldn't be stopped. So, dear Belle, we did deliver London for the king." His eyes glittered rather than twinkled. He was edgy, not joyful. He couldn't look Luke in the eye, nor Luke him. Neither was sorry that Master Chaucer stood between them, his writing box under his arm.

"Dulcie's well. I retrieved both the horses, and Granada and Dobs are back from St. Denys," Walter said.

"I'm glad," I said.

Somebody in the crowd began to dance.

"Come home with me," I said, because I couldn't think of anything else.

"We'd be delighted," Master Chaucer said at once. "Now, we can't walk four abreast in this crowd, and Luke and I've been together so long that Luke needs new company. You walk with me, Walter, and would you mind carrying my box?" Walter took the box. "We know the way, Belle," the Master said. "You're just next to the Tabard. Isn't that right? On you go." As Walter brushed past, he cast a pleading glance. He didn't have to remind me. I knew what he didn't want me to say to Luke. I wouldn't break that promise.

Luke and I walked behind. There was so much to say. I could say almost nothing. "Your bruises are healing," I said at last.

"Yes."

"What exactly happened?"

"The monks found a song and teased me with it. I fought them. I was expelled."

"Luke, please look at me."

He turned slowly. I didn't know what he was reading in my face, but behind his glasses those gray eyes melted from steel into cloud. "I'm sorry, Belle. It was just a shock, in the courtroom. I knew you'd marry Walter. I just didn't expect . . . didn't expect"—he crunched his heel hard into the mud—"I didn't expect to find him in your bed so soon."

Without breaking Walter's confidence, I could have said that I'd lied. But that would lead to more questions, and, in the end, Luke would inevitably draw the right conclusion. I couldn't allow that. I felt every bit of happiness drain away. We walked in silence. The Master and Walter disappeared.

At the top of our street I stopped. "I'd forgive you," I said.

He frowned and took his glasses off. His hair, cut by the monks, was growing back, but he still looked shorn

and very far from my Helmetless Knight. I didn't care about that. I wanted to touch his hair, to smooth it down, to feel his scalp again.

"You'd really forgive me?" he asked.

"Yes."

He fiddled with the arm of his spectacles. "Then you can't love me very much."

We reached our front door. I opened it. Luke stepped inside.

Master Chaucer was in the back with my father. Walter was with the widow, who, thrilled, was extolling my virtues to him. Had Luke not been there, it would have been very comic. As it was, it was insupportable. I cut in. Crestfallen, the widow went back to the hearth but was soon humming into her pot.

We heard laughter. "Come and see my father's workshop," I said. We went through.

My father was showing the Master how his calipers worked. The Master was stroking his chin. His foxy look was quite returned and he filled his clothes again. "Genius," he said, "the hinges especially." He tapped them. "Joiners are of much more use than writers." He inspected Luke and me closely. "Be that as it may, I've some little presents, and I think now's the time to give them out. Would you mind, John?" My father shook his head. "Well then." He reached inside his jacket and brought out several sheaves of parchment, all cut to the size of a schoolbook.

"I've written a story for you," he said, handing them to Luke. "I know it's not quite traditional with presents, but I wonder if, before you take the story away, you could make a fair copy? You'll recognize the beginning. It's a story we began on our journey." He gestured to my father's table. "There's space enough there for the writing box. Set it down, Walter."

Walter did so. Luke, mute, opened the box, cleaned his spectacles, prepared a quill, and began.

"Now to you, Belle," the Master said. He seemed slightly less sure. "Your present involves asking a favor." He coughed. "I've got such an idea, but some of it comes from you and I want to use it as my own. I want to write about our pilgrimage." My eyes widened with alarm. He continued quickly, raising his hand. "Just a collection of pilgrims telling stories to each other on their way to Canterbury—a way of passing the time. Each story will be different. Some may have little morals. Others will just be stories that I already know and adapt for my pilgrims to tell." He paused to look at Luke, who was no longer writing, only reading.

"Where's the favor in that?" I asked, puzzled.

"Remember the anecdotes you wove?"

I remembered very well. "Some of them were unkind," I said, "and yet the same people were kind to me."

"That's true," the Master said. "Luckily, few people recognize themselves in books." He glanced at Luke again.

He was still absorbed. "I'd dedicate the whole work to you, naturally, in gratitude for your inspiration and for other things"—he gave me a very meaningful stare—"and it'll take me some time to write. In principle though, do I have your permission?"

"Of course you do," I said.

"You weren't thinking of writing such a work yourself?"

"No," I said. "Not a work like that." I hesitated. "The story I write will be a love story."

Master Chaucer held my gaze. "Yes," he said. "That's what great writers write."

"It'll be a tragedy," I said.

His smile was quizzical. "Always difficult to tell how a tale is going to finish before you get to the end."

There was a movement from the table. "Ah," said the Master. "What did you think of that, Luke?"

"It's a good story," said Luke slowly. "I hope I've understood it."

"What's it about?" my father asked.

Luke didn't look at my father. He looked at me. "It's about a girl who's almost unfaithful to the man she loves." He paused. Nobody spoke. "It's about forgiveness," he said, and in front of everybody, without any hesitation at all, he kissed me like a knight who, after a long journey, is claiming what is rightfully his.

# 18

*And thus with every bliss and melody*
*Palamon was espoused to Emily,*
*And God that all this wide, wide world has wrought,*
*Send them his love, for it was dearly bought . . .*

Adventures would be much more enjoyable if you knew that everything was going to turn out well in the end. As it is, I don't think you enjoy them at all except in retrospect, and even then you have to be careful. Once Luke and I were married and he began to help my father in his business, it would have been easy to turn the pilgrimage into something greater than it was, and to depict ourselves as heroes and heroines, with everybody against us as villains and crooks.

I hope I haven't done that. Just as the summoner was not completely a crook, so the Master, Walter, and I were not heroes. Only Luke, perhaps, deserved that epithet because he was the only one of us who didn't lie. And my father, of course. And the widow.

I kept Walter's secret; at least I didn't tell Luke in so many words. I know he guessed part of it on our wedding night. You'll know how. Not that he said anything directly. It was just that when Walter came a few weeks later to tell us he was going on pilgrimage to Jerusalem, Luke embraced him very warmly. I saw Walter close his eyes as Luke held him, and I knew just what he was feeling.

He brought Dulcie for me. His sister, he told us, had never returned, but he hoped the visit to Jerusalem might help. One bit of good news, he said brightly. His father had lined up a girl for him to marry when he got back. I knew, at that moment, that Walter would never come back. He was not capable of perpetrating such a deceit. Before he left, we had an afternoon alone together, just talking and remembering, and I cut a lock of his hair. I thought my heart would break when he rode off and Luke never reproached me for my torrent of tears. I still think of him every day. Sometimes, when I walk, I pretend he's beside me. You see, I didn't really lie about that in the courtroom. Walter's my other love, and the only person, apart from you, my reader, who knows everything that happened.

The king's story, of course, is well known. His triumphant entry into London was a momentary flicker that came to nothing. In the end, just as Master Chaucer feared, he was deposed and probably starved to death. I sometimes remember him in my prayers. Like most of us, he was a mixture of good and bad, but if you're king, that's not what counts. Richard wasn't canny. That was his downfall.

For a few years, there was an annual pilgrimage reunion party at the Tabard, instigated by Dame Alison. Sometimes those reunions prosper, sometimes not. Ours didn't. Memories of that courtroom killed it. After a while I heard news of the pilgrims only occasionally; a death usually, or a faint scandal.

Master Chaucer was a firm and faithful friend. He came to Southwark regularly until he was made clerk of the king's works and became too busy. Though I missed him, the appointment pleased me. It showed that he still had the king's favor. Sadly, he never completed his tales, and when, about a year after King Richard was deposed, the Master died and his son Thomas, acting as executor, offered them to me to finish, I declined. I had my own memories of the pilgrimage and didn't want to muddy them. However, the Master's death did spur me to make this record, although now I've finished it, I'm nervous. To this day, just as I've never told Luke the whole truth about Walter, so I've never told him the whole truth about the Master. Even though he understands and forgives all my faults, and I doubt he'd hold an unwilling conspiracy against the man who brought us together, I think the revelation would disappoint him. Perhaps I'll let him read this, perhaps not.

You may want to know what happened to the summoner. I've no idea. Nothing, I expect. Only in stories do the wicked get their just deserts.

There's nothing left to say now except that I love Luke with all my soul, and he loves me, and that the more I think about it, the more our love seems the miracle of this tale. That I, with all my imperfections and compulsions, should find my best peace in the gray eyes of a boy I only met properly because he spoke before I'd counted to three, needs more than luck. Perhaps God was at work. Perhaps St. Thomas. I don't know. Sometimes I feel I should care. Other times, I just sit with the lock of Walter's hair around my neck, counting my blessings in the litany of the bells. Luke remembers all their names, together with their weights and volumes. He laughs now when he thinks of the time he wanted to be a writer, though he never thinks it was a waste. "It brought me to you," he says when we're lying together, and the way he says it almost stops my heart.

I live an ordinary life these days, with no more life-in-the-head. I don't need it. My love makes the ordinary extraordinary, and, as Walter might say, that's the loveliest kind of love. Dear Walter. Dearer than dear. As I lay down my quill, I hope that wherever you are, either in heaven or on earth, you're happy.

# AUTHOR'S NOTE

In the English-speaking world, we are taught that Chaucer (c. 1342–1400) is the father of English literature. His *Canterbury Tales* are staples of the school curriculum. But let's be honest: many readers' hearts sink a little as they contemplate even the beautifully bawdy "Miller's Tale" in the original Middle English. Somehow, having to look up every other word in a glossary strips Chaucer's stories of all the pleasure we're assured we'll find in them. Even so, at my convent school I remember being entranced by an erudite and very serious-minded nun reading "The Franklin's Tale" aloud and with unexpected feeling. As we, like Dorigen, contemplated those "grisly rokkes blake," the barrier of the language evaporated. But more than that, I suddenly realized it's not Chaucer who's dull, it's certain ways of teaching him.

If you really want to enjoy Chaucer, remember four things: first, you're allowed to laugh—he's very naughty and very sly; second, if he were alive today, he'd be writing for comic soap operas, some to be shown only when children are in bed; third, the way he pokes fun at clerics and pompous officials means he's not just the father of English literature, but also the father of stand-up comedians; and fourth, father of English literature or not, he led a rowdy life that outdoes anything he actually wrote.

It was, indeed, more his life than his tales that inspired *Belle's Song*. All Chaucer biographies will tell you he was an author, poet (I quote some of his poetry in my story), philosopher, bureaucrat, deputy forester, member of Parliament, comptroller of customs, clerk of the king's works, courtier, and diplomat. Not all will tell you that he was a spy—euphemistically referred to as "working for the king"—and possibly a criminal too—in 1380 he was cited in an "incident" against a woman. Gloomy scholars seem to want the father of English literature to be a saintly man with an unblemished reputation, not a real man of his time, with a wart or two to his name.

Yet hurrah for the warts because they turn Chaucer from an author of stories into a character in *Belle's Song*, and when you add to Chaucer's own warts the grisliness of the fourteenth century with the plague, England's peasants revolting, and King Richard II not being able to cut the mustard, as we British say, I felt the same kind of stirring as Chaucer himself must have felt as he prepared his vellum for his magnum opus. There are, of course, many differences between Chaucer and myself, but my favorite is that I finished my book and he never finished his . . .

# Selected Timeline

1342 Geoffrey Chaucer born

1367 Richard Plantagenet (later Richard II) born

1368 Chaucer sent on a mission to France by King Edward III

Among other literary works, Chaucer writes a fragment of *The Romance of the Rose*

1370 Chaucer runs royal errands to France

1376 Chaucer in France on royal mission to negotiate peace

1378 Edward III dies. Richard II, aged ten, succeeds the throne

1380 The case against Chaucer for *raptus* (which might mean rape, kidnapping, or seizure) is dropped; Chaucer begins to write *The Parliament of Fowls*

1381 The Peasants' Revolt: Richard II bravely meets the mob, promises them much, saying, "I'll never go back on my word." He does not keep this promise

1386 The Duke of Gloucester and the Earl of Arundel complain of Richard's extravagance and his policy of peace with France. A controlling council—the commission—is imposed on the king, much to his humiliation

Chaucer begins to write *The Canterbury Tales*

1387 Chaucer's wife dies

1393 Richard II gives Chaucer £10 for "services rendered"

1394 Richard II grants Chaucer an annuity of £20 for life

1397 Richard II takes his revenge on the commission but his position is very shaky

1398 Richard II grants Chaucer a "tonel" (252 gallons) of wine, to be delivered every year for the rest of Chaucer's life

1399 Henry Bolingbroke (later Henry IV) lands in England and claims the crown of England

1400 Richard is taken prisoner and dies in Pontefract Castle, probably murdered

Chaucer signs a receipt for his tonel of wine and probably dies soon after